Worth the risk

CAROLINA REBELS SERIES

LINDSAY PAIGE

First Edition: February 2018
Library of Congress Cataloging-in-Publication Data

Paige, Lindsay
Worth the Risk (a Carolina Rebels Series novel) – 1st ed
ISBN-13: 978-0998195582

Raelynn

"**Y**OU'RE FIRED."

My mouth drops. "What? You can't do that!"

"We need people who are dependable, and you are not," my jerk of a boss says calmly.

"My son was sick, and I'm the only one who can be with him. What was I supposed to do? You can't fire me over this."

"I just did."

He hangs up on me like the bastard he is and I lean forward, clutching the steering wheel. This can't happen to me. My eyes water with tears and I take deep breaths because I can't cry. No matter how badly I want and need to. It's been one bad thing after the other for months and now, I'm jobless *and* homeless.

"Momma," Jackson's soft voice says from the backseat.

I take a quick deep breath and turn to look at him. "What's wrong, baby?"

"I don't wanna go to school."

We sit in the school's parking lot. There shouldn't be a reason why he doesn't want to go. I unbuckle my seatbelt and lean over the console to reach him in the backseat, resting my hand on his knee. "Why? What's wrong?"

He frowns. "I don't feel good."

I touch his forehead with the back of my hand; he doesn't have a fever. He was sick earlier this week, but he's been doing better. "Try and if you feel really bad, tell Mrs. Solomon, okay?"

He nods. I get out and walk around to his door. He unbuckles himself because he's a big boy and Momma can't do it anymore. He hops out and I reach in to grab his book bag. I have until he gets out of school for the day to find a job and a place to live.

He holds my hand and we walk up the breezeway and into the school. The closer we get to his classroom, the closer Jackson walks next to me. He's always been a quiet kid, but when it comes to new people, he's super shy. It's only ever been the two of us, so it takes some adjusting when new people come into the picture. He has been in school for about three months, but he still refuses to walk in without me.

Mrs. Solomon smiles when she sees us and crouches to be eye level with Jackson. "Hey, Jackson." She holds out her hand and after a few seconds, Jackson takes it. He walks away, glancing over his shoulder to wave goodbye to me. The tears can't be helped now. I wait until he takes his seat before I leave. Not that I have anywhere to go. I was already trying to find another job because my boss is a sleazy bastard. I put in applications everywhere I can think of, but nothing has panned out so far.

I get in my car and break down like I've wanted to do for the past few months. The sobs rip through me, tearing me apart so easily while this voice in my head berates me for letting things get this bad in the first place. How could I let Jackson down? What kind of mother loses her job and home in one day? A terrible one. That's me. How did I become like this?

I've been a strong person for so long, but life has finally broken me. Everything I own is in this dingy car. It's loaded down with what few possessions we own since we had to be out today. What am I going to do now? Why does everything have to be so hard for Jackson and me? We've managed to get by just fine until a few months ago when everything started going wrong left and right and sucked my money away faster than I could make it.

You'd think in the five years I've been on my own, I would've made some friends and have someone to help me, but it hasn't worked out that way. I'm as alone now as I was when I left the hospital with a newborn in my arms. My parents were strict, hypocrites of preachers. They told me that I made the bed, and I would lay in it. They had as much issue with the fact that I was pregnant at sixteen as who the father was.

My parents got on my nerves so bad and stressed me out so much during my pregnancy that I nearly had him early twice. I went into labor on my seventeenth birthday and Jackson was born early the following morning. Everything was set. I had a job and I was able to move out and in with a family friend. As soon as I scraped up enough to move away, I did. I went across state lines and never looked back. My parents don't know where I live and haven't ever seen their grandson.

I've had to grow up, learn how to be not just a parent, but a single parent completely on my own, and survive for the two of us. I've managed to do it. There's been a lot of ups and downs, but my son has always been fed and had a place to sleep.

Until today.

I can't fail my son now. Something has to give. There's only seventy bucks to my name. My son needs a place to sleep and I need to be able to feed him. I wipe my tears and sniff a few times. The time for Raelynn's pity party is over. I need to move forward for Jackson's sake. First, I stop by the public library, type up a résumé, and print off fifty copies. Hopefully paying the library to use their printer lands me a job before I go broke. With résumés in hand, I visit places of business and with more confidence than I actually have, demand to speak with whoever is in charge of hiring new employees and plead my pathetic case.

Like how I'm currently in a quilt shop faced with a pretty blonde and a tall, intimidating man. With a quick, steadying breath I hope they won't notice, I hold out my hand, which the woman takes. "Hello, my name is Raelynn Woods. I'm sorry if I bothered you while you were busy," I glance to the man, his black eye and busted lip particularly, but force the words to continue out of my mouth, "but I wanted to make sure I talked to the person in charge." I find my résumé in my purse and hand it to her. "I don't know if you have any positions open, but I'm in desperate need of a job, so if one opens up, I'd appreciate it if you'd keep me in mind."

She tells me what everyone has told me today. "I will. I don't have anything right now."

My shoulders fall. Is it too soon to give up hope and cry again? I'm nearly out of résumés. Someone *has* to have job opening. Someone has to be willing to hire me.

"Are you open to any kind of job?" the man asks, surprising me. He seemed content to stand and hang around.

"Yes." If he's offering, I'll take it. I don't care what it is, I'll do it. I'm desperate.

"What about as a nanny?"

"I can do that. I have references, experience, and I'm CPR-certified." The words can't leave my mouth fast enough. At this point, I'll take what I can get and figure out details later.

"Stay here for a second," he says.

"What are you doing?" the woman asks him.

He says a name as he steps away with a phone in his hand. I watch him talk on the phone, hoping that this is my chance. The one that will ease the tension in my muscles, that will start me back on the up and up with Jackson. I don't know how being a nanny will work, considering I have my own son, but surely it's just babysitting during the day and maybe late at night, right?

Before I can worry too much, the man is back.

"Here's the deal. I have a friend who is a single parent and he needs a nanny to help with his little girl, Bree.

She's almost nine months old. He can explain everything to you during the interview, which he'd like to do as soon as you can make it to his house because he's in between interviews right now. Deanna, where's a pen and paper?" She walks around the counter to grab him what he asked for and he asks me, "Can you go now?"

My anxiety returns as it hits me. It's a single father? I don't know any of these people. "To this man's house?" I manage to say. I'm supposed to go to some random guy's house? Is he insane?

"He's a good guy. I can go with you if you're uncomfortable going alone; that's totally understandable," Deanna says.

Is a potential job worth this? Her reassurances help, but I don't know. I glance at the man. What if his friend looks like him? I'm being a judgmental bitch right now when I have no choice, but I also have no clue what he does or what I'm walking into here.

"Can you read that?" He holds out the piece of paper with his handwriting and I nod. "Are you going? He doesn't have all day." Deanna slaps his arm from across the counter. "What?" he asks.

"Don't pressure her. She doesn't know us and you're trying to send her to a man's house and she doesn't know him either. And you got beat up at work, so you look a little sketchy." What kind of work does he do where he walks away looking like that?

He frowns. "I'm not pressuring her." He glances at her. "I look sketchy?"

"Intimidating," I correct, using the word I first thought of when I saw him.

He smiles. "That's a better answer." He looks at me.

"We're all good people, but Deanna can go with you if you want. Here." He pulls his phone back out and after a moment, he turns it toward me to show off a picture of a little baby girl. "That's his daughter. How dangerous does she look?"

Okay, he has a point. I debate it while the two banter until I hear Deanna ask, "Anyway, would you like for me to ride out there with you?"

"You don't mind?" It would make me feel more comfortable, if she's willing.

"Not at all."

"His mom is probably there too," the man adds.

I nod. That works for me. I follow Deanna outside and then to this man's house. It's a nice house in a nice neighborhood. I could never afford to live here, that's for sure. The house almost reminds me of a doll house from the outside. I wonder what this man's job is.

I glance into my rearview mirror. I look frazzled and out of place. I tried to freshen up in the bathroom at the library, but obviously, I did a bad job. No wonder people don't want to hire me. With a deep breath, I run my fingers through my hair again and get out to meet Deanna. It's now or never. Deanna and I walk up the pebbled walkway. There's a sign on the door.

Sleeping baby. DO NOT RING DOORBELL. Knock. Quietly.

Deanna raps her knuckles on the door softly. I want to ask her what his name is again, but he answers before I can.

"Hey, EJ," Deanna says. "This is Raelynn Woods." She looks at me. "Are you good?"

I nod and she waves as she leaves. EJ is a handsome

7

young guy in jeans and a T-shirt that flaunts strong arms covered with tattoos. He appears to be not too much older than myself if I had to guess.

He sticks out his hand. "EJ Bertuzzi. Nice to meet you."

I shake it. "You too." No need to repeat my name when he already knows it. He steps aside for me to walk in.

How does a guy this young afford a place like this? Much less a nanny. Maybe he's into something shady with all of those tattoos. *Shut it, Raelynn. No judging.* I follow EJ through his gorgeous house and into the kitchen. It feels rude to gawk at his house, even if he can't see me, so I stare at his back. It's broad and leads to a huge ass and thick legs. Damn. I shake my head. No ogling the potential boss either!

"Have a seat." He motions to the dining table. "Would you like something to drink?"

"No, thanks. Does EJ stand for anything?" It's a stupid thing to ask, considering he's supposed to be interviewing me, but I can't help it. I see a name like that and I'm always curious.

"Elias James, first and middle name, but only my mother calls me that. Most of my friends just call me EJ."

Elias. That's a pretty name. He seems more like an Elias to me for some reason. "So, I could call you Elias?" I ask.

He shrugs as he grabs something for himself from the fridge and then sits down across from me. "If you want. I don't care." He's a bit intimidating between his size and those tattoos. What is it with intimidating men today? "Okay, here's the deal," he starts, getting down to business. "I haven't liked or trusted anyone I've interviewed so far, and I'd like to finally find someone so my mom can return home. If I like you and I think you'll work out, then I'll give you a chance. Do you happen to watch hockey?"

I'm so thrown off guard by his question that it takes a second to shake my head. I'd need something other than an antenna to watch that.

"Well, that's what I do. I play for the Carolina Rebels. I travel and have a rigorous schedule for most of the year. I need someone I can trust to be with Bree and who is willing to keep in contact with me while I'm on the road. You'd live here, and you'd be paid well. We can go over specifics if I decide I like you. So far, what do you think?"

I'd have to live here? Oh, boy. I wasn't counting on that. He's going to shun me the moment I tell him I have a little boy. But maybe if he likes me enough first, then we can somehow work out an arrangement? I don't know. But I find myself saying, "I think I'm still interested."

Elias smiles. It's such a pretty smile. "Great. Other possible duties would be tidying up. Your number one priority would be taking care of Bree. You'd have vacation time during the offseason and—"

"When is that?" I interrupt, curious. "Sorry, I don't know much about hockey. Or anything about it at all, really."

"It's okay. Season ends in April, unless we make it to playoffs. So, let's just say late June to early September. You could take that entire time off or as little as two weeks. Up to you. I get one mandated day off every week during the season; that can be your day off, but if for some reason you need another day, let me know with plenty of advance notice if possible."

Elias goes on and on about his schedule and things he'd want from me. Maybe Jackson and I could live here with him while I'm a nanny. That would solve both my job problem and living arrangements. But is that the right decision? Should I even contemplate that? Would Elias?

Soft cries comes from a nearby baby monitor and Elias jumps up.

"She's awake," he says with a crooked smile. The man just got hotter.

I shake those thoughts from my mind. "Can I come with you to meet her?"

If possible, his grin widens. "Sure. Come on."

I follow him up the stairs. "You have a beautiful home," I say what I've been thinking since I walked in.

"Thanks," he mumbles. "My mom had a hand in decorating."

The room we enter is a pink explosion fitted for a princess. Elias picks up his baby and rocks her gently. I step next to him.

"She's beautiful," I whisper, even though she's awake.

"That she is."

Elias seems enthralled by his daughter and it tugs at my heart. Bree reaches her arm out to me.

"Can I hold her?"

He hesitates, but then nods, handing her over to me like she's his most prized possession.

"Hey, pretty girl," I coo. She smiles. Holding her makes me wish Jackson was still a baby. Bree makes baby noises and I laugh when she tugs on my hair.

"You're a natural," Elias says. "You seem like you

know more than I do," he chuckles.

I shrug it off.

"Come on."

I follow him out of the room, but in the opposite direction of the stairs. He walks two doors down and opens the one on the opposite side of the hall.

"This would be your room. If you'd rather have your own things in here instead, I can move this stuff to storage, no problem."

I nod, my stomach churning and tying in knots. I need to tell him about my son. Elias leads me back downstairs to the kitchen. Bree has dozed off again with her head on my shoulder, so he lets me continue to hold her.

"Any questions or concerns? Because I'm ready to make an offer."

"I have the job?"

"If you want it."

The relief at hearing those words overwhelms me and I squeeze my eyes closed to stop the tears. I will them away. This isn't a sure thing yet. "Um, yes, I do have some concerns."

Elias frowns, not expecting that. "What are they?"

Bree stirs and I take the opportunity to look at her instead of him. "I...I'm a single mom of a five-year-old. If I accept the job offer, if you're still offering, then it would be my son and myself moving in."

"How old are you?"

I lift my head. He doesn't think I could be the mom of a five-year-old. "Twenty-two," I answer curtly. I hope like hell he tries to judge me. That is one thing that brings out my inner momma bear. Judge me for almost anything else, but not that.

"Oh, man. I wasn't expecting the kid."

My heart sinks and my inner beggar makes an appearance. "*Please.* I need this job. I'm completely qualified seeing as how I've been taking care of my son for five years by myself. He's in school for most of the day, and he's a good kid, I swear. I can do this job and take care of your little girl. You wouldn't have to worry about feeding him either. I can buy the food for him." Elias said he would cover the grocery bill for me. "Please, don't let this cause you not to hire me. I *need* this job. *Please.*"

Elias just stares at me. That can't be a good sign.

EJ

DAMN. I DIDN'T see this coming at all. Not to have a hot as sin woman knock on my door to be Bree's nanny, sort of recommended to me by Brayden, or the fact that she'd be a single mom. Raelynn looks at me with these big, watery green eyes. All I thought I was getting was a new roommate, but adding a kid to the mix makes things trickier, doesn't it?

There's a buzz from her pocket and she winces.

"I'm sorry. I need to pick him up from school." She carefully hands Bree back to me. "I'm sorry for wasting your time." She moves for the door the moment my princess is securely in my arms.

"Wait," I call out, standing to follow her. "You threw me for a loop. I wasn't expecting that. You're the first person I've interviewed who I've liked and actually seems interested. I need someone to hire, too. The job is yours if you want it. We'll figure the rest out as we go."

I've never seen such a heavy tension leave someone before, but I swear, it's like I lifted the world from her shoulders.

"Can I start this afternoon?"

"Yeah, sure. Come back here once you pick up your boy."

She surprises the hell out of me by coming over and hugging me, careful not to disturb Bree. "Thank you so much. You have no idea how much this means to me." The sincerity is obvious.

I nod as she pulls away with embarrassment. "Hey, what does he like to eat?"

She chuckles to herself. "Hotdogs and mac and cheese are his favorites. He likes to drink water or apple juice, too."

I nod. Raelynn leaves. I cancel the remaining interviews just in time for Bree to start whining, so I feed her, change her, and gather her up to run to the store. Hotdogs and mac and cheese are not regular items in my kitchen. Once I'm back home, I sit on the couch with Bree in my lap and play patty cake, which causes her to giggle constantly. My mother also returns. I sent her out for a spa day because I felt like hiring a nanny needed to be something I did on my own.

Now that I have a nanny, Mom will be able to move back home. She was home over the summer, but she came back once the season started. Mom has been helping me adjust to becoming a dad and learning how to take care of a baby, but she can't stay forever. Hence, the nanny search. It's taken way longer than I thought possible.

"Well?" Mom asks.

"We have a nanny."

"Oh, yeah? Do you think she'll be good?"

"Yeah. Her name's Raelynn. She's younger than I am, but she knows what she's doing. She's actually a single mom. She seems to have had a rough time; she has no one but her kid."

"Wait. They're both moving in with you?" Mom frowns at this and I know she is feeling the same thing I was when Raelynn told me about her son.

"They should be here soon. Her son is five, so he's in school during the day."

"Are you sure about this, son?" Mom interrupts.

"Yeah. Bree likes her and Raelynn seems perfect for the job. I have a good feeling it'll work out like it should." That's the only reason I still hired her. My gut told me the second she held my daughter that this girl was the one. I can't waste any more time looking for other okay nannies when I know I've found a fantastic one.

Mom is quiet for a moment. "Okay then. I'm going to stick around for a few days and make sure she passes my inspection."

"Ma." That causes her to glare at me. "You might make her nervous."

"And? She's going to be caring for my granddaughter. I need to make sure your instincts are correct."

Before I can argue with her further, there's a knock on my door. I forgot to take down the sign about the doorbell. I open the door with Bree in one arm and Mom hovering behind me to find Raelynn and the spitting image of her in the form of a little boy. He has his arms wrapped around her thigh as he hides behind her, peeking out with one eye.

"Hey. Come on in. This is my mom, Alice. She's been helping me so far and she'll be here until you get settled in."

I step aside. The boy stays glued to Raelynn's side as she and my mom shake hands. We go into the living room and he climbs onto Raelynn's lap.

"Hey," I say gently. He glances at me. "What's your name?"

He ignores me and Raelynn rubs his back. "Jackson's shy when it comes to new people." She glances down at him. "Jackson, this is Mr. Bertuzzi. Don't you want to tell him hey?"

Jackson looks over with his head still resting on his mom's shoulder and mumbles, "Hey."

"My friends call me EJ; you can too." No way that kid should have to say Bertuzzi if he ever does talk to me. "Want to watch cartoons with my mom while I talk to your mom in the kitchen?"

Jackson shakes his head. Raelynn whispers something in his ear. "Any cartoon will work," she tells me. Jackson moves to his own seat on the couch. "I'll be right in there, okay?" she tells him as she stands. I place Bree in my mom's lap and we go into the kitchen.

We hammer out the details of her pay, and she thanks me like three more times for giving her the job.

"What's your story?" I finally ask. She's definitely got one.

A wry smile appears as she glances into the living

room. "Which one?" Raelynn shakes her head. "Most recently, stuff happened back to back to back to make making ends meet that much harder; I lost my job and apartment this morning, and everything I own is in my car. If you hadn't given me this job, the last of my money would've been spent on dinner for Jackson and a very cheap hotel room."

"You don't have any family? Or friends?"

She shakes her head. "It's just Jackson and me." Raelynn clears her throat. "Can you watch him while I get our things and put them in our room?"

"Sure." Then I realize she said *our* room. "Actually, I have another spare bedroom, the one next to yours. Jackson can have it." There's a twin bed in Bree's room, so I'll sleep in there and let Mom have my room until she leaves.

"Oh. Thank you."

I feel like I should help her, or do it for her, but she may want to move her things herself. She goes outside and I return to the living room. Jackson's eyes widen as he watches his mom walk out the door.

"It's okay." He whips around to look at me. "She's getting your stuff out of the car. She'll be right back."

"You aren't going to help her?" Mom asks.

"She seemed to want to do it herself. Go move your things into my room."

She purses her lips, but gets up to do it, leaving me alone with the boy.

Jackson sits on the edge of the couch and seems to be anxious as he waits for his mom. Then he looks at me. "You're a Rebel."

My eyebrows rise. "Yeah, I am."

"You were at my school." His little legs swing,

bumping into the couch each time.

"I was?"

He nods. Oh, maybe I was. We went to some of the local schools in September, right before training camp, for this reading program thing. We read to a few classes and then played ball hockey with the older kids.

"What's hockey?" he asks as if he's been dying to ask this question ever since I went to his school.

"It's a game. Like baseball or basketball, but you play on ice with skates."

Raelynn walks back inside, her arms loaded with stuff. She smiles at Jackson before continuing up the stairs. Bree cries, so I pick her up from where Mom placed her in the pack 'n play and sit on the couch. Jackson and Bree eye each other. Bree leans over and tries to grab Jackson, but he leans away from her.

"Who's that?" he asks.

"This is Bree. I'm her dad."

"She drools a lot."

I laugh. "Sometimes. I bet you drooled a lot when you were a baby."

Jackson doesn't seem to like that idea. "Momma," he says when she comes back down the stairs.

"Yeah, baby?"

"Did I drool when I was a baby?"

She laughs. "Yep. All babies drool." She kisses the top of his head before going back out to her car.

"Mr. EJ, I'm thirsty."

Part of me wants to correct him and tell him he can just call me EJ, but if his mom has told him to say mister, then I don't want to overstep. "What would you like to drink?"

"Apple juice."

"You're in luck. I have some of that. Come on." He follows me into the kitchen. "Do you drink out of a big boy's cup?"

"Yep," he answers, popping the p just like Raelynn did earlier.

I find my smallest plastic cup and pour him some juice. I hear the door open and close, and then footsteps up the stairs. I carefully watch him and I'm kind of impressed when he drinks out of his big boy cup without spilling his juice. I so have a ton to learn about kids. Raelynn appears in the kitchen a moment later, some papers in her hand.

"Momma, look! No straw!"

"I see. Did you tell Mr. EJ thanks for fixing you something to drink?"

"Thanks," he quickly says.

"Welcome, buddy."

Raelynn looks uncomfortable for a second. "Um, mind if we use your table? He's got some homework."

"In kindergarten?" I ask with disbelief.

She laughs. "Yep."

"Go ahead. I'll start dinner." I put Bree in her seat and get busy while listening to Raelynn help Jackson focus on his homework. "Are you guys allergic to anything?" I ask as Mom appears in the kitchen.

"No."

Good to know. I let Raelynn know that there's an extra carseat in the garage and that she can park in there starting tomorrow. I'll run out to get an extra key made in the morning. I'll need to write down the code for the alarm system, too. I give her my cell, Mom's cell, and the number of some people within the organization in case of an emergency. I'll give her the full house tour tomorrow morning.

Jackson is delighted about having hotdogs and mac and cheese. I feel like an oddball in my own house as Raelynn asks him about his day and the apparent upcoming field trip. Jackson can be a chatterbox if he's talking to someone he likes. Raelynn offers to clean up, but I decline her offer. I go upstairs to change a stinky diaper, something I didn't think I would be doing at twenty-four, that's for sure. Raelynn and Jackson are cuddled on the couch, watching TV when I come back.

We watch cartoons before Raelynn declares it's bath time. Bree is fast asleep on my chest, so I show Raelynn where everything is after laying her down.

"I like her," Mom declares. "She seems like a good mother and that means she'll be a great nanny."

"Told ya."

She rolls her eyes. "I'm going ahead to bed."

I follow after her to get what I need from my room, so I won't disturb her later. Afterward, I check on Raelynn and Jackson. The bathroom door is open, showing it's empty, so I peek into Jackson's bedroom.

"I wanna go home, Momma. I don't wanna stay here. Why can't we go home?"

"This is part of Momma's new job, baby. Isn't this better than our home? You even get your own room here." *He didn't have his own room before?* "You know how Peter Pan goes on an adventure? That's what we're doing. We're on an adventure."

Jackson seems to think about this. "Is Mr. EJ Captain Hook?"

Raelynn laughs. "No, he's not. Think you'll be okay

in here by yourself?"

"I'm scared."

She crawls into bed next to him, her back facing me. "I'll be right here while you fall asleep, okay?"

He must nod because they don't talk anymore. I quietly move away to stop eavesdropping. I can't imagine how bad things might've been for her, or what it must be like to raise a kid without any help or a lot of money. Kids are expensive, and mine isn't but nine months old. With Bree down for the count, I quickly jump into the shower. Afterward, I head downstairs to turn off the lights, lock the doors, and set the alarm.

Jackson is all alone in his room, I peek into Bree's room, and then stop outside of Raelynn's. The door is cracked. I'm about to knock when I hear soft cries. Oh man. I've never been good around crying chicks. Do I knock or leave her alone? Before I can think better of it, I push her door open.

"Raelynn? You okay?"

She's lying on her side, her back facing me, and she hasn't yet changed into any pajamas. Still, I can see her quickly wipe her eyes. "I'm fine. I was tired, so I'm going to bed early."

"Okay. Well, um, I'll be across the hall in Bree's room if you need anything. Otherwise, I'll see you in the morning." I wait to see if she'll say anything, but she doesn't. "Good night, Raelynn."

"G'night, Elias."

With that, I close her door and retreat to my temporary bedroom. Bree was a surprise that entered my life. I was a carefree guy who played the sport he loved for a living. Then, all of a sudden, I'm a single dad with an unfamiliar set of responsibilities. I've never worried so much in my life. I don't know what I would've done if my mom hadn't dropped everything to come help me. I still don't know what I'm doing half the time, so I'm relieved to have Raelynn, an expert practically like my mom, around to take care of Bree when I'm not here, but to also help me out.

I fall asleep in the pink room, worried that I'm going to somehow mess my little princess up.

Something pokes my shoulder and then I hear, "Mr. EJ. Mr. EJ. Mr. EJ."

My eyes creak open to see Jackson standing next to the bed. "What's wrong?"

"Where's my momma?"

I toss my sheets aside and am surprised when Jackson takes my hand. "Her bedroom is right next to yours," I whisper as we cross the hall to her room. Raelynn is on her back, her arms above her head, and she's sound asleep.

"Momma," Jackson whispers, poking her in the ribs before I can say her name.

Her eyes fly open and she quickly sits up. I've never seen someone wake up so fast. "You okay, baby? What's wrong?" She glances between us.

"He found Bree's room by accident. He was looking for you."

"He didn't wake her, did he?" I shake my head. "I'm sorry he woke you, Elias."

I shrug. "I live with a baby. It's okay."

Jackson lets go of my hand to crawl in bed with his mom. She seems able to handle the situation, so I turn to leave. "Momma, I wanna sleep with you," I hear Jackson say. "It's too dark in that room."

"Okay, come on."

I make a mental note to find the kid a nightlight when I get the key made in the morning. Since I'm up, I peek into Bree's crib. Her eyes are open and I'm surprised she's not crying. "Hey, princess," I whisper, reaching my hand inside her crib, smiling when she grabs a finger. I pick her up and settle into a recliner that's in her room. I rock her gently until she falls back to sleep.

My life has been turned upside down. It's been hard and exhausting and more often than not, I feel like a dumbass. But it's been worth it. Bree has made it worth it.

Raelynn

BREE STAYS HOME with Elias and his mom while I take Jackson to school. I may shed a few tears on the way home because for the first time, my baby wanted to walk by himself to class. I walked him to the entrance of the school, and then he left me without a backward glance. It was almost like the first day of school all over again. I had to go inside anyway to update his files with a new home address.

When I return, Elias goes straight into showing me every nook and cranny of the house practically before having another round of discussion in the kitchen with his mother nearby with Bree.

"I won't be home until kinda late because we have a game tonight," he continues. "Lock the doors if you go to bed before I get home, but if you set the alarm, make sure you do the silent alarm. That way it won't go off when I come in and wake the kids. I have to run out and get a key made for you before I head to the rink. Is there anything you or Jackson need me to pick up? Do you want me to go ahead and set up her carseat in your car, so you don't have to do it later?"

"I don't think so, and if you want. It doesn't matter."

"I'll do it." He nods to himself. "And here's a credit card you can use in case you decide there is something you need or would like to have here."

He holds out the card, but I stare at it, flicking my gaze to see a disapproving look from his mother. "Um, that's okay. We'll be fine." It doesn't feel right to basically have my employer's credit card to use at my disposal for things for Bree or Jackson and me. It's worse that his mother watches my every move, waiting for me to mess up so she can convince him to fire me. It feels that way, at least.

"Raelynn, take it. I said I'd provide groceries for y'all. There's a road trip coming up around Thanksgiving. You'll need this. I'm not always going to be here or have time to go shopping." Reluctantly, I take it, and he adds, "You don't need to ask before you use it either, but Mom will show you where to put the receipts. Need anything else before I go?"

I think about my car, which is low on gas. I think about my phone bill, which is due today and will likely wipe my account of what money I have left. "Could I get this week's pay already?"

"Yeah, sure." He disappears upstairs and returns a minute later with a check.

I've never made so much money in one week before. I almost feel like I should argue about the amount since I'm living here rent free, utilities free, and grocery free, but I'm not. This was the amount he offered and I could definitely use the money.

"Thank you," I say softly.

"Just don't let me down." He walks over to his mother, kisses her cheek, and then leans down to kiss Bree's forehead, causing her to have that goofy baby smile. "Love you, princess." It's so sweet to watch Elias interact with his daughter. It also makes me wonder how he ended up with custody; he's yet to mention her mother. I'll have to ask about that later. I don't want to be unprepared in case someone shows up. "I'll be back shortly, Raelynn," Elias tells me before heading out the door.

With her son gone, Alice interviews me with far more questions than her son did. I answer them completely. What harm is there in telling her that Jackson and I have struggled and the only reason I'm here is because I needed a job and Elias was offering? She asks me if I'm trying to take advantage of him, but when it becomes clear that I'm not because I had no clue I could take advantage of him, she accepts that. When she asks of my past, I politely shut her down. My past is my own and has no relevance.

Alice hugs Bree in her arms. "Take good care of my granddaughter, okay? I have complete faith that you will, but I have to say it anyway."

"I will take care of her as if she's my own," I promise. Today is a big day for a couple of reasons, one of which is Alice leaves to go home.

"*I'm* also here to take care of my daughter, Ma," Elias tells her. "She'll be fine. Unless you don't trust us?"

"I trust you. That's how I'm able to leave."

It's been nice to have Alice around. She's helped me adjust to things here, learn my way around, and feel comfortable, somewhat. It's nice to know she's giving me her official stamp of approval.

Alice kisses Bree's cheeks until Elias takes matters into his own hands and takes Bree away, giving her to me.

"It's time to go, Ma. We don't want you to miss your flight."

"Fine. Fine." Alice hugs me, kisses Bree one last time, and says, "Tell Jackson I said goodbye."

"I will." He's already at school, so he's missing the goodbye session. Alice did say goodbye to him this morning, but I'll be sure to pass along the second goodbye.

Elias leaves to take his mother to the airport and I focus on a new milestone I must cross. Elias is about to leave for his first road trip with me as his nanny. I'm slightly terrified, especially since his mother is gone. To stay calm, I've been doing what I'm doing right now: sitting on the floor, playing with Bree, so I don't have to think about it.

"Hey," Elias says as he comes into the living room. "Feeling good about being on your own?"

"Yeah," I lie. I mean, I can take care of my own baby, no problem, but it's giving me serious anxiety to be left alone in someone else's house with someone else's baby and with someone else's credit card to use as I see fit.

What if I mess up? What if I do something that's not up to his standards? I don't feel like I know Elias well enough to know boundaries yet.

"Good. I, uh..."

At the sound of Elias sounding nervous, I glance up. "Is something wrong? Did I do something?"

"No," he quickly says. "I feel like a jackass, but I'm not sure what's the polite way to tell my nanny to give me my baby and sort of leave me alone until I have to leave."

I laugh. "You say, 'Raelynn, I'm about to leave for a few days and I'd really like to spend some time with my daughter before I go. Shoo, please.'" I stand, picking Bree up as I go, and hand her to him. "There you go. I'll be in my room."

Elias's smile slowly disappears. "You don't have to hole up in your room."

"I don't mind," I say, meaning it. "Pretend I'm not even here." I walk away before he can say anything else.

This is another thing I haven't figured out yet. When and how to give him space. I live here, but I'm also an employee. Maybe I'm overthinking it, but I don't want him to feel like I'm constantly intruding on his space or on his time with his daughter, like I almost accidentally did just now. That's one reason why the other night, when he texted me after a game, mentioning how the guys were going to a bar and he was debating going with them, I told him he should go. The kids were asleep. Why should he rush home? To keep me company? Ha.

I need to figure out a game plan to combat this. This, as in, a way to make sure he's free to do as he wishes in his own home, and even out of it. I guess Jackson and I could always hang out in our rooms or outside when he's home. We'd always be out of his way if we did that.

Despite my nerves and uncertainties, this job has been such a blessing. I've been able to do some schoolwork when I manage to snag some free time. Thankfully, Elias has internet, so I don't have to go to the library to get my work done. I've been slowly working through earning a degree online. I've been lucky to receive grants through financial aid to pay for the expenses. I normally do my work when Elias has a game or once everyone has gone to bed.

I've been getting my baby fill, too. Every now and then, I'd wish I could find someone only to give Jackson a little brother or sister. He's such a shy kid who sticks to himself. Maybe a sibling would help. I was an only child and I hope that one day I can give Jackson siblings. One day when I'm better off financially, which means it'll be a long time before I can entertain the idea. Well, I'd need a man, too, but that's not the point.

This is the only drawback to a job like this. I love babies. Jackson was a good baby. Then again, I was so in love with him, he could've cried twenty hours out of the day and I would have thought he was a good baby. Bree is also a good baby. She loves to interact and play. She naps during the day. She cries and makes a fuss when she wants something. She's crawling up a storm and loves for us to walk around the house together. She's adorable.

After awhile, Elias calls my name because it's time for him to leave. He's been great, too. It's been sweet to watch him with Bree, but also because my second day here? When he was out getting a spare key made for me, he bought Jackson a nightlight. He refused to let me pay him back for it, but it was sweet that he decided to do that for Jackson.

As he hands Bree to me and I say, "Say bye bye to DaDa," I see the nerves on his face for the first time. That's not reassuring in the least, especially when Bree hiccups and whines a little, reaching for him. She knows what bye bye means. She also knows who DaDa is.

"Take care of my princess, please," he says softly with his eyes on her.

"I promise I will."

"If she says a coherent word that's not DaDa, don't tell me." At that, I laugh and Elias looks at me. "Okay, tell me anyway." He smiles easily and kisses her forehead once again. "I'll see you soon. Call me if you need me."

"Go," I whisper. He's wasting time unnecessarily. Elias nods and then he's gone.

Bree and I play the day away until it's time for her afternoon nap. She wakes up just in time for us to leave to pick Jackson up for school. Jackson has settled in okay; he's taken a great interest in hockey all of a sudden. We watched a game on TV last night for the first time, but saw a player get hurt. Not so much fun. However, I've never seen Jackson take so much interest in something before. He keeps asking me about things, but I don't know anything about the game.

"Momma, Bree is looking at me," he says from the backseat on the way home. He hasn't quite gotten used to her yet.

"She's curious about you. Why don't you talk to her? Or sing to her?"

Jackson decides to talk. He does so for a few minutes, but then asks, "Is Bree really a princess? She doesn't look like a princess and Mr. EJ calls her princess."

I smile and say, "She's his princess. Like how you're my baby."

"So, she's not *really* a princess?" he asks, not letting it go as I pull into the driveway.

"It doesn't really matter."

"Definitely not a princess," he mutters. "Where's Mr. EJ?" he asks once we're inside and it's clear we're home alone.

"Mr. EJ is on a road trip. The team goes to other cities to play games."

"Can we watch the games?" he asks hopefully.

"Maybe."

Later that night, my phone vibrates with a video call from Elias. Before I answer, I pick Bree up from where she's playing on the floor and say, "Want to talk to Da-Da?" Her face lights up with a smile, and I'm pretty sure it's only because I said DaDa. I swipe across on my phone and hold it away from us.

Bree is looking at me with her smile, patting my chest, until she hears Elias say, "There's my princess." Her head swivels toward the phone and she squeals.

Jackson leans over from next to me, his eyes filling the screen. "Hey, Mr. EJ."

Elias laughs. "Hey, J-man. Did you have a good day at school?" My heart warms a little at him entertaining Jackson, even though he only called to see his little girl. It's already sweet that he has a nickname for my son, too.

A foul smell tickles my nose as Jackson answers him. "Jackson, hold my phone for a second, and you don't have to hold it so close to your face." I peek into Bree's diaper and find the source. "Talk to Mr. EJ. Elias, I'm changing her diaper real quick and then she's all yours, I promise."

"No rush," he says.

Bree is pretty easy to change. She likes to play with her feet. As long as you talk or sing to her, she's happy and lets me clean her up and change diapers rather quickly. Jackson has gone quiet on Elias by the time I return, leaving him to do all the talking. Sometimes, he talks to him just fine. Others? He reverts to being shy.

"Thanks, baby," I say, kissing the top of his head. Jackson doesn't waste a second saying goodbye to Elias and handing the phone back to me. "No coherent words so far," I tell him, causing him to smile.

"Good. How'd today go?"

"Just like every other day," I speak over Bree who wants to talk just as much in her gibberish. Elias doesn't seem to know who to focus on: me or her. I decide to be quiet and let her talk, making sure I smile and laugh when she seems to want a reaction.

"She really likes you," he says quietly, bringing my gaze back to my phone. "She cried a little when you left the room today; that was when I knew. She doesn't do that for just anyone."

I can't tell if he's happy about this or not, so I'm not sure what I should say. "I really like her, too," is what I settle on.

He talks to her for a little bit before it's time for me to lay her down for the night. He doesn't hang up, though. Oh, no. I have to take her upstairs, place her in her crib, and then let Elias say goodnight. She cries as I walk out of the room and Elias frowns.

"I always hate when she does that, even though I know she'll stop within a minute or so. It took my mom a long time to convince me not to stay by her side all night."

"It's nice that you had a good support system to help you learn the ropes." It took forever to become semi-confident in my actions as Jackson's parent because I was so young and didn't have a clue as to what I was doing. A question seems to be on the tip of Elias's tongue, but I don't want to talk about me or my past. "I'll let you go. I need to get Jackson ready to wind down for the night as well and tidy up the house."

Elias nods and says goodnight, hanging up a moment later. I take a deep breath and peer into Bree's room. She's still lying down. I've caught her standing up a few times after I've walked out. I'll check on her later to see if she's asleep.

The next day, Jackson watches cartoons while Bree sits on my hip. She's been a bit fussy, so I've been dancing around the house with her, singing, much to Jackson's annoyance. Bree has loved it, though. There's a knock on the door and I freeze, mid-step. I should have no guests with Elias gone. What if it's her mother? I still don't know if she may pop up at some point. Damn it, I should've asked Elias!

With a deep breath, I slowly walk over to the door and open it. My eyes nearly pop out of my head. Never thought it would be this guy. "Brayden, right?" The man from the quilt shop. Elias told me his name is Brayden. He's one of his teammates and Deanna is his girlfriend.

"Yeah. Sorry to drop by like this, but I needed to get out of the house. Can I hang here for a while?"

"Um." Why on earth would he want to do that? Why is he even here? Then, it hits me. He was the guy who was injured in the game Jackson and I watched. I glance over my shoulder at Jackson, who watches with interest with his chin resting on the top of the back of the couch. This guy was nice to me. He's friends with Elias. "Sure," I say, not totally confident in this answer.

"You can say no, you know. I just wanted to see Bree, but if you're not comfortable or whatever..."

"No, that's okay. Come in." I won't take it back now. I step aside and Brayden doesn't give me a chance to change my mind again.

"Hey, Jackson," he says as I close the door.

He knows my son's name? Jackson looks as surprised as I feel. Elias probably told him.

"This is Mr. Brayden, Jackson. He's friends with Mr. EJ." Jackson, my shy, shy boy. He turns around and focuses on the TV. "Sorry. He's shy around new people." That's what I always say. "Did you want to hold her?"

"Yes, please." He holds his hands out for Bree and I let him take her, watching as he walks into the living room as if he's been here before.

For a moment, I worry if this is the right decision. Would Elias want him over here while he's not here? Would he want him to play with Bree? Does Elias know he's here? But then, I remind myself that this guy helped me get this job, so Elias has to trust him.

"Do you mind if I catch up on some chores?" Might as well take advantage of the unexpected babysitter.

"No, go ahead," he says. "I'll find you if we need anything."

"Thanks." I glance down at Jackson. "I'll be in the

kitchen, baby." He doesn't look up at me. "Mr. Brayden plays hockey with Mr. EJ, so you'll be fine," I add, hoping that relaxes him. He finally glances at Brayden when I say that.

Feeling better about things, I leave the three of them to clean up the house. I scrub and clean the kitchen until it's sparkling before I return the living room to check on my guest.

"How is it going in here?" I ask.

"Is there a place I can lie down for a minute?"

He wants to lie down? I nod, hoping I didn't look too surprised. Brayden and Bree are behind me as we walk upstairs. "You can lie in here if you want," I say as he lays Bree down in her crib. "But if you'd rather have a bigger bed, you can have your pick of Elias's or Jackson's, I guess." I'm certainly not offering mine, even if he does seem nice enough.

Brayden seems confused for a moment, which worries me, but then he says, "I'll lie in here. I'll be out of here soon."

"Let me know if you need anything."

The moment he nods, I leave the room, pulling the door until it's almost closed. I could use a break for a while, so I go sit with Jackson. He and Brayden apparently talked about hockey. Jackson shows me what he's learned, which is mostly what the referee's signals mean.

He, of course, wants to watch the hockey game tonight and I don't think I can deny him. He won't be able to stay up for all of it, but he can watch some of it. The game comes on and I keep glancing at the clock. Where is Brayden? It's getting kind of late. I wait and I wait, but when eight thirty rolls around, I walk upstairs.

He's lying on the bed with a pillow over his head. Oh, man. I have to wake him up. He probably wants to go home. With a deep breath, I shake his shoulder. "Brayden? Brayden?" He lifts the pillow and winces immediately. "I'm sorry to wake you, but it's getting kind of late and I thought you might want to wake up."

"What time is it?" he grumbles.

"Eight thirty."

"I'm sorry."

He rubs his forehead before standing and sighing. When he has to blindly reach out for the wall to steady himself, I worry about what happens if I have to support him. This is a big, tall man. I am not even average height for a woman. He'd probably crush me if I had to help him down the stairs. He'd lose his footing and then we'd fall and I'd die either from the fall or him landing on me.

"Are you okay?" I ask.

"Yeah." He pats his pockets and then pulls out a phone. "I'm going to make a phone call."

He seems to be fine. Bree stands in her crib, so I pick her up to take her with me downstairs. She's not used to people in and out of her room and talking, or to going to sleep as early as she did. Tonight will be a long one with her; I just have a feeling.

I reclaim my seat next to Jackson on the couch and Bree pulls on my hair. It's her favorite thing to do. She doesn't really pull too hard. She likes to tug while her fingers try to make knots form in my hair.

Brayden's footsteps are heavy down the stairs. "Someone's coming to pick me up," he says. I nod as he takes a seat in the chair, looking absolutely miserable. He leaves with a quick thanks and a see you later once he sees his ride is here.

With him gone, I focus on getting Bree back to bed. With Elias gone for a few days and Jackson out of school until next Monday due to Thanksgiving, my plan is to take him shopping. He's in desperate need of new clothes and now, I have some money to buy him some. It'll be interesting to shop with both him and Bree, but I'm sure I'll manage just fine.

EJ

WE'RE IN MONTRÉAL, our second stop on this road trip, and it's the day before Thanksgiving. Some of the guys are getting together to eat, but I'm meeting with an old buddy of mine, Derek Novak. He's also a professional hockey player and we always meet up if we have time whenever one of us is in the other's town. We played hockey together when we were younger and he's one of my best friends. Whenever we get together, we always seem to pick up where we left off.

"You get a nanny yet?" he asks as he slides into the booth.

"You're late."

He shrugs. "It's just you, so it doesn't matter. Please tell me that your ma isn't still taking care of your kid."

"I have a nanny."

"Since when?" he asks in disbelief.

"About a week."

His eyes narrow. "I've talked to you since then. Why didn't you tell me?" I shrug, and he ignores it. "Is she good? Is she taking care of the baby like she should?"

I glare at him. "For someone who self-appointed himself as my baby's godfather, 'the baby' is a girl and she has a name."

Derek rolls his eyes. He refers to Bree as *the baby* all the time just to piss me off. "Fine. Is she taking care of Bree? How is she?"

Before I can answer, the waiter walks up to take our drink orders. My phone buzzes with a text as he walks away. It's a selfie of Bree and Raelynn with a message that she wants to talk to me if I'm not busy. I tap the picture and turn it to Derek.

"She looks fine, doesn't she?"

He snatches it from my hand to hold it closer to his face. "Who the fuck is holding the baby?"

"My nanny, Raelynn."

Derek's gaze lifts to meet mine. "This woman?" His eyes drop again. "This 'hot as hell, I'd totally fuck her in a heartbeat woman' is your *nanny*?"

My jaw clenches, my eyes narrow, and I wish I could punch him. "Don't talk about her like that."

He looks at me again. "When you said nanny, I expected someone like your mom. Middle-aged, maybe older, motherly, but not someone who when you see her, she gives you an instant hard-on. No wonder you didn't tell me about her. You have the hots for your nanny, don't you, EJ?"

I yank my phone from his hand. "*No*," I snap with too much denial. "She's just a woman taking care of my princess." I glance down at the photo, but somehow, it's trying to start a video call with her. Derek opens his mouth, but I hold up my hand as she answers.

"Hey, Elias," Raelynn says. "Hold on." Her face disappears and now I see the ceiling. *Elias?* Derek mouths, trying not to laugh. "No no, Bree," I hear her say. "Come on. You can look at your DaDa while I talk to him."

I frown as Derek slides out of his side of the booth and moves next to me, so he can view the screen, but stay out of sight.

"Is everything okay?" Raelynn asks, bringing my eyes back to the phone. "Where are you?"

"In a restaurant. Is everything okay there?" Bree tries to grab her phone, so I add, "Hey, princess." She gives me a big, goofy grin.

"Yeah. I, ah, just wanted to let you know that Brayden stopped by last night. He said he just wanted to see Bree. He hung out for a bit, fell asleep, and then left. I felt like maybe you'd want to know he stopped by."

"Okay. That's fine." Also might explain the text I got as I was walking into the restaurant. He wanted to know if she would be alone for Thanksgiving and if so, could he have her number so he could invite her over to his house. "He might text you and invite you to his house for Thanksgiving. You should go."

Her eyes widen a little. "Oh, okay. Well, you should be eating or whatever. If you want to talk to Bree later, call me back." She pauses and then adds with a slight smile,

"Still no coherent words."

I laugh a little. "Good to know. She's probably saving them for when I come home."

Bree reaches for the phone again. Raelynn isn't fast enough and Bree disconnects the call. Derek moves back to his side of the booth. He eyes the menu and doesn't say a word. That's bad. So, so bad that he isn't talking yet. The waiter returns with our drinks and takes Derek's order. I decide to order the same thing as him since I didn't really look over the menu that well.

"How did you even find her?" he eventually asks.

"She was looking for a job, and she went into Brayden Hayes's girlfriend's workplace. He was there and got her an interview with me. She's just a twenty-two-year-old single mom who happens to be my nanny."

"Wait. She has a kid?"

"A five-year-old," I say with a nod. "It's just the two of them."

He whistles quietly. "Well, that puts a spin on things." He folds his arms and leans forward on the table. "Are you seriously trying to tell me that you don't find her attractive? I mean, you've seen what she looks like, right? She's even your type."

"I don't have a type," I quickly dismiss.

"She has brown hair, green eyes, and do I really need to go into detail about her rack? She'd be perfect for you looks-wise if she's short." At that, I look down at the napkin and fiddle with it. "Holy shit. She's short!" Derek laughs.

"Anyone is short compared to me." Not anyone, but most women. I'm six feet two inches. Raelynn's lucky if she's five foot four, if I had to guess. And I really don't

41

have a type. Brown hair is common. The green eyes thing has been a total coincidence and it hasn't happened every time. I think back on girls I've seen before. He *may* have me on the short girl thing. Not saying I'll dismiss a girl based on height, but I don't know. He's fucking with my head now. Bree's mom was average height, so he can suck on that.

"You're in denial," he says with a chuckle.

"Leave it alone, Derek. Nothing's happening. Nothing's going to happen. I need her as my nanny more than I need to..." My voice trails off as I struggle with what to say.

"More than you need to fuck her or have a relationship with her?"

"Yeah, whatever. What are you doing for Christmas?" I ask. Sometimes, he'll spend it with my family.

"What are you doing? Is Christmas at your place or Ma's?" Yeah, he's been around too much since he calls my mom Ma like I do. "Is Raelynn going to be there?" he asks in a sugary voice.

"I don't know on all accounts. Ma will probably want us to go there, but I don't know if I want to fly with Bree yet, especially over a holiday." That just sounds horrible. If I have time off during the season, why would I want to spend any of it in an airport or on a plane? Especially considering it's just a few days, such a short time period, and I don't know how Bree will be on a plane. I haven't taken her anywhere yet. "Christmas will be at my house," I decide right then. "You're more than welcome to come and sleep in Bree's room or on the couch."

"Thanks. I'll book my tickets soon."

I ask him if he's seeing anyone, getting the conversation far away from Raelynn. Talking to him, though, has unfortunately made me realize I need to start thinking about Christmas. This will be Bree's first Christmas. I don't want to go too crazy, considering she'll be ten months old by then and let's face it, she won't know what the hell is going on, but there's a bit of a weight on my shoulders. If I want to start any traditions with her, this is the year to start, especially if later, I want to be able to say, "I've been doing this since you were a baby!"

I wonder what traditions, if any, Raelynn has with Jackson. The only one Mom and Dad really had with me was buying an ornament for me every year. That'll be a good one to pass down. There's still time to think about it, though. The bigger issue is that it looks as if I'll have a full house for a few days in a month. I'm actually looking forward to it.

When someone is out of the game, the lack of his presence can be felt by everyone, especially when it's a prominent person like Brayden. He may not be the most talkative guy and he can be a bit rough on the surface, but he has a confident, reassuring presence nonetheless. People look up to him. They listen to him. They follow his lead. With him at home, dealing with a concussion, Scotty is the one who seems to make the best attempt at filling his shoes.

Once we skate onto the ice, it doesn't take long to feel and see that our start will be another shaky one since losing Brayden. Shaky starts aren't fun, but it's nothing to be concerned about right now. We just need to get our minds focused, get our legs going, and tally a few goals. We can repeat what we did the last game. Start on the wobbly side, but finish strong and with a win.

They score first and second. Both times, the puck seemingly makes an easy path past Liam 'Savage' Irving, our goalie in net. The rest of the first period is scoreless, but there's a lot of back and forth up and down the ice as possession of the puck changes hands from their team to ours.

The second period starts off much better. The Kessy twins are on the ice with Sergey Orlovsky, the trio of forwards who have been working well together lately; they rush down the ice. Serge has the puck, but there's a defenseman on his heels, so he passes it to Collin, who is in the middle of the ice. He slaps it to his brother and from his place along the boards, he slaps the puck toward the goalie with a quick release.

The entire bench holds their breath for a moment.

Waiting.

We exhale as we stand, fist bumping and cheering for Thing Two's goal. We're on the board and now only one goal behind.

The next chance comes with about five minutes left in the period. I just swiped the puck from a player and send it gliding along the boards and behind the net, right to where Nathan 'Donny' O'Donnell waits to scoop it up. The goalie squares up to him, but Donny shoots and the puck wiggles its way between the post and his shoulder, knocking into the back of the net.

Tie game.

The third period seems to be the most intense. Everyone wants to score the next goal, to take the lead, and maybe even have that goal be the one to secure the win by the time the seconds count down to end the game. Ian 'Bruiser' Rhett draws a penalty. While one of their players sits in the sin bin, Scotty charges down the ice with the puck after gaining it from the face-off. He sends it right through the five-hole.

And not another goal is scored.

Rebels win.

I'm finally home. It's late and the house is quiet, except for my footsteps. I walk up the steps and peek into Jackson's room first. He's sprawled out on his stomach, sleeping soundly. Across the hall, my princess has her arms up above her head and her legs stretched out as she sleeps. She's too fucking cute. Lastly, I walk to Raelynn's room. The door is halfway closed, but a light is on.

"Hey," I say, expecting her to be awake when I push the door open.

She's not.

She lies on her stomach, her cheek is smushed against an open book, and a laptop sits next to her. What is she doing? Another book sits by the one she's using as her pillow and I pick it up. It's a textbook. Why would she have a textbook? Raelynn hasn't mentioned being in school. Then again, Raelynn doesn't talk much about herself.

I set the book on the dresser and then the laptop, closing it. I gently shake her shoulder, remembering how easily she wakes up.

Raelynn rolls over and squints at me. "Elias?"

"Hey. I figured you may want to use a real pillow."

She glances down at her textbook. "Oh. Yeah. Thanks." Raelynn closes it and I take it from her so she doesn't have to get up to put it on the dresser with the other one. She sits up, criss-crosses her legs, and grabs a pillow to hide the fact she's braless. "Good trip?"

"Yeah." I sit on the edge of the bed, briefly wonder if I'm crossing a boundary, and then ask, "Are you in school?"

Raelynn grabs the hem of the pillowcase and twists it around her fingers. "Yep. I've been working on a business degree for practically forever. I don't know what I'll do with it, but at least I'll have a degree." She rubs her eyes. "What time is it anyway?" There she goes again. She gave me more than I was expecting, which was a simple yep, but it didn't take long before she deflected the subject away from her.

"Late enough. Go back to sleep; I was just checking in on everyone." I stand and walk to the door. "Oh." I turn around to face her. "My parents, maybe my sister, and a friend of mine are coming here for Christmas during my time off. I only have a few days, but they'll be here. If it's okay with you, I thought Jackson could stay in here with you, so my parents could sleep in his room. Derek will sleep on the couch, maybe, so my sister can sleep in Bree's room. I think that'll work. What's the matter?" I ask since she's frowning, but the moment I ask, it disappears.

"Nothing. Your parents can have my room. Derek or your sister can have Jackson's. We won't be here."

"You won't?" I ask with surprise. Where is she going? Before I can ask, she speaks again.

"I think I'll see about visiting a very old friend of mine who I haven't seen since I left home." She twirls a strand of her hair. "Yeah, we'll do that."

"Oh, okay. Well, you're more than welcome to stay here with us."

Her hand drops from her hair as she nods. "Thanks for letting me know. We should get some sleep. G'night, Elias."

"Yeah, good night, Raelynn." I leave her room and cross the hall to mine. Well, I learned a few things about Raelynn tonight. She's earning a degree. There's a possibility she isn't from here if she left home, as she said. And I don't think she likes the idea of me being home for Christmas.

That bugs me a hell of a lot more than it should.

Raelynn

The next morning, I find out when Elias's Christmas break is and book a hotel room for Jackson and me during that time. The idea of being here during the holiday and intruding on his family time nearly made me sick to my stomach when he told me about it. I didn't even know he had a sister because he hadn't mentioned her. Just like I need to ask about Bree's mom, but for some reason, I haven't done that yet.

I felt horrible wasting my money on a hotel room, too, but I can't imagine being here during that time. It was a bit awkward spending Thanksgiving with his teammate. Nice, but I felt out of place. I can only imagine how much worse it will be if it's a holiday with Elias and his family.

"Hey, Raelynn?"

I look up at a nervous-looking Elias and am immediately on guard. "Yeah?"

His mouth opens and closes. "I want to ask you something, but I don't know how without sounding rude."

"Oh. Just ask then."

"Are those all the toys Jackson has?"

My cheeks flush with embarrassment. Thankfully, I've always been tan enough that it's hard to tell when they're flush. "Yep," I say, popping the p like usual and trying to sound nonchalant. "He lost a few during the move, but we normally play pretend or build a fort or read books." Damn it. Maybe I should've bought Jackson some more toys while Elias was on his road trip, but I didn't think about it. I went with what he needed.

I want to save up as much money as I can with what Elias pays me. Who knows when I might lose this job or need that money for a rainy day. My current rainy day fund is nonexistent, so it definitely needs to be built back up. Jackson hasn't even asked for anything lately. Have I been too distracted by Bree that I've neglected him somehow?

"It's fine, Raelynn," Elias says as if he can read the panic on my face. "Can I pick him up from school today?"

"Why? No." I shake my head before he can tell me why he wants to do this. "He won't know to look for you and it might freak him out."

"Like it's freaking you out right now," he lightly teases me. "I just want to pick him up and take him somewhere. You and Bree can come."

"Where do you think you're taking my son?" My

heart beats wildly in my chest as if he told me he planned to kidnap him. I'm officially crazy.

Before Elias can answer, the doorbell chimes a sound throughout the house. He stands and goes to answer it, Bree on his hip.

"Is Raelynn here?"

My body freezes at that voice. It's older, manlier, but it sounds like...no. It can't be.

"Raelynn?" Elias calls.

I don't move. It can't be. How did he find me? What would he want?

"One second." Footsteps sound as Elias walks into the living room and crouches in front of me. "Raelynn? What's wrong?"

"I think...it sounded like Jackson's father," I whisper.

His eyes widen. "Is this bad?"

I nod. "I haven't seen him since I told him I was pregnant. I don't know how he found me either. I never told anyone where I planned to go."

Elias's face hardens. He holds out his hand. "Come on. Let's see what he wants."

Reluctantly, I take his hand and he pulls me up to stand. He leads me to the still-open door, never letting go of my hand. I squeeze the life out of it and wish I could hide behind him, much like how Jackson likes to hide behind me, when I see Henry. He looks practically the same, but all those boyish features have molded into a grown-up, manly version.

"How'd you find me?"

"I can't come in?" he asks.

"Answer her question," Elias demands.

Henry glances between the two of us and our joined

hands. I don't care what he thinks. I just want to know what he wants. "I hired a private investigator." He leaves it at that. "I want to talk to you, Rae." I flinch at hearing him shorten my name like he used to. "Can I come in?"

I step aside and Elias follows suit. Henry steps into the house, going no further than he has to, waiting for me to lead him in a certain direction, but I'd rather send him back out the door. Elias taps the door closed with his foot since I have no plans of letting go of his hand. He walks into the kitchen.

"Sit." He motions to the dining table and looks down at me. "I'm going to lay her down for her nap," he says. "Do you want me to come back?"

Do I want the surprising strength he gives me to not panic and collapse at having my ex-boyfriend show up or do I want privacy?

I pick strength and nod. I let go of his hand and sit at the table.

"So, we have a boy," Henry starts. "Jackson Alan Woods."

I glare at him. "How do you know that?"

"Birth records, Rae."

Of fucking course. "Don't call me that," I snap. "What are you doing here, Henry?"

"I live here now."

That causes me to stand and pace and breathe a little faster. Why would he live here? His family and their fortune are back home in Virginia. I don't need to think like that. Virginia isn't home anymore. North Carolina is.

"I want to be in my son's life."

I grab the counter, ready to faint. My vision comes and goes for a few seconds. He can't be serious. Jackson doesn't even know he has a father! This is bad. So, so bad. I can't let it happen.

"Raelynn?"

Elias's voice snaps me out of my panic and jump-starts my rage. I whirl around to face Henry, but Elias is in my way. I sidestep him. "He is *my* son. Not yours. Not ours. No one's but *mine*. I gave birth to him in a hospital without any family or friends. I left home with only him. I raised him by. My. Self! Don't you dare show up five years later and tell me you want to be in *your* son's life! It's not happening, Henry Davenport! Never. Not even over my dead body. Get the fuck out of this house and don't you dare come back."

Henry infuriates me further when he calmly folds his arms over his chest. "I've been here for six months, Rae."

"Call me that again and I'll slap you," I warn him. Elias stands behind me and attempts to calm me by rubbing my arms.

"Right. Anyway, I've been here for six months, settling in, getting a job, and making this place my new home. All so when I finally come to talk to you, you'd give me a chance." I scoff, but he continues to talk. "I'm not going anywhere, Raelynn. I'm not sixteen anymore. I'm not the same person. I'll do this however you want to do it, as long as I can be in his life. Please."

"No."

His jaw nearly pops out of place he's clenching it so hard. "No because of how you feel toward me or because you don't think I could be a good father to him?"

"Both."

"Raelynn—"

"I'm not changing my mind," I interrupt. "Jackson

doesn't know he has a father. You can't just turn his world upside down. You don't know what he's like; I do. And I wonder why that is!"

"Okay." Elias comes around and steps in front of me. "Take a deep breath. You keep yelling and you'll wake Bree up."

My shoulders slump and I feel a little guilty.

"What's the situation here anyway? What are you doing here, Rae?"

That's it! I dodge around Elias and raise my hand, but an arm is around my waist, lifting me into the air and away from Henry before I can hit him.

"Raelynn," Henry corrects. "Sorry. Old habit." He doesn't sound sincere, though.

"She's my nanny," Elias answers. "Get your phone out," he adds to him. He's still holding me, making me feel like a toddler since he's obviously keeping me from going somewhere and my feet can't touch the ground. "Here's my number." My mouth drops in outrage when Elias spouts off his number. Why does he need that? "Text me so we'll have your number and get out of my house before I unleash her on you."

"What are you doing?" I ask him. "We don't need his number."

"Be quiet," he orders me.

I can't believe this! Henry nods to Elias, gets up, and leaves. The moment the door closes behind him, Elias sets me on my feet again.

"Okay, you need to tell me the full story."

"Excuse me? This isn't any of your business."

Elias stands up straighter to tower over me more than he already does. He holds up one finger. "He came to my house." Another finger. "You asked me to come back down here instead of giving you privacy." And another. "You said it's always been you and Jackson. Sounds like it's time you've added some friends. We already trust each other because otherwise, you wouldn't be here. Talk to me."

He may trust me, but I don't know if I trust him as much or if I even trust myself all that much. With a sigh, I move to sit at the table and Elias follows. I don't have much choice.

"I was sixteen when I got pregnant. My parents immediately disowned me. They were pissed that I was pregnant and that he was the one who knocked me up. My family thought his family had no morals because they didn't go to church every Sunday. My parents told me to go live with them and they could help me since they're well off. Well, Henry freaked and bailed on me. I was stuck with my parents, who gave me hell every day, until I gave birth the day after my seventeenth birthday. I was at the hospital by myself."

I stop and shake my head as if that could rid the memories. "I was able to stay with a friend for two months and then I left to come here. My parents don't know their grandchild is a boy or what his name is or where I live. I haven't spoken to them in five years. Same went for Henry. Aside from that brief time at a friend's house, where I basically just had a place to stay, I've been on my own. No one has reached out. No one has popped into my life."

"Until now," Elias says.

"Exactly. And I'm sorry, but he's not getting anywhere near Jackson. He can't appear out of the blue five years into his life and demand I let him into it. What if this freaks Jackson out? How would I even explain it? What if he tries to take Jackson from me? What if he's terrible? He doesn't deserve it." My eyes water and I quickly wipe away an escaped tear.

Elias rubs his jaw with the back of his fingers while he thinks. "What if he's a good father? What kind of impact would it have on Jackson to have another parent in his life?"

"Are you saying I'm not enough for him?"

"Not at all," he quickly says. "I want to play devil's advocate. Like, what are you going to say when Jackson does start asking about his father? What if when he's older, he wants to get to know his father and he finds out he could've known him all along, but he didn't because you didn't want him to? Especially if it turns out that Henry is a decent guy now. I think you're too lost in your panic over him showing up to make a decision either way. If you want me to watch Jackson for you to get to know who he is now before he meets Jackson, I'll do that for you, too."

"I can't ask you to do that," I immediately object.

"You aren't. I'm offering. We're friends now, Raelynn. Remember that." He glances at his watch. "Why don't you stay here with Bree? I'll pick Jackson up and take him to the rink. I want to take him skating."

"He doesn't know how."

Elias rolls his eyes. "He doesn't need to know. He'll be with me. I can help him and get him going. He seems to love hockey, so he'll be thrilled about this. You can stay here and let everything sink in."

I want to say no so badly. It's stupid and crazy. It's not because he's essentially wanting to do something for Jackson and me, but because after seeing Henry, I don't want Jackson with anyone but me. I nod, though. I'd feel so guilty if I was the reason Jackson didn't get the chance to skate when he does seem so interested.

Elias's grin is bright, as if I just made his day. He looks ridiculously handsome when he smiles like that. He stands, grabs my hand, and squeezes. "It'll be okay, Raelynn."

"Thanks."

I tell him where Jackson's school is, where the kindergarteners stand, but that maybe he should park and go get Jackson. Elias could always tell one of the many teachers who he's picking up, but I'd feel better if he did it my way. He leaves to pick Jackson up before I can change my mind about staying behind.

If Elias wants to be friends now, then I need to learn how to do a few things. Like trust him more. Trust myself more. Figure out how to stop panicking because Jackson's and my world is expanding. That's a good thing, and I need to remember that. Well, it may not be because things could go wrong and we could get hurt, but there's only one way to find out.

But what am I going to do about Henry?

I used to wonder what it would be like to have him in our lives, but it was difficult to picture. How could the Henry I loved in high school be the same person who would walk away from me and our baby? Anytime I pictured those scenarios, I saw the Henry who walked away, not the Henry I fell in love with. The fact that he's here, five years later, and seemingly wants something to do with Jackson blows my mind.

What changed his mind? How are his parents reacting? They were as unhappy as mine when they found out, and I'm certain they played a part in Henry acting as if I didn't exist anymore. Does Henry really plan to stay here in North Carolina, doing whatever it is he does now, so he can be in Jackson's life? How will all of this work?

How the fuck am I going to tell Jackson about Henry? I never told him he didn't have a father, but I didn't exactly tell him he had one either. It's been the two of us and Jackson hasn't asked why he doesn't have a dad around, so I've been able to avoid that topic. Until now. Thanks, Henry. And poor Jackson is so leery and shy around new people, he may not take this well at all. Hell, I'm not. He probably gets this crap from me.

My world has been closed off for so long. Things have been terrifying at times while I struggled to make things work. And now? Now, I have to open up. Be willing to trust others. Climb over the walls I built myself. I have to do it for Jackson. If Henry is serious and can be a good father to him, then I can't be the one to stand in the way of that.

But I'm still not sure where my hunky, handsome boss fits into this. Maybe we shouldn't be friends. There needs to be a clearly defined line because I can't lose this job, especially now that Henry is back in the picture. I'm already failing at this whole trust others, opening up, and letting go of my fears thing.

Bree giggles. "Oh, Bree," I say as she looks up at me. We've been walking laps around the couch together ever since she woke up. She loves to walk, though she hasn't quite conquered it on her own yet. "What am I going to do?"

EJ

WHEN JACKSON SEES me walking toward him, he frowns. That's not exactly the reaction I'm hoping for.

"Hey, J-man. I get to pick you up from school today." I nod to one of the teachers standing around and look back down at Jackson.

"Where's my momma?"

"At home with Bree."

"Why didn't she come? She always picks me up from school." Jackson peers around the other kids to look at the line of cars. "Are you sure she's not coming?"

Raelynn wasn't kidding. You can't just throw his

world upside down, and I think that's what I'm doing right now. He's like Raelynn. He's so used to it being the two of them that it freaks him out when something changes.

"She's not, but only because I want to take you somewhere. It's a surprise," I say, hoping it'll entice him. I hold out my hand, which he takes. Thankfully. One of the teachers eyeballs me like I'm about to kidnap him in front of everyone.

"A surprise?" he questions. "Does Momma know? She said you could?"

"Of course."

"But why isn't she here too?" Jackson sounds seriously worried now, and that worries me. I get him into the booster seat I bought for him earlier today, so I could have one in my car.

"We're having a guys afternoon. Here." I pull my phone out and dial Raelynn. "Why don't you talk to your mom and see for yourself while I drive?"

He takes the phone and holds it to his ear, but when Raelynn doesn't answer, Jackson panics. "She didn't answer! If someone at school calls my momma, she always answers."

"She's probably playing with Bree or changing a dirty diaper. Try again." I tell him where to push and he calls until she answers, three calls later.

"Why didn't you pick me up from school?" he demands when she answers. She most likely explains what I told him and I hear him ask, "Why didn't you answer your phone?" His bossiness makes me smile, though I hate the little guy was worried. "Okay," he says. Then, he grumbles, "Yeah, you can tell her I said hey." Just like that, he's back to being totally fine. "Do you know what the surprise is?"

He talks to Raelynn for a few more minutes before they hang up. Seeing him panic a little just because I picked him up instead of his mom does make me worry about how he'll react with a new person entering his life on a possibly permanent basis. He seemed to transition okay to living with me, but maybe that was because he recognized me from when we visited the school and he's been curious about hockey.

"What's this place?" Jackson asks me as I pull into a parking space.

I put the car in park and twist to look at him. "How would you like to do a little skating with me today?"

His eyes widen to the size of saucers. "Like, on ice? Like you do? I can do that? Momma said I could?" The hope in his voice is unbelievable. He wants this so badly.

"Yep."

Jackson doesn't wait for me to say another word. He makes a go at unbuckling himself, causing me to laugh and get out of the car to help him. He skips and hops and jumps next to me as we walk inside. We have a little while before any classes start, so the place is mostly quiet at the moment. I get Jackson a pair of rental skates, put them on him, and then put on my own.

He listens attentively, nods his head, and pays close attention to everything we do as I instruct him on what to do. His hands squeeze my fingers for fear of falling, but he doesn't hesitate at all. He could totally be a little hockey player in the making. What seals it for me is when he glances up at me. Pure wonder, fascination, and excitement shine through his eyes.

"Can we do this again, Mr. EJ?" he asks before we're

even done.

"If you want, J-man, absolutely. You're doing really great."

"Can I let go?" His hands tighten around my fingers.

Raelynn would kill me if he fell, but...

I nod and make sure I can easily grab him if he looks like he's heading for the ice. Jackson's five-second solo causes him to beam with pride. "Did you see me?" he asks, as if I haven't been right here next to him this entire time. "I did it all by myself!" You'd think he did a lap around the ice with all of the excitement he has.

"You sure did. Good job, Jackson."

Once the ice rink is busier, I decide it's time to head home. We return Jackson's skates, mine go back into my bag, and then we're on the way with Jackson asking once again when we can come back. The moment we get home, he races to Raelynn, nearly knocking a hot casserole dish out of her hands in the process. She lifted it up just in time.

"Whoa, baby. Where's the fire?" she teases him.

"I went skating! And Mr. EJ let me do it by myself!"

Raelynn frowns and glances up at me.

"He was fine. He did great. I brought him back without any scrapes, cuts, bruises, or broken bones." There's nothing to be upset about.

She smiles at Jackson. "I'm glad you had fun. Go wash up. Wait!" she calls as he runs out of the kitchen. "Did you thank Mr. EJ?"

"Only a billion times on the way home," I answer for him. Jackson grins and scurries on his way to the bathroom to wash his hands.

"Thank you for doing that for him."

I shrug. "I knew he'd enjoy it." I pick up Bree and

kiss her cheek. "How are you doing with everything?" I ask Raelynn.

"Fine. Thanks for helping me with that, too."

"No problem. Any time."

Jackson jogs back into the room and we sit down at the table to eat. The sense of accomplishment and pride I feel when Jackson talks to me like he normally talks to Raelynn is odd, but I don't care. He can talk his head off to me all he wants. I'll listen because that means he's more comfortable here and around me.

Later, Raelynn and I sit next to one another on the couch. Bree has one foot on each of our legs and Jackson is somewhere behind the couch, popping up in random places as he plays Peek-a-Boo with her. While he does that, Raelynn tries to get her to say her first word.

"Come on, Bree." Raelynn points to me with her free hand. "DaDa. DaDa. DaDa, DaDaDaDaDaDaDaaaaa!" she sings, causing Bree to giggle and speak some gibberish. She tickles her stomach and says, "Bree, Bree, Bree, Bree, Breeeeeeee." My princess claps her hands and jumps a little. Jackson pops his head up between us with a "Peek-a-Boo!" shout, absolutely thrilling Bree. "And there's Ja-Ja-Ja-Jackson!" Raelynn finishes.

Jackson crouches behind the couch again and Bree leans toward where he disappears. "Ja-Ja! Ja-Ja!" she squeals.

My eyes widen. I take her completely and hold her up into the air. She grins because she can see Jackson again. "Did you hear her? She just said her first word!"

"What?" Jackson asks with confusion, walking around the couch.

"She said your name!" I exclaim.

"She didn't say Jackson," he argues like I'm a huge idiot.

"She said Ja-Ja. That's you! Didn't you hear your mom? Ja-Ja-Ja-Jackson?"

His eyes widen for the second time today as he looks between the three of us. "I'm her first word? Momma? Did you hear that? I'm Bree's first word!" He points to himself in wonder.

"Yeah, baby. That's awesome." Raelynn's lackluster response makes me realize she doesn't seem as excited as the rest of us. "Say goodnight to Bree and Mr. EJ. It's time for your bath."

Jackson loses a bit of his smile, but he does as Raelynn asks. A moment later, they head upstairs. I focus on Bree.

"Now, time to say DaDa, princess." She yawns. Figures. I'm obviously not as exciting as Jackson. "We'll get there," I reassure her. I stand and take her upstairs because it's about time to get her ready for bed, too. Bree said her first word. I can't believe it. Sure, it wasn't DaDa and it was only part of Jackson's name, but I'm counting it as a legitimate word. I'll have to call Ma tomorrow and tell her.

Bree takes a little while to fall asleep. By the time I'm walking out of her room, Raelynn walks out of Jackson's room.

"I am so sorry, Elias," she whispers.

I frown as my brows pull together. "For what?" Did I miss a major mishap?

"Her first word should not be associated with us. I'm just an employee here and it seems wrong that—"

"Raelynn," I interrupt, not caring where exactly she's going with this. "Her first word could've been 'no' or baba or anything else and I wouldn't have cared. I'm just happy she said something we understood. You don't need to be sorry about anything. You and Jackson are going to make an impact on her life because of how much time you spend with her. It's inevitable. Don't feel bad or whatever when something like this happens. It doesn't bother me."

"Are you sure? Because I'm pretty positive it would bother me."

"I'm sure."

She nods. "I'm sorry for being so crazy-like. I worry too much."

"It's okay. Come on."

Raelynn follows me downstairs and into the kitchen, where I plan to have a snack. "Can I ask you something?" she says.

"Sure." I open the refrigerator doors to scan the shelves.

"You haven't mentioned this, and I've been meaning to ask, but what am I supposed to do if Bree's mom shows up?" I freeze. "Is she allowed to see Bree? Or...I don't know. I don't mean to pry, I swear, but I don't want to be unprepared or do something wrong either."

I close the doors of the refrigerator and take a deep breath as I face a nervous-looking Raelynn. "You won't ever meet Bree's mom." Her eyes widen a bit at this. "She's dead."

"Oh, I'm so sorry." Raelynn plops into one of the seats at the table, looking a little lost and upset.

Forgetting about my snack, I take the seat next to her. "I dated her on and off, just saw her here and there. She dropped off the face of the earth one day and then in February, I find Bree on my front porch with a note from

Vicky. I knew where she lived, so I drove over there, freaking out obviously. You can't drop off a one-week-old baby at my house, tell me she's mine, and that I'm now solely responsible for her without expecting me to ask questions.

"When I get there," I take a deep breath, remembering all the sights and sounds from the horrible part of that day, "she had been found dead of an apparent overdose. I didn't know her that well, so I had no clue she had a drug problem. It seems she was able to stay clean long enough to have Bree and that was it.

"My mom had to fly down here because we were about to leave on a road trip. I didn't want to leave her, but at the same time, it was too fucking crazy to wrap my mind around, so I didn't mind losing myself in my job for a little bit. Anyway, I probably should've told you sooner, but it's not something I enjoy talking about."

Raelynn gives me a little smile. "That I completely understand." She sighs. "I guess you should give me Henry's number."

"I'll text it to you. Have you figured out how you'll do it?"

She shakes her head. "I know I want to talk to him one-on-one first. But as far as introducing them? No idea. Jackson sounded freaked when he called me today and I just keep thinking Jackson isn't going to know how to process this or he'll want nothing to do with Henry or," her eyes water, "he'll like Henry more and then Henry will steal him from me."

Without thinking too much about it, I reach over and take her hand. "Raelynn, that won't happen. You've been his entire world for all of his little life so far. He isn't going to give you up for someone new. I mean, maybe he would for me because I took him skating today and he really loved it."

She laughs. "If you take Jackson, then I'll just steal Bree from you," she warns.

"Okay, okay. Let's keep our own kids." Her smile has me smiling. She's way too freaking pretty to live in my house all the time. I'm even attracted to her complex personality that I haven't even begun to figure out yet. And for some reason, at this exact second, I hear Derek in my head, *You have the hots for your nanny, don't you, EJ?* I shove that thought out of my head. "If you need help with anything, let me know."

"Thanks, Elias." As if she suddenly realizes we're holding hands, she pulls her hand out from under mine. "I should do some schoolwork. I'll see you in the morning."

"Good night." With a lingering gaze, I watch her walk away.

Brayden returned, and then we left for two games. Now, it's Sunday, we're home, and there's another game tonight. Raelynn, Bree, and Jackson are going. Jackson is beyond excited. Right now, though, I'm enjoying some time with Bree. We all sit on the floor. Jackson and Raelynn play with Legos while Bree and I play with blocks. We've been mostly quiet. As quiet as we can be with a nine-month-old and a five-year-old.

"I have a meeting tomorrow," Raelynn says out of the blue.

I look up at her and she glances at Jackson. "Oh? Do you want me to go with you?"

She shakes her head. "I was hoping Bree could stay here with you."

Oh. That makes more sense. She doesn't need me or Bree there while she's meeting with Henry. "Yeah, of course. Take the day if you want it." We're about to leave for another trip this week anyway. If she wants a day off, tomorrow will be a good day to take it.

"Thanks. I might."

"Are you nervous?" I ask, though it's a dumb question to ask. Of course she is.

Raelynn nods. "I have a lot of questions for him. It'll be good to get some answers. He's using his lunch break to meet me, but I don't know if an hour will be long enough."

"If you need me to watch Jackson for you, I will."

"Thanks. Is your family excited about coming for Christmas? Where exactly is home for them?"

She stuns me for a moment, just by being curious about me and my family. I don't miss that she changed the subject, but that's okay. "They're excited," I answer. I called Mom earlier this week to finalize the plans. "I'm from Canada, Thunder Bay specifically."

"Wow. So, they're flying all this way just for a few days? That's awesome."

"Yeah." I pause for a moment, wondering if I should ask the question I've been thinking about and then decide to go for it. She'll either answer or she'll deflect. "How do you two normally spend Christmas?"

Raelynn doesn't get the chance to answer before Jackson, who has been listening, decides to do it for her.

"We decorate a little tree with lights and ornaments and tinsel. On Christmas Eve, we make cookies and build a special fort and sleep under it while we wait for Santa." Jackson leans forward and whispers, "Sometimes, we eat some of the cookies for Santa. Momma says he doesn't mind." He leans back and speaks normally again as he continues, "In the morning, I open presents in our fort and we eat any leftover cookies for breakfast."

"What about your mom? Does she have presents to open?"

Jackson shakes his head, slightly confused by my question. "I'm her Christmas present every year. Right, Momma?" He looks at Raelynn for confirmation.

She nods. "Yep," she says, popping that p at the end again. "Best present ever."

He grins and focuses on whatever he's building. Raelynn smiles while she watches him. Her Christmases since he's been born have been just the two of them. They have their own traditions and ways to spend the holiday. While she probably doesn't mind that no one has looked after her, or has been there to give her a present in that time, it makes me want to figure out what she'd like and buy it for her. I already have an idea of what I'd like to do for Jackson.

"Maybe we could go shopping before or after your meeting tomorrow?" I suggest.

Raelynn looks surprised, but she nods. "Yeah, that should be fun."

And maybe I'll catch her eyeing something I can buy her for Christmas.

Raelynn

ELIAS PULLS INTO a parking space at the restaurant and I spot Henry standing by the door, waiting for me. Even in work clothes, he manages to have this arrogant, filthy rich, high class air surrounding him. Maybe it's the way he stands, all tall and confident, at ease, and somehow looking as if he owns the place.

"Are you ready for this?" Elias asks.

"No."

He chuckles. "You'll be fine. Make him buy your lunch and I'll be back in an hour unless you text me sooner."

I nod and get out. Since we're shopping afterward, he

thought he should bring me and hang around the area until I'm done. I don't know what he and Bree are doing while I'm here, but I have other things to worry about.

"You came," Henry says as I stand in front of him.

"Of course I did. Let's get this over with."

He opens the door for me and we walk inside. The silence between us is awkward amongst the noisy fast food restaurant. We came just in time for rush hour. The line is long, people's voices clash with one another as they talk and order, and as we shuffle closer to the counter, Henry's arm brushes against me here and there. I cringe each time.

When we finally sit down at a small table in the back corner, I take a moment to watch Henry. To wonder how he ended up here. How will this go? I'm about to find out, I know, but am I ready?

"What happened?" I ask, deciding not to wait.

Henry's shoulders drop ever so slightly. "Can we ease into this first?"

"You only have an hour."

He nods. "I know. Why don't you tell me how things have been for you before we get into my side of things?"

I frown, glancing down at my food. "Why? So you can hear how much I've struggled? How until I started working for Elias, Jackson and I barely got by most of the time?" My eyes water and I shake my head. "You don't get to hear that." Maybe he should. Maybe he should know exactly how hard it's been for me so he can feel terrible for not being there and helping me, but I can't stand the thought of telling him any of it.

Looking up at Henry, his eyes are full of shame and guilt, his face contorted in agony. "Tell me about Jackson then," he says so softly, it sounds more like a question than a gently delivered command.

"He's a good kid. Smart. Shy. He has a good imagination, but we play pretend a lot, too." There's no need to add that's partly because I can't afford to buy him a bunch of toys. "He's probably a little too attached to me, but I think he's branching out a little since we've been living with Elias. I don't know how he'll react to you because new people and situations make him nervous and you might freak him out as much as I freaked out."

Henry props his forearms on the table and clasps his hands together, leaning forward a bit. "Rae," I flinch and he corrects himself. "Raelynn, just so we're clear, I have no plans to dictate or suggest how this should happen. You're in charge. You decide how it happens. If you want to go through the courts to set up an official visitation schedule and child support payments, I have no problem with that. Whatever you want, I'll do. I just want to get to know Jackson and be in his life."

"Where were you five years ago, Henry? Why are you here now?" I sit up straight as a terrifying thought occurs. "Do our parents know you're here? Do they know where I am?" It's not like they'll come looking for me, but I suddenly realize how much I like them not knowing anything about my life anymore.

"They don't care, Rae," he says softly with a built-in apology in his tone. "Before I left home, I went to see your parents. I asked them if they wanted to be in contact with you if I found you and they said no. So, no, they don't know where I am or where you are. My parents?" He shakes his head in disappointment. "If they want to know, then they'll find out, but I didn't tell them."

"What happened?" I ask. What happened five years

ago? What happened for him to change his mind about Jackson? What happened, period?

His voice is thick and choked up as he mutters, "I'm sorry." He clears his throat, staring with the most sincere look he's ever given me. "I have to say that first. I'm sorry, Rae. I panicked when you told me, I know, but when I told my parents, they gave me an ultimatum. If I stayed with you, they were going to take my trust fund and my future position in Dad's company."

Wow. I knew they didn't like us together, but I didn't think they'd ever go that far.

"And you know how much I wanted to make my dad proud and follow in his footsteps." Yeah. It would've killed Henry not to be a part of their company. "But I had a plan, Rae. I thought I could get around it. I would do what they wanted, still have the money, and at the very least, send you some of it to help. But then, you had the baby and left."

Henry pinches the bridge of his nose and squeezes his eyes closed. "I didn't put in the effort to find you and still help," he says, opening his eyes. "The guilt has eaten me alive, Rae. Not knowing what happened to you or Jackson, how you were doing, and knowing that I completely abandoned you after all.

"Eventually, I gave it all up. I learned how to do my current job with the electric company, which I love, and I began to plan how I would find you and get into Jackson's life. My parents are pissed and aren't talking to me right now, but I still have my trust fund. So, if you need money—"

I cut him off before he can dare finish that offer. "I don't need any of their money."

He nods as if he expected as much.

We're quiet for a few minutes as I soak in what he said and we eat. He seems remorseful enough. Knowing he planned to help somewhat doesn't change my opinion on his abandonment at all. He still did it and he obviously didn't care for me that much back then because not once did he mention how he wanted to stay with me. Oddly enough, it doesn't bother me as much as I thought it might.

"What are you thinking?" Henry asks.

"I'm thinking about how you chose money and a career that would've been handed to you over your son." The words tumble out of my mouth before I realize it. I almost regret it seeing the emotion that crosses over Henry's face because I'm right, but it's the truth. The truth hurts and it can't be changed. Henry decided money and a job was more important than being in his son's life. He even said part of his plan was to send me money, not to come join me and help raise him. Rage bubbles and boils under my skin at how he could do such a thing to my baby.

"I was young and stupid."

"So was I," I argue, "and yet I've been raising him for the past five years. I guess it's easier to walk away when you didn't have to carry him in your body or give birth to him or walk out of a hospital with him."

"Rae," he starts.

"Stop calling me that. I'm not your girlfriend anymore." He never called me Rae until we started dating. "If you want to be in Jackson's life, then okay. I'll allow it. But once you're in, you're *in*. If you hurt him, I will hunt you down and kill you. Understand? And you don't mention anything about our lives to your parents or anyone else from back home." They've stayed out of our lives so far, I don't need them putting their noses where they don't belong just because Henry is here.

He nods. "What if my parents decide they want to meet him?"

My muscles tense. "You think they might want to? How would they treat him if they still hate me enough that they aren't talking to you?" I shake my head. "No. No. No." My son will not be around mean people like that and if anyone is going to steal Jackson from me, it would be Henry's parents. Just to be assholes and to get Henry back without having me. "I need to go." I stand and gather my trash, but knock over my drink in my distress. Those mean old bastards can't be in the same state as my son, much less within five feet of him. I won't allow it. It can't happen. Ever!

"Rae, calm down." He stands and touches my shoulder, but I jump back from him and bump into someone else.

"Raelynn? Are you okay?"

I whirl around at the sound of Elias's voice and relax a little. Bree is in his arms and she reaches for me. "Can I?" I hold my hands up to take her and he lets me.

"What's going on?" Elias asks. There's an edge in his voice as he takes in my slightly panicked state, the mess on the table that Henry cleans up, and how I'd much rather focus on Bree right now.

"Nothing her employer needs to be concerned about," Henry answers.

Elias narrows his eyes at him, his lips flattening in an instant. He looks kinda hot when he's irritated. Henry throws our trash away and looks between us before settling his gaze on Elias.

"Can you give us a second?"

"No."

Henry looks at me for help. "Rae," he says with irritation.

"Didn't she tell you not to call her that?" Elias reminds him. He grabs my purse, hands it to me, and rests a hand on my lower back.

Henry sighs heavily and decides to ignore him. "I was only asking in case they change their mind. There's no reason to panic. If they ever did meet him, they would treat him like their grandson, and they would be nicer to you, too." I snort, not believing that, and the sound makes Bree giggle and tug on my hair. "Just let me know when I can meet Jackson, okay?"

I nod and he turns to leave. The moment he's gone, my body relaxes and leans into Elias.

"You're okay, Raelynn." His hand rubs my back for a moment. "Come on. Let's get out of here." When we're in the car, he asks, "How did it go?"

"Overall, okay." I rehash most of the conversation with him, needing to tell someone about it. "I freaked out because he brought up his parents possibly wanting to meet Jackson in the future. Maybe it's crazy and irrational for me to think someone will take him from me, but it's always been the two of us and he's all I have. I didn't have to worry about anyone else interfering with our lives, you know? And now, Henry's here. And if anyone is going to screw us over, it'll be his parents. They'd do it just to get me out of Henry's life again."

"Do you really think they would?"

I give him a look. "They made Henry choose between Jackson and his trust fund and his position within their company," I tell him. "Yes, they'd do that. They also have way more money than I could ever dream of having. They could pull strings and snatch him from me in a heartbeat, I bet."

Elias reaches over and takes my hand, interlocking our fingers together. "You're his mother and the only family he knows. No one would hurt Jackson like that. And my gut tells me Henry wouldn't let them either." He glances over at me. "My gut is never wrong. Don't worry about it, Raelynn."

Stressed by this entire thing, I decide we need to change the topic, so I raise an eyebrow. "You listen to your gut?"

He grins. "All the time. That gut instinct is why you got this job. When I don't listen to it, bad shit happens."

He's intrigued me now. "Like what?"

"One time, I woke up and had this feeling that I didn't need to go to school that day. I went anyway and got into a wreck on the way there."

Whoa. That's kinda freaky. Elias arrives at the mall, gets Bree's stroller out, and as we head inside, he asks, "So, what do you want for Christmas?"

I frown. "What?"

He smiles at me. "You see, Raelynn, on Christmas morning, people open gifts. Most people make a wishlist. I'm asking what would be on yours."

"I don't have a wishlist. I don't need anything. Jackson is the only one who gets presents." And he only gets a few because money has always been tight. "What are you getting Bree for her first Christmas?"

He shrugs. "I don't know. Something to kick off our Christmas traditions is all I know for sure. She doesn't really need anything and at this point, she can unwrap an empty box and it'll make her laugh. It seems a little crazy to buy a soon-to-be ten-month-old Christmas presents, right?" Elias glances down at me for confirmation.

"Well, I guess it depends. Her first Christmas is more for you than her, so if you buy her five presents, then you get to watch her open those presents and see what happens. I think it's more about that experience than what you're buying her."

He nods. "Are you still going to visit your friend now that Henry is here? Or will you stay so he can see Jackson for Christmas?"

Crap. My plan is experiencing some issues already. Elias leads us into a children's store. "I don't know." Considering we're only going up the road to a hotel, Henry can still see Jackson. "We'll have to see how things go between now and then. I need to decide how to introduce them."

"You'll figure it out."

We walk around the mall, making small talk mostly while picking up some gifts. I buy Jackson's Christmas. Elias gets things for his family and a few things for Bree after all. Spending time with him isn't so bad. I keep smiling when I glance over and watch him push Bree's stroller. If he catches me, he'll raise his eyebrows at me, but I always find something particularly interesting in the store to look at.

I peek another glance at him. He's almost a foot taller than me, probably. But what makes me smile is seeing this man in dark jeans and a hoodie that hides his tattoos pushing this stroller that looks so small in front of him. It's freaking adorable and a little comical.

"Why do you keep smiling like that, Raelynn?" he finally asks, amusement coloring his tone.

I laugh and say, "You pushing the stroller." He glances down, clearly not seeing why that would make me smile. "Here." My fingers graze his hip as I push him aside. "I look mostly normal with it in front of me. I probably look too small for it, but whatever. My point is that when you push it," I grab his hand and pull him back behind it, "the proportions don't add up. You look too big for it."

He laughs and shakes his head. "Let's pick Jackson up. We have one more thing to do today."

"What are we doing?"

"Picking out a Christmas tree."

"A real one? Shouldn't that be done without us?"

Elias gives me a look that shuts up the rest of my protests. "Yes, a real one, and no. You'll be enjoying the tree, too. Don't you think Jackson will enjoy it?"

Well, darn. He has me there. Jackson might have fun picking out a live tree. We leave the mall and pick up my little boy, who talks all about his day as Elias drives to a tree farm. I decide to carry Bree while we walk around and Jackson holds onto Elias's hand. The wind bites into my skin and I double check that Bree is covered well enough.

But that causes me to lose the boys.

"Where is DaDa and Jackson, Bree?" I ask her. She rests her head on my shoulder with a yawn. She missed her afternoon nap with our shopping. I weave in and out of the trees until I hear Jackson's voice.

"These are all so big. Our tree isn't this big. It fits in a box."

"Trees come in all different sizes, J-man. And some

78

you can buy at the store in the box or here on the tree farm. Which one do you think we should get?"

"One as tall as you!"

Elias laughs. "Okay. We can do that."

I peer around the tree to see him holding Jackson now. They examine the branches on one of the trees. Elias glances around, but doesn't see me.

"Hey, Jackson," Elias says. "Would you like to get your mom a present this year?"

What is he talking about? What is he doing?

"I'm her present," Jackson automatically responds.

Elias smiles. "Yeah, I know. A good one, too. But if you could get her something as like a bonus present, would you want to do that?"

Jackson seems to think about this. His legs swing on either side of Elias's body. "I could get her a present?"

"Yeah. I'd help you find it or make it. We could wrap it up and put it under the tree, so she'd have something to unwrap on Christmas morning, too."

"Okay."

Elias grins. "Okay. But it's a surprise." Jackson nods. "Let's find us a tree then."

Before they can step away, I come out of my hiding place and Elias glances over, his eyes softening a little when he sees Bree asleep in my arms.

"Hey, there you are."

Here I am. And I have no idea how to feel about him helping Jackson find a present for me. Other than a warm fuzzy, gooey mess because that is seriously too sweet.

8

EJ

JACKSON DOESN'T KNOW what to do with himself. He is absolutely thrilled about having a big, living tree. I hold both him and the lights, and we walk around the tree, laying the lights between the branches. He wants to help, like he does with his tree, and I don't care how the tree looks, so I'm pretty much letting him do most of the work.

Raelynn and Bree sit on the couch. Raelynn claps Bree's hands togethers and each time, she says, "DaDa. Let's say it, Bree. DaDa." Bree either giggles, mumbles some nonsense, or says, "Ja-Ja." If Bree says DaDa anytime soon, it'll be because Raelynn has been relentless.

"Momma, maybe she just likes me better," Jackson tells her, causing me to laugh.

"Maybe you're her best friend," I say.

His brows pull together, like they often do when he's thinking about something. "That's why she made me her first word?"

I grin. He thinks Bree made a choice. And he thinks she chose him. "You play with her, don't you?"

He shrugs and stuffs some lights into the tree. "Sometimes."

"And she seems happy?"

"Yeah."

"Then I think you're her best friend."

Jackson looks over my shoulder at Bree. "Does that mean she's my best friend? How many can I have?"

"As many as you want, and if you want her to be."

He decides to let that topic go while we finish putting the lights on the tree. Raelynn helps once she puts Bree to bed for the night. Jackson has the most fun with the tinsel. He grabs a handful and runs around, throwing it on the tree. Raelynn looks like she wants to tell him to be more direct with his throwing since part of it falls onto the floor. I don't want to ruin his fun, though. I grab some tinsel, just a few strands, and throw it at her.

She looks at me with surprise and a little smile.

"He's fine," I whisper.

"Mr. EJ, I can't reach the top. Will you help me?"

"I can," Raelynn says as she stands, but Jackson shakes his head with an expression as if she's crazy.

"Momma, you can't reach either." The *duh* is silent, yet loud and clear.

I chuckle, which earns me a quick glare from

81

Raelynn. "I can still lift you up, Jackson." He clearly doesn't believe her, but she picks him up anyway. He's nearly as tall as she is. He's only like two feet shorter. I'm surprised she can pick him up still. Just as I think it, I hear her grunt when he leans forward. I walk over and before I can say anything, she grinds out, "I'm fine."

"Either I take him, or I pick you both up."

Her hair flies out as she whips her gaze over to look at me with wide eyes. I'm dead serious, too. I can easily pick them both up. There's no need for her to injure herself. Or drop Jackson.

Jackson leans too far to the right while Raelynn eyeballs me, probably wondering if I'd really pick her up. He falls forward, which pulls Raelynn in that direction. I snake an arm around her waist and lean her upright again.

"Sorry, Momma," Jackson says softly.

She kisses his cheek. "Don't be, baby." She takes a deep breath. "You're growing up is all. Mr. EJ will help you with the rest."

I briefly rub her back before taking him from her to help him toss tinsel onto the top portion of the tree. When he's done, I set him on his feet and take a few steps back with my hands on my hips. "Well, J-man. What do you think? Is it finished and perfect?"

Jackson walks over to stand next to me, mirroring my stance. He eyes the tree and then nods. "Yep."

Raelynn laughs. "Time for bed, Jackson."

He follows her upstairs and I tidy up a bit. I was worried how the transition would be. For me to have a nanny. For my mom to be gone. And then for there to be another kid in the house. After all, I went from living alone to having a baby and now to having a house full. My peace and quiet alone time is almost nonexistent now, but this new part of my life? It's not bad at all. I thoroughly enjoy it.

Not to say I haven't been enjoying life since Bree came into it, I have, but things seem to have settled down now with Raelynn here. It's a new, different kind of peace.

I eye the crazy tree. The ornaments are nearly hidden from all of the tinsel Jackson put on it. That's definitely going to be a tradition for Bree and me. It's too fun not to be. I flip the switch to turn the outlet off and thus, turning the lights off on the tree.

"Elias?"

I turn around at the sound of Raelynn's voice, sounding close by.

She throws her arms around my neck, her entire body leaning into me as she hugs me. "Thank you," she whispers.

"For what?" I hesitate for only a moment before sliding my arms around her waist. The action pulls her body closer to mine. A body that while smaller than mine still manages to fit perfectly. A body with curves and breasts and warm, soft skin. Fuck. I need to get laid. I'm so distracted by her hug and the temptation to wrap her legs around my waist that I nearly miss what she says.

"For being so good to Jackson." After a brief pause, she adds, "And nice to me." She pulls away, her hands sliding down my shoulders to my arms since I can't seem to let her go yet.

"You don't have to thank me for that." Would her lips get pinker or turn more of a reddish shade if I were to kiss the hell out of her?

"I do. It's all part of me trying to expand our world and allow people in." She frowns and tenses in my arms as some thought occurs to her. "He likes you a lot, so please don't ever hurt him."

"I wouldn't."

Her eyes flick to her hands, which must be what makes her realize we're in this position because she quickly steps away from me. My arms have no choice but to fall to my sides. It's probably a good thing, though. I definitely don't need to fuck my nanny.

Right?

Even if she was interested?

And with Raelynn, I can't tell. She's too closed off of a person to tell if she's attracted to me. I know she's more comfortable being here, living here, and being my nanny, but that's about all I've gathered about her so far. Except for how she feels about Henry being around. She definitely isn't thrilled about that.

But is she attracted to me? As attracted as I am to her? Do sexy thoughts about us filter past the Do Not Think About sign in her mind like they do in mine? Is she tempted? Does she wonder what it would be like?

Because the longer I'm around her, the more attracted I am to her. The more I wonder what it would be like. The more tempted I become, even though it seems like a huge no-no. As much as I hate to admit it, Derek was right. Physically, if I have a type, Raelynn is it. Living with her and being platonic might become torture at some point, especially since she's a really good person on top of that. A person I like. A person I'm pretty sure I want to fuck.

Damn it.

Raelynn tilts her head. "Why are you looking at me like that?"

"Like what?"

"Like you want to get inside me."

I blink. She can't know I was thinking that.

"My head!" Raelynn quickly corrects. "You looked like you were trying to get inside *my head*. Oh my god." She turns away and covers her eyes for a moment. "I need to go to bed. G'night, Elias." She runs up the stairs before I can call after her.

I need to find a way to get Raelynn out of my head because I can not think about fucking with her.

It's Saturday. We're on a California road swing and at our last stop before we go home. I think I've devised a plan for Raelynn. I don't know if it's going to work. One-night-stands or casual flings aren't my thing. Not after what happened with Vicky. And since I can't stop thinking about Raelynn, my bright idea is to set her up with someone.

The purpose is two-fold. Raelynn could probably use some fun. A date will give her that. Considering she hasn't had too many days off, I can also use this to make her take a day off. Secondly, if she's out with someone else, then surely I won't think about her.

Plot holes everywhere, but it's all I've got. I most certainly can't take her out and make sure she has fun. However, I can find one of the guys to do it and watch Jackson for her while she's gone. That's another thing. I know she'd leave Jackson with me. The only other person she might do that with is Deanna since they apparently had lunch earlier this week and are friends.

Convincing Raelynn will be another issue, but I'll worry about that later. Right now, I need to find her a date. I've been thinking about all the guys on the team and I've narrowed it down to two. I don't know what I'm thinking, but they seem like the least likely to be jackasses. With a deep breath, I walk over to the table where the Kessy twins are having lunch and sit down.

"Hey, EJ," they say together, a quirk they've been doing since around Thanksgiving to get on everyone's nerves and to creep some of us out.

"Hey. How's it going?"

"Good," Cal answers.

"How's Bree?" Collin asks.

"She's good." The guys exchange a look and I say, "I need a favor."

"Told you," Cal says, causing Collin to roll his eyes. "He'll do it."

"We don't even know what it is," Collin argues. "I might not want to do it."

"Both of you shut up and listen." I wait in case they decide to argue with me, but when they don't, I say, "Would one of you like to take my nanny out on a date?"

Cal laughs. "Collin will definitely do it. I'm not. If you have to get a date for the girl, that's bad news."

"She doesn't need my help," I argue. "I just want her go out and have some fun." I focus on Collin since he may be my only hope. "Only once. No obligations other than to make sure she has fun."

"You don't have to do it, Collin," Cal tells him.

He seems on the fence, so I pull out my phone and show him a picture of her. "Just one fun date," I repeat.

"Yeah, okay. Fine. But only because she's hot."

It takes a lot not to frown at his comment. "Thanks." I spot Brayden walking in, so I say goodbye, get up, and join him at the table he claims. "Hey."

"Hey. What's up?"

"Just setting Raelynn up on a date."

He eyes me with mild surprise as he picks up the menu and the waiter comes over to take our drink order. We get waters and when the waiter walks away, Brayden asks, "Why are you setting her up?"

I shrug, not sure if I should reveal the real reason. However, my shrug makes him suspicious.

"EJ, is something going on with your nanny?"

"No." Which may or may not be the problem. Brayden watches me for a moment longer before switching his focus to the menu, deciding to let it go. "If you had a nanny, you wouldn't fuck her, right?" I blurt out.

Brayden laughs, but doesn't look up from the menu. "Depends on if it's worth the risk, especially for you considering how long it took you to find a nanny you liked. You sleep with her and it goes sour, she leaves and your mom has to come back."

That's the thing. My gut feeling? It's totally on board with this. I don't think it would turn out badly, but Raelynn is a loose cannon and that's where all of my hesitation comes in. Who the hell knows where that girl's head is? I'll stick with my game plan of sending her on a date with Collin and then reevaluate after that.

Later that night, we're getting our asses kicked just a little. The first period ended with a three to zero score and not in our favor. The second period? Well, it starts by a sleazy bastard scoring thirty seconds in. Savage's expression is completely blank, almost stony. He reminds me a lot of Brayden right now.

It's Serge and the Kessy twins who get us rolling shortly after Bruiser has a go with a player. Serge plants himself right in front of the goalie, who looks around him, expecting the shot to clearly come from Thing One or Thing Two. But Collin shoots wide, the puck bounces off the boards toward Serge, and he redirects it to the net. We all stand because the goalie tries, but fails to keep the puck out.

Throughout the rest of the game, we try. We're relentless. We do our best to take advantage of their turnovers, of every time we have possession of the puck, of every shot, but their goalie shuts us down every fucking time. That's the only goal we Rebels manage to score.

This game is almost like how my life is going with Raelynn. Things are happening, we're both doing our best, but it's not going quite as expected. Hopefully, things turn out better when it comes to my life and the slight issue of me wanting to be with my nanny.

Raelynn

"**G**O SHOWER AND get dressed."

I frown at Elias. He's been anxious all day and now, he's giving me orders? "Why?"

"You have a date tonight."

Jaw, meet floor. "What? No, I don't." I haven't been on a date since high school! No way in hell am I going on a date today!

"Yes, you do. I set you up with a teammate." Elias stands, takes my hand, and pulls me to stand as well. "Go upstairs, shower, and get ready. He'll be here in an hour."

My head shakes back and forth in protest. "No, Elias.

No. No. No." He glances at Bree in her pack 'n play and Jackson, who watches TV, and then pulls me up the stairs since I won't move. "No! I don't want to go." Yet, I follow along helplessly anyway. "Why would you do this?"

"Because I thought you could use some fun."

"But my last date was with Henry!"

Elias pauses outside of my bedroom with concern finally filling his features. "I didn't think about that. Look, it's nothing serious, okay? Just two people going out for some fun. That's it. You can do that, right?"

With one of his teammates who I don't even know? "Why can't you take me out for fun or I can go out for fun by myself?"

His eyes widen a little with surprise. "I'm watching Jackson for you and because we both know you wouldn't go out by yourself." His thumb brushes over my knuckles. "You'll be okay, Raelynn. I wouldn't put you in a bad situation."

I nod. "Okay. Fine. I'll go." Like I have much of a choice! I move past him and to the bathroom. If I have to go out with anyone, I'd rather it be with Elias. His reassuring gesture just now reminds me of our hug the other night. He's been a little handsy lately, but not in a weird or uncomfortable way. There just seems to be more touches between us and it's blurring the line.

I should not want to go on a date with Elias.

Or think about his well-built body.

Or want to kiss him.

He pays me to take care of his daughter. He's my friend. That's it. That's all there should be. I need this job and the money he pays me more than anything else. My greatest fear where Elias is concerned is losing this job.

It's the best job I've ever had, certainly pays the best, and Jackson and I need it too much for me to screw it up by acting on the fantasies I have about my boss.

Who knows? Maybe this date will work out better than we expect.

But my nerves continue to build through my shower, as I half-dress because I decide I don't like my shirt choice, and finish getting ready in all other areas. I stand in front of my closet and flick through what few choices I have. Maybe I need to spend some of the money I'm making on new clothes for me. I wouldn't have to go crazy, but I should at least have something to wear on a date!

A light knock sounds on the door. "Raelynn? He's here."

"Shit," I curse under my breath.

"Can I come in?" Elias asks.

I glance down at my bra before quickly grabbing my towel and covering my chest. "Yeah."

He steps inside. His eyes land on my chest before averting elsewhere.

"I don't know what to wear," I confess.

"I figured. You mind?" He points to my closet. I take a step back, my cheeks flushing with a bit of embarrassment because there seriously isn't much in there. He fills the space with that big body of his immediately, distracting me. I really have to stop thinking about his body and how hot he is. For the most part, I'm able to ignore it, but damn, it's hard sometimes. A moment later, Elias turns around with a shirt in hand. "This one."

He rushes out of the room the moment I take the shirt from him. I quickly slip the purple V-neck over my head. The only thing left to do now is go downstairs to meet my date. With a deep breath, I leave the safety of my room.

EJ now holds Bree and talks to a guy about as tall as he is. The guy stands with his hands in his pockets, looking a little nervous. Maybe he doesn't really want to be here either.

"Are you leaving, Momma?" Jackson's worried question stops their conversation and alerts them to my presence.

"Only for a little while."

"I'll put my shoes on." Jackson turns, but Elias's voice stops him.

"J-man, you're staying here with me."

"But—"

"I'll be back before you can miss me," I interrupt him, crouching down. "Give me a hug."

"But I always go where you go, Momma," Jackson says with confusion as he hugs me.

"You can't go with me today. Mr. EJ needs you to show him how to build a fort." Hopefully, Elias won't mind, but I know Jackson would look forward to doing that.

"I wanna go with you," he whispers in my ear in this tiny voice that kills me. His arms tighten around my neck until I almost can't breathe.

I glance at Elias and my date, who both look like they feel bad for Jackson. "Not this time, baby." I kiss his cheek. "Build a fort with Mr. EJ and think about how many books you want to check out from the library tomorrow, okay?" He nods and finally pulls away. "I love you."

"Love you."

I stand and hold my hand out to my date. "Hey, I'm Raelynn."

"Collin," he replies as he shakes it. "Ready?"

Nope. Not at all. But I nod and we walk out the door. Once we're in the car, the silence is super awkward.

"I'm sorry you're here," I blurt out. "I didn't know Elias was doing this until about an hour ago."

"It's okay."

Silence.

Heavy, awkward, uncomfortable silence again.

"What are we doing?" I ask.

Collin laughs. "No fucking clue. I didn't realize EJ wanted me to do this today until a few hours ago." He glances over at me before focusing back on the road, apparently driving nowhere in particular. "What do you want to do? EJ said he wanted me to make sure you had fun."

I frown. "You're only here because Elias basically made you take me somewhere, right? Not because you want to be on a date with some girl you don't know?"

Collin winces. "Can I be honest?"

"Please."

"EJ came to me and my brother, said he wanted one of us to take you out, make sure you had fun. My brother offered me up. I don't really know what EJ wants out of this or why he couldn't take you himself, but whatever. I don't really think it's a date, but I don't know. You're hot." He shrugs. "It boils down to being whatever you want it to be and us doing whatever you want to do. I'm already here, so I'm down for whatever."

"You're one of the Kessy twins." That's what occurs to me first. Collin nods. "Jackson is a bit fascinated by the two of you. Not as much as he is with Elias, but... Did he recognize you?"

"Yeah. He's a cool kid."

Everything sinks in. This doesn't have to be a real date. That relaxes me a bit. "We can do whatever I want?"

"Anything as long as I don't end up in jail." As an afterthought, he adds, "Or you. EJ would kill me."

I laugh. "Is there a game on tonight?"

"Most likely."

"Take me to a sports bar."

Collin doesn't ask me why. He just switches directions. I've been meaning to learn a little more about the game since Jackson is obsessed, but Elias is always *in* a game when we're watching one. Why not learn from a player while I'm being made to spend time with one?

Collin parks in a parking garage downtown and then we get out and walk. The place he brings me to doesn't look appealing at all, but it's full of people already. He finds us seats at the bar, makes the bartender change the TV to a game, and then looks at me.

"Now what?"

"Teach me the rules. Well, at least what stuff means when it happens. Jackson loves hockey, but I don't know anything. He is always disappointed by my ignorance. He'll be so impressed if I know what's happening."

"Okay. I can do that."

We order food and drinks. I order alcohol for the first time in my life. It makes me nervous, but then, so does being on my first date since high school. Might as well add something else new to the list.

Collin laughs when I make a face after taking a sip of my Long Island iced tea.

"Don't laugh. I've never had a drink before."

His eyes widen. "You don't need to start with me. EJ will kill me if I bring you home drunk."

I roll my eyes. "You'll be fine. I don't plan to get drunk either, so relax."

He doesn't look like he believes me, but he lets it go. Collin focuses on the reason we're here. He explains each position and the basic setup of the game. I switch to regular sweet tea after finishing my drink because while good, I really don't want to drink more than I already have. During a commercial, I look at Collin.

"I'm never going to remember all of this, Collin," I whine a little dramatically.

He laughs. "Yes, you will. It's for Jackson."

"Do you know what I've noticed?" I say as a picture of some hot hockey player is shown on the screen since it's intermission and they're talking about him.

"What?"

"There are a *lot* of hot hockey players. That guy, Elias," I turn to look at him, "you." Collin shakes his head with a slight smile. "Do you like playing with your brother? What's that like?"

"Yeah, I like playing with him. I don't know if I could do it without him."

His seriousness makes me frown. "Why?"

He points to the TV. "It can be overwhelming. Cal helps ground me." He shrugs. "Do you like being a nanny?"

I nod. "Bree's sweet and Elias is the best." I sigh. "He's a really good guy."

"Rae?"

My muscles lock and I swivel slowly to see Henry, who eyes Collin. "What are you doing here?"

"I was going to ask you the same thing. Where's Jackson?"

"Is there a problem here?" Collin asks me.

I shake my head, though I want to say yes. "Go away, Henry. It's bad enough I have to see you tomorrow." When Jackson will officially meet him.

"Who is Jackson with while you're here?" Henry pushes.

"He's with Elias. Why does it matter?"

"He should be with you."

I don't know how it happens, but one minute my drink is in my hands, and the next, I throw it at Henry. How dare he tell me I have to be with Jackson twenty-four-seven. This is the first time since he was born that I've left him with someone else to go out.

"Okay." Collin stands, takes my cup and places it on the bar, and then pulls me away from a shocked Henry. "We're leaving."

I go to the bathroom while he pays our bill. I don't see Henry when I meet back up with him, which is good. There will likely be hell to pay for what I did.

"Can you take me home?" I ask Collin when we walk outside into the cold air.

"Not yet."

He takes my hand and we walk another block or two before he pulls me into what looks like an arcade, but there's a bar and it's full of adults. Collin pulls me to the first empty game we come across. It's one of those dance-off games.

"You're supposed to have fun with me, Raelynn. If you can't have fun here..." He lets the sentence trail off as he gets the game started.

"You're going down."

He grins. "We'll see."

We play a few rounds, all of which Collin wins, before stopping by the bar for a drink, sweet tea for me and water for Collin. I spy an air hockey table and that's where I drag Collin off to next. We're a bit more evenly matched in this one. Well, almost.

"Stop cheating!" I shout, making him laugh.

"I'm not."

"Yes, you are! You're using your freakishly long arms to your advantage." He reaches across the table and hits the little red disk just as it reaches the halfway point to cross over onto his side. Not even fair. I can't reach like that.

"Okay, whiney baby. We'll play by your rules."

My rules help me win, too. After I win two in a row, I raise my arms in the air and then take a few bows.

"I've had fun. Can you take me home now?" I'm starting for feel guilty about being here.

Collin doesn't argue me with this time. My mind wanders to Elias and if he built that fort with Jackson while I was gone as Collin drives me home.

"Are you going to tell EJ you had a good time?" Collin asks as we approach Elias's house.

"Yeah, why wouldn't I?"

He shrugs. "Are you going to tell him about that guy? Henry?"

I sigh. "Are you?" I don't know that Elias really needs to know.

"Should I?"

"That's the question, isn't it? What is he doing?" I ask when he pulls into Elias's driveway and we see him standing outside his front door with his arms folded over his chest.

"I don't know."

We get out and the moment we're close enough, Elias goes off on Collin. "Where the hell have you been? You were supposed to take her out for like two hours tops. I already put Jackson in bed without her, and it nearly gave the kid a heart attack."

I'm so confused. "Elias, why are you upset?" Granted, I feel horrible for not being here to tuck Jackson in and that he had to deal with that, but this whole thing was Elias's idea.

Elias opens and closes his mouth a few times. "He wasn't supposed to keep you out all night," he finally sputters.

"It's not that late," I defend. He's overreacting. I look at Collin, who seems amused by all of this. "Thanks, Collin. We'll see you later." He nods and waves goodbye as he retreats to his vehicle. I grab Elias's hand. "Let's go inside and unruffle those feathers."

"You had fun?" he asks almost as if he's hoping I'll say no.

I smile when I see a blanket fort in the living room. I toe out of my shoes, drop my purse, and leave Elias to crawl under the blankets, held up by the couch and chairs. There are more blankets and pillows lying on the floor. Jackson taught him how to built a fort after all.

"Raelynn?" Elias calls as he crawls in after me and then lies next to me. "You had fun?"

I shrug. "We ran into Henry. I decided to drink alcohol for the first time. And Collin took me to this arcade place afterward so the night wasn't completely ruined. We would've been back sooner if not for that."

Elias frowns. "Are you going out with him again?

What happened with Henry?"

I laugh. "This wasn't even a real date, so no, there probably won't be another one." I close my eyes and lean my forehead against his shoulder. "Henry's a jackass. That's what happened. I don't want to talk about it. I want to lay here in the fort." Once I've had a moment of peace, I lean back a little to look at him. "Don't send me on any more dates, especially if you're going to get mad at them for doing what you asked."

"Trust me, I won't."

"Good." My gaze drops to his lips, which rise into a smile, and I realize how close we are. I should probably move back some.

"You ever think about kissing me, Raelynn?"

My eyes snap up to Elias's. "What?" My heart hammers in my chest, ready to break out and run far, far away.

Elias's hand rests on my hip and he repeats, "Do you ever think about kissing me, Raelynn?" I can't answer that! "Would you be upset if I kissed you?" Nope. Not at all. But that doesn't mean we should. I don't think it's a good idea. All I can do is stare at him. His head inches closer to mine.

"I...we..." Where are the rest of my words to protest this fantastically bad idea?

"Should totally kiss?" Elias says with a grin. He's so close now his nose touches mine. "Close your eyes."

If I do it, he'll kiss me.

If my eyelids close, I'm giving him permission and saying I want him to do this.

Against my better judgment, I close my eyes. The second I do, his lips press to mine, gentle, soft, and perfect. Our tongues slide against one another as the kiss deepens. Elias pulls my body on top of his while rolling onto his back. There's nothing fast or frantic about this. But the sensuality and need in the kiss has my arms moving up to rest on either side of his head and my fingers curling into his hair.

Elias's hands slip underneath my shirt. They glide up and up and up until he reaches my bra. Then, suddenly, he rolls us over so he can hover above me. It takes me a second to realize he's stopped kissing me.

"Good?"

I nod.

And just like that, his mouth is on mine again. My skin flushes. My body comes alive with every kiss, every stroke of his hand down my side, and every push of his hips against mine. My nails scratch him as I grab his shirt, wanting to take it off.

"Raelynn?" Elias pulls back. His breath hits my mouth and I don't want him to talk. I don't want to think about what we're doing. I don't want to second-guess myself here. "Do you want to go upstairs?"

I nod before I can say no.

He knocks the blankets down so we can stand instead of crawling out. He pulls me up after he stands and I follow him up the stairs, my heart thudding and echoing with every step. Holy shit. This is happening. I'm about to sleep with my boss. My deep breath is loud enough that Elias glances at me as he closes the door to his room.

"Changing your mind?" He doesn't look mad with his question. Mostly curious and maybe on the verge of being slightly let down.

"What if this messes things up?"

"I don't think it will, but if it does, we'll fix it. You

want to stay and I don't want you to go anywhere. That's why we'll fix it."

I nod, reassured by his words. Elias walks further into his room and I follow him. "What happens afterward?" Do things go back to normal? Do we sometimes sleep with one another? What?

Elias sits on his bed, reaches out, and pulls me to stand between his knees. "What would you like to happen? For this to be a one-time thing? For it to happen again? For me to take you out on a date instead of that prick, Collin?"

A giggle escapes before I can help myself. Elias smiles. "Collin's a prick now?"

He nods. "I only sent you on a date with someone because I was hoping it'd make me stop thinking about you. It backfired big time." He slowly pushes my shirt up, my muscles tensing in anticipation as his fingers graze my skin. "Do you want to take the risk with me, Raelynn?"

"Yep."

His grin leaves me breathless. It's the first of many times tonight he takes my breath away. Being with Elias is not as scary as I thought it would be, considering he's the first person I've been with since Henry, since having Jackson. It's seamless and feels like one of the best decisions I've made in a long time.

EJ

WAKING UP WITH Raelynn makes the morning a little brighter than usual. I kept waiting for her to say no last night, but she never did. It almost seems surreal. Are we sure last night happened? That she's here in my bed right now? I close my eyes and open them again.

Yep, she's still here.

I set my alarm before we went to bed and it went off a second ago. I kiss Raelynn and she hums.

"Time to wake up."

"No," she grumbles. "It's not fair that your bed is this comfortable."

"Yours isn't?" I've never slept in that room, obviously.

"Not this comfortable." She sighs and opens her eyes. "I should get up, though. The longer I stay, the worse it'll be, right?"

My lips dip in a frown. "What do you mean?"

"You know. It's better to suck it up, face the cold air, and rush to the bathroom for a shower than to stay here and think about it while being underneath the blankets."

Oh. For a second, I thought she was somehow talking about us. Raelynn rolls away from me and gets out of bed, snatching a T-shirt to pull over her head. She pauses after she picks up the rest of her clothes.

"Whatever we're doing, let's not do in front of Jackson, okay? For now, at least."

"Yeah, no problem."

"Thanks." She scurries out of my room with that covered.

I might as well get up as well. Part of what Raelynn said bugs me. The *whatever we're doing* part. I thought we settled it last night that we'd see where things go with us. That means dating, not "whatever we're doing." Maybe she was simply nervous at the idea of me kissing her in front of Jackson and that flubbed her words. Either way, I want to make sure she knows I don't want this to be a one-time thing.

If Henry wasn't coming over, I'd take her out tonight. Tomorrow, we have a game. Maybe Deanna and Brayden will watch the kids Wednesday or Thursday for me to take her out. He always complains I never let him babysit. Now, he can.

By the time Bree and I make it downstairs, Raelynn is

in the kitchen with Jackson, making breakfast.

"It's not game day, J-man," I say when I see he's wearing his jersey. He got it last week when Deanna took him to a game for Raelynn. He usually tries to wear it on game days, as long as Raelynn doesn't make him change into something else.

He shrugs. "I know. But maybe if I wear it today *and* tomorrow, you'll score two goals." Jackson thinks he and his jersey are my good luck charms since I scored a goal when he first wore it.

"You're not wearing it two days in a row, Jackson," Raelynn quickly shoots him down.

"Please? It's for Mr. EJ!"

"You can wear it for the game tomorrow, but not to school."

Jackson frowns, but doesn't argue with her anymore. He looks at me. "Do you think it'll still work?"

"It might." He'll be disappointed if I don't score two goals tomorrow and he'll think it didn't work, that his good luck is fading. Who knew the most pressure I'd feel would come from a five-year-old? "Do you need help, Raelynn?"

"No, I've got it. Thanks."

She normally turns me down unless she's running behind. I get busy feeding Bree.

"Will today be the day, princess?" I ask her. "Are you going to say DaDa? Or stick with Ja-Ja as your favorite?" Bree smiles at me. "DaDa," I say, pointing at myself.

"DaDa!" she shouts, slamming her hands on the table. I stare, stunned. She reaches over to where Jackson is and continues talking in her baby language. But hold the phone. My baby just said DaDa! Laughter racks my chest as I stand and pick her up, holding her in the air above me. She laughs now.

"Say it again." She doesn't. I bring her down and look at Raelynn, who smiles. "Did you hear her? She said it! She said DaDa!"

"Yeah, I heard her. She yelled it to shut you up," she teases.

I laugh. "Don't try and ruin my moment."

Not much can take this away from me. I ride on cloud nine for the rest of the day. We don't have practice today, so I have to settle for texting Brayden the news. I'll have to tell everyone else tomorrow. I hang out with Bree and don't do much else. Well, I watch Raelynn do schoolwork and worry herself.

"It'll be fine," I tell her for the fifth time. With Henry coming tonight to meet Jackson, Raelynn is wound up tighter than I've ever seen her.

"I have a bad feeling. Maybe my bad feelings are like yours." She closes her laptop and steals Bree from my lap.

"Well, I have a good feeling, so there. And I'll be here, lurking in the background, ready to jump in and be prince charming to save the day if needed."

Bree rests her head on Raelynn's shoulder as Raelynn gives me a smile. It's time for my princess to take a nap and she knows it.

"You'd make a good prince charming."

"Think so?"

She nods, rubs Bree's back, and laughs a little. "And I'm the perfect example of a damsel in distress."

"No, you're not." I completely disagree with her. "You've raised Jackson for five years on your own. No one swooped in to save you. You're still kicking ass."

Raelynn looks down at Bree as she shakes her head. "When I met you, we were essentially homeless that day."

"But you made sure you found a job and a place to live. You are like a reigning queen, Raelynn. You might not always have your shit together, but no one singlehandedly saves you."

She's quiet for a moment before chuckling and looking over at me. "A queen? You're delusional, Elias."

I roll my eyes hard, which makes her smile. "So, would you be okay with Deanna and Brayden watching the kids Wednesday or Thursday?"

"What for?" she asks. Her confusion would be cute if I didn't feel the reason should be obvious.

"For our date."

Her eyes widen briefly in surprise. "Um." Raelynn stands and I follow her as she heads upstairs to apparently lay Bree down in her crib. "I don't know, Elias."

"Why?" Is she changing her mind already?

She doesn't answer me. Not right away at least. She lays a sleeping Bree down, watches her for a moment, and then takes my hand to lead me out of the room. "I already left Jackson once this week. I don't know what's going to happen today either. I just worry it might be too much happening all at once for him."

I relax a little, knowing she's only worried about Jackson.

"And if Henry finds out about this—"

"What does Henry have to do with it?" I interrupt.

She sighs and leans forward, resting her forehead on my chest. "When we ran into him? Collin and me, I mean. He kept asking where Jackson was. I told him, but was stupid enough to ask why it mattered. His answer was because he should be with me." She looks up at me. "I threw my tea on him."

"Raelynn," I start to say something, but she cuts me off.

"I don't know what came over me except anger. It was the first time I've been out without Jackson and he says that to me? Him of all people?" She shakes her head. "I can't have Henry thinking I'm a bad mom," she finishes in a whisper. "Or making me feel like one."

Have I mentioned I don't like Henry? Because I don't. While I don't think he'll cause major problems, he's obviously making waves with Raelynn. I pull her against me in a hug. "You just need to show Henry who's boss until he figures out how to co-parent with you. Until he figures out how to be a parent, period. Don't let him make you feel like shit, Raelynn. Do you know the best way to do that?" She looks up at me with questioning eyes. "You go out with me this week."

She smiles. "You're relentless."

I take a step forward, which causes her to take one back. I keep doing this until we're in my room. "That sounds like a yes."

"It's a maybe," she counters. "What are we doing in here?"

"Bree's napping. Jackson doesn't have to be picked up for an hour." I grin. "Whatever shall we do with that time?"

"Talk. Get to know each other." Her smile matches mine and she lifts my shirt for me to take it off.

"We can do that when the kids are awake and present." I dip my head to kiss her. We only have an hour and I plan to make good use of every second. I want to hear her moans, her sighs, and feel her body tense and relax beneath me. I want to get to know her *this* way, connect with her on this level, and get her even more comfortable being here.

Because here is right where I want her to be.

At exactly five thirty, the doorbell chimes throughout the house. Raelynn and I both stand. She might want to answer the door herself, but this is my house and I don't like Henry, so I want to make sure he feels my presence. Raelynn stands slightly behind me as I open the door.

"Hey, Henry. Come on in."

He steps inside and closes the door behind him. Raelynn grabs my shirt at my back, but quickly releases it. That's the only sign she shows of her nerves.

"He's in the living room," she says, turning on her heel.

We follow after her. Jackson eyes Henry as Raelynn sits next to him. I sit next to her, picking up Bree, and Henry sits in the chair.

"Who are you?" Jackson asks.

Raelynn opens her mouth, but Henry replies first with, "I'm your dad."

"Henry!" Raelynn shouts at him. Jackson frowns with confusion and crawls into Raelynn's lap, hiding his face in her neck. "My way, Henry," Raelynn reminds him. "My way or you can leave right now." I want to kiss her for the steel resolve in her voice.

Henry nods and I'm glad he looks uncomfortable with

Jackson's reaction.

Raelynn takes a deep breath as she looks down at Jackson. "Baby, look at me for a second. We have to talk about something." Jackson does as she requested. "That is your dad; his name is Henry. It takes a mom and a dad to have a baby, but sometimes, the baby only grows up with a dad, like Bree." At this, Jackson glances over at me. "Sometimes, the baby grows up with only a mom, like how you've done so far. Sometimes, the baby always has his mom and dad. Sometimes, the baby grows up some and meets his mom or dad later, like you are right now. So, now, you have me and your dad, okay?" Jackson just stares at her.

"He's going to have dinner with us tonight and you can get to know him. Does that sound like fun?" Jackson shakes his head no. "You don't want to tell him about all the things you like to do and play with? Maybe he likes the same things." Raelynn's eyes widen in horror. "He might not know how to build a fort." She gasps. "He might not even know what a fort is!"

Jackson doesn't give a fuck what she says. He leans forward and hides his face again, making Raelynn sigh and look helplessly at me.

"Ja-Ja!" Bree leans over and slaps his back. That gets his attention.

"Maybe you should tell him about that," I suggest. "That's pretty cool."

Jackson holds Bree's outstretched hand, which makes her happy. He stays silent, though. This may be a disaster if we can't figure out how to get Jackson to talk.

"You like hockey?" Henry asks him, deciding to take an initiative. "Whose jersey are you wearing?" If he doesn't watch hockey, he might not know it's mine. Plus, I can't remember if I ever told him my last name.

Jackson sends him a look, but I can't see what kind it is. "Mr. EJ's."

And we have contact!

Henry glances at me, but he keeps his face passive. "Is he your favorite player?" Jackson nods. "That's cool. I bet you know more about hockey than I do. They use a ball, right?" He can't be that stupid. And he's not, because he gets Jackson talking finally.

"It's a puck," Jackson corrects. "There are three periods." He slowly turns and angles toward Henry as he fills him in on all he's learned about the game since living here. Raelynn leans back into the couch, relaxed now that things are transitioning the way she hoped.

Eventually, they move to the floor to build with Legos. Raelynn takes Bree from me, so I can cook the dinner we're supposed to have. I decide since Jackson's had a rough day, we can have his favorite: hotdogs and mac and cheese.

Raelynn appears with Bree as I get his plate ready.

"Everything going okay still?"

"Yeah. I was really worried for a second there."

"You and me both."

"Momma," Jackson says as he comes into the kitchen with Henry trailing behind. "Are we going to the game tomorrow?"

"I don't know, Jackson. It's a school night."

"Please? If I can't wear my jersey to school again, then I have to wear it to the game for the good luck to work. Right, Mr. EJ?" His eyes are so hopeful.

"Don't bring me into this, J-man. You going to the

game is up to your mom."

"But if I go, you might score *two* goals." He even holds up two fingers for emphasis.

I laugh and Raelynn says, "I'm sure your good luck will reach him from here, baby. We'll watch it on TV until it's your bedtime." Jackson frowns. "Don't pout or we won't go to a game this weekend. Why don't you and Henry wash up for dinner?"

Jackson tells Henry to follow him and they leave to wash their hands in the downstairs bathroom. We set the table and everything is ready by the time they return. We start eating and things seem to be going fine.

"Is he moving in?" Jackson asks, pointing to Henry.

Raelynn drops her fork. "What? No. Why would you think that?"

"Bree lives with her dad," he points out.

"Yes, but you live with me and Henry has his own house. He will come over here to see you and visit with you."

Henry opens his mouth, but a glare from Raelynn causes him to shut it. Jackson accepts that answer and a few minutes later, he looks at me. "When can we go skating again?"

I briefly glance to Raelynn, but say, "Maybe one day this week." I don't know how to schedule time with Jackson when I don't know how often Henry will want to see him. My answer already has Henry frowning, so I suspect he wants to see him as often as possible. "Maybe your dad can come with us."

"I can't skate," Henry says.

"Neither can Jackson," I reply.

"Mr. EJ is teaching me," Jackson adds. "I skated by

myself some last time," he says proudly.

I'm not exactly thrilled about the idea of Henry tagging along, but I didn't invite him for me. Jackson may be talking to Henry now, which is a good step up compared to when Henry arrived, but when Henry goes to leave and Henry asks for a hug, Jackson hesitates. He wraps his arms around Raelynn's leg instead. I've learned that's one of his go-to moves when he's uncomfortable. Henry offers a fist bump instead and Jackson doesn't hesitate to give him that.

Jackson comes with me to read to Bree while I rock her to sleep and Raelynn says goodbye to Henry in private. I almost want to stay to make sure he's not an ass to her, but I feel like she can handle him on her own.

I'm sitting in the recliner in Bree's room with Bree in one arm, a book rests on my knee, and Jackson sits on my other side with his legs stretched out on the arm rest. I read about a chicken who thinks the sky is falling. By the time I finish, not only is Bree asleep, but so is Jackson. I'm stuck in place until Raelynn comes in; otherwise, I'll wake one of them up.

While I wait and rock in the recliner, my mind wanders to Raelynn. Maybe she'll at least sleep in my room again tonight. I've been with her for twenty-four hours and I already can't get enough.

Raelynn

MY HEART SWELLS and bursts at the sight of how cute Elias looks, sitting in the recliner with Bree asleep in one arm and Jackson asleep with his head on his shoulder. Elias grins like he knows I'm stunned stupid from how adorable they look.

"Can you help me? If you get her, I'll take him," he whispers.

A small pain twists my heart because my baby is too big for me to pick up and carry anymore without it being a serious struggle. I walk over to pick up Bree. She continues to sleep soundly as I lay her in the crib. I follow Elias over to Jackson's bedroom. My son doesn't stay asleep, which is fine by me. We get him ready for bed and changed into his pjs. Before Elias can leave the room, so I can tuck him in and say goodnight, Jackson says, "Mr. EJ, will you read to me tonight?"

Elias flicks his gaze to me, almost looking like he wants permission to say yes. I nod. We sit on either side of Jackson while Elias reads him a Dr. Seuss book. He falls asleep two pages before the end. I kiss his forehead and we sneak out of his room.

"Tonight wasn't too bad, was it? You okay with Henry coming with us when we go skating?"

I smile and nod. "It's sweet you offered. Henry wants to see him every day for a while." I shake my head as Elias slips his hand in mind and leads me back downstairs. "I'm torn. I see why he does, but then if Jackson gets used to seeing him every day, is he going to be upset when that slows down? I feel like we should get on a schedule and make it more like it will be in the future." Elias sits on the couch, but pulls me onto his lap. "He's jealous of you."

He raises an eyebrow. "Me?"

"Yep. He thinks Jackson might like you more than him. He also questioned whether my job is healthy for Jackson." And that got to me because while I don't want to lose this job, I don't want Jackson to get hurt if something were to ever happen either. Jackson is bound to get attached to Elias, just like Bree is bound to get attached to us. Her first word was Ja-Ja, for goodness sake!

Elias's hand rests on my cheek for a moment before sliding up into my hair and then resting on the back of my head. "Raelynn, listen to me very carefully because I'm only going to say this once and you should only repeat what I say to Henry once. If you decide to stop being

Bree's nanny one day or if things don't work out between us, Jackson and me? We're still going to be friends. Just like if you still wanted to be in Bree's life, I wouldn't stop you, especially if she was Jackson's age and was used to having you around.

"You want to expand your and Jackson's world, remember? Well," he grins, "I'm now a part of your and his world. Henry can suck it up. Jackson will like him eventually. You need to stop letting him make you second-guess yourself."

"I'm not second-guessing myself that much," I defend. "Bree will get attached to us just as much as Jackson will get attached to you, so I worry about them both." His eyes soften at this.

"You don't need to worry about my princess because *I'm* not worried. I only let her around good people."

I can't help it. I smile.

"There you go," he murmurs. "Smile. Relax." He grins. "Kiss me."

I do kiss him. It still surprises me that I'm this comfortable around him. I always thought that whenever I started dating again, I'd feel awkward and so nervous, but it hasn't been nearly as bad with Elias. As he begins to run his hands up and down my thighs, his fingers digging into my skin as I now straddle him, I pull away.

"What was your life like before Bree?" I ask. "What did you do with your free time, I mean." Elias spends almost all of his free time now with Bree. But since we're about to go on a date, I wonder what he likes to do with his spare time.

Elias shifts his hips to relax further into the couch with his head leaning against the back of the couch, and I have to swallow hard at the feel of his cock through his jeans. "I'm boring," he says with a chuckle. "My favorite thing to do was stay home and watch movies."

"That doesn't make you boring."

"Yes, it does, Raelynn. I'm just on the road so much and busy with work that it sounds like heaven to stay at home and watch movies for a few hours, you know?" I nod and he smiles. "But that's only during the season. I like to be a beach bum and fish during the offseason. I didn't go this past summer since Bree is so young. I didn't want to take her to the beach yet. Maybe next summer. Or I might get a pool."

"That sounds nice." Jackson would probably love a pool, too.

"What do you like to do?"

I shrug. "I'm a mom and Bree's nanny. I'm also a student. I don't have free time." Okay, so I have a little and I use it to do something, but I'm not so sure I want to tell Elias this. I haven't been able to do much of my little hobby since I moved in here anyway.

He frowns. "There must be something you like to do and are able to do."

"I've gotten hooked on a soap opera since I've been taking care of Bree," I say, hoping that will appease him.

It doesn't.

"Do you have a nice dress?"

His change of topic confuses me for a second. What does that have to do with what I do in my spare time? "No," I answer him anyway.

"You need to go shopping, then."

"Why?"

"It's for our date."

116

My eyebrows shoot up and Elias smiles. He's taking me somewhere really nice then.

"I'll take Jackson and Henry skating Wednesday, and we'll go out Thursday," he adds.

"Sounds good. Why don't we watch a movie?" If that's his favorite way to unwind during the season, then I'd like to do that with him. Elias seems to love this idea as well based on the smile on his face. He reaches for the re-mote to find a movie. We also move to lie on the couch on our sides with me in front of him.

This is all so bizarre, being here with Elias like this, but at least now, I don't have to worry so much about not ogling him and thinking inappropriately about him. About thirty minutes into the movie, Elias pulls my hair out of the way. He kisses my neck. My breathing shallows im-mediately. His hand slips underneath my shirt, his finger-tips trail up and down my side.

"What do you hope your future has?" he murmurs against my skin.

He wants me to think while his hand and lips are touching me? Doesn't he realize I'm basically like a teen-ager right now? I swallow hard and think of an answer. "I want to graduate, figure out my dream job, and one day, give Jackson a sibling."

Elias's movements stop. He turns me a little so he can look at me. One of his eyebrows arches. "You didn't men-tion a relationship," he points out.

"My last one left me pretty scarred." I shrug because maybe those words aren't as true today as they once were. "I care more about taking care of Jackson, I guess."

Elias smirks. "How do you plan to give him a sibling if you don't have a relationship at some point?"

"That's kinda the problem with my plan," I say, causing him to laugh. "Especially since I don't want to have a kid with just anyone. I learned my lesson with Henry." At this, his expression sobers. "Do you want Bree to have a sibling one day?"

"I don't know. I wouldn't be opposed, but I'm like you. I'd need to find someone I'd want to make a baby with."

All this talk about making babies causes me to look back at the TV.

"Momma?"

I spring upright to see Jackson's feet descending down the stairs. He didn't see me with Elias, which eases some of my nerves, but he doesn't usually wake up in the middle of the night. I stand and head toward the stairs. "Yeah, baby? What's wrong?" I walk up to him.

"I heard a noise in my room at the window."

What? That scares me a little. "Elias? Don't you want to come with us?" When I turn, I see him already at the bottom of the steps to follow us. I take Jackson's hand. "Come on. We'll make sure everything's safe and get you back to sleep."

The light is on in his room when we get there. I get a reluctant Jackson back in bed while Elias peers out of his window and double checks that it's locked, even though we're on the second floor. Jackson says it sounded like something hit the window, but Elias tells him there's nothing outside. He turns the light off and stands by the door, waiting for me.

"Everything's okay now. You can go back to sleep." I kiss his forehead.

He frowns. "You aren't staying with me until I fall

asleep?"

"I can if you want me to." I never turn him down when he's scared; it's the one thing I've never been able to do. Jackson holds his arms out for me and with that, I lie on the bed next to him. I don't sing to him like some moms might. Sometimes, I just hold him. Sometimes, like tonight, I run my fingers through his hair with one hand and soothe away the wrinkles on his forehead with the other. Running my fingers across his forehead and down the bridge of his nose always relaxes him.

He falls asleep within minutes. I slowly ease out of bed to find Elias in the same spot; I figured he'd leave once Jackson asked me to stay. We carefully and quietly leave Jackson's room.

"I'm sorry."

"For what? Being his mom and doing mom things?" Elias rolls his eyes. "Don't apologize, Raelynn. Not for something like that." As he tugs me in the opposite direction of the stairs, I realize it's dark down there. Maybe he did leave to turn off all the lights and turn on the alarm. "Will you sleep in my room tonight?" he asks.

I glance back at Jackson's room. He'll panic if he wakes up again, checks my room, I'm not there and clearly, I'm not downstairs. I don't want him finding me in Elias's room either.

"I'll lock the door. If he wakes up, he'll come to my room when he can't find you. I can answer, escort him back to his room, and you can slip out, like you were in the kitchen or something," Elias supplies, reading my worry. "Or you can stay in your room." He releases my hand. "I don't mean to pressure you."

"I think I'll stay in my room tonight." I don't know

why I say these words or why I feel like I should be in my room instead of his.

Elias nods, not looking disappointed at all. He simply accepts my decision, which makes me relax. He kisses me softly for only a moment and we go our separate ways. My stomach twists like I made the wrong decision as I get ready for bed. What's the big deal if I stay in my own room and give us some space? I wince to myself. We don't even need space.

I'm settled in bed, my blankets resting over my breasts, and all I can think about is being in Elias's room. My bed feels lumpy, though it's not. It feels hard, though it's not. What it is is not nearly as comfortable as Elias's bed. Is he asleep already? What would it be like to simply sleep with Elias? Would he hold me? How? An arm around my waist? One under my neck? Would his legs tangle with mine? Would my head rest on his chest? Or would we barely touch, each on separate sides of the bed? I toss and turn for another thirty minutes with these damn thoughts in my head.

That's it. I can't take it anymore. I toss my blankets aside and tiptoe across the hall. Elias left his door halfway open. Maybe he knew, or hoped, I'd change my mind. I stand in the doorway, not able to see into his dark bedroom, despite the nightlight Elias put in the hallway for Jackson.

"Are you just going to stand there, Raelynn?"

A whoosh of air pushes through my lips. He's awake and can see me. "Can I come in?"

A moment later, the lamp next to his bed illuminates his room. "Everything okay?"

That's not a yes. "If it's okay with you, I'd like to

change my mind."

His grin is slow and brilliant. Elias pats the spot next to him, wordlessly telling me to come on. I walk across the room, around his bed, and slide underneath the sheets he holds up for me. He flicks off the lamp and I lie on my back, suddenly stiff as a board. This is probably the first time I've truly felt nervous around him.

"Look at me, Raelynn."

I turn my head his way, but it's so dark in his room. "I can't see you," I point out.

He chuckles. "That's okay. I'm about to kiss you." He waits two seconds for me to object before I feel him shift. My heartbeat trips over itself in an effort to pound faster in my chest. His lips graze over mine. I suck in a breath just as his mouth presses harder and his tongue enters my mouth. My body turns toward his, his hand clutches my hip, and my leg is way more forward than I am, tossing itself over his hips. Elias pulls away. Whether it was his intention or not, his kiss relaxes me.

"Thanks," I breathe.

His lips still against mine rise. "Welcome. My alarm's already set to wake you up."

"You knew I'd come in here?"

"No. I hoped you'd change your mind, though."

Now, we're both smiling like idiots. We stay as we are, giving ourselves a little space as we rest our heads more comfortably on our pillows. I worry that I'm not a cuddly person. I normally sleep on my back. People don't really care about this sort of thing, do they? If I wiggle out of Elias's arms at some point to sleep on my back, he won't care if he happens to wake up and find me like that?

I need to talk to a girl friend and squelch some of

what I'm sure are stupid anxieties. Maybe I can confide in Deanna soon. That'll be something else that's sort of new for me. I haven't done that since high school. Most of my high school friends dropped me so fast once they found out I was pregnant. Any I had left disappeared when I left town.

A deep breath fills my lungs. This is a big week. Henry will hang around. Someone else will be watching my baby for a night. I'll go on a date. Daydreams of what that date may be like lull me to sleep.

Deanna has blown me away. She texted me, all excited about the fact that she is watching the kids for us *and* because Elias and I are going on a date. When I mentioned how Elias said I need a dress and how I need to go shopping, she took the day off work and came with me. Having a friend again is so *weird*. Having someone I trust to watch Jackson is weirder.

"Are you excited about the date?" she asks as she flicks through the rack. She told me to leave it up to her to find the perfect dress for me, and I have no problem doing so. It allows me to keep a better eye on Bree.

"Yes, but I'm nervous, too."

"That's understandable. I will say that EJ must be a great guy all around. Brayden has friends on the team, of course, but EJ is probably his best and most legit friend. He wouldn't be friends with a jackass. And he'd probably eventually get annoyed by anyone else if they sent pictures of their kid so much," she adds as an afterthought.

122

"I have no doubts that he's a good guy. I can tell from how he is with his daughter and Jackson." And the fact that he still gave me the job. All signs point toward Elias being a good guy, but it doesn't make me any less nervous. Just because he's a good guy doesn't mean he's the good guy for me or that this will end in a happily ever after. "Can I ask you a question?" It seems like the perfect one for Deanna because to me, she has this air of confidence cocooning her and I want that for myself.

"What is it?" Deanna stops looking at dresses to give me her full attention for a moment.

"How can I be more confident and less insecure with myself?"

Her mouth opens and closes a few times, like I've stunned her and she's unsure what to say. "What are you insecure about?" she finally asks.

"Stupid stuff. Like he asked me to sleep in his room the other night and for some reason, I told him no, but I ended up in his room anyway. Then, I worried about whether or not I was cuddly enough because I felt like I'd end up sleeping on my back and away from him. I worry about some of the bigger things too, especially now that we're sort of dating."

"Like what?"

"Like not intruding on his space. We live there. Before I was just someone who worked for him and helped take care of Bree. I tried to find and respect the boundaries and make sure he had time alone with Bree. Now, we're doing this."

"Have you talked to EJ about this?"

"No, but I think he wants the boundaries too. He's asked for time alone with Bree before." I have a sudden need to get my secret off my chest about Christmas, but for this, I don't quite trust her not to tell Brayden and for him to keep this from Elias. We haven't reached that level of trust yet.

"Has EJ complained about anything? Is he pretty vocal with you?" When I nod, she says, "Maybe you can try relaxing and let him sort of lead. Let him tell you if you're doing something wrong." She winces. "I don't like the way that sounds, but you know what I mean."

I nod.

"Ja-Ja!" Bree shouts, rattling her toy.

"He's at school, Bree. We'll see him and DaDa later." Her eyes light up as if she knows exactly what I'm saying. She talks some more and soon, Deanna ushers us to the dressing room with an armful of dresses. I hope we find one that makes me feel confident and beautiful and tempting to Elias Bertuzzi.

EJ

"**I** HAD A feeling you wouldn't be able to resist," Derek says with a grin. I stupidly decided to meet up with him since he's in town for the game tonight and I just told him I'm now officially dating Raelynn. "Why can't we eat at your house?"

I shake my head. "You can meet her another time. It's too soon and you're too annoying."

"Have you told your ma yet?"

"No. I'm going to wait until Christmas for that."

He nods. "Is Nicole coming too?" he asks, referring to my sister.

"She finally said she would. She wanted to stay behind and with a friend, but she changed her mind." I'm glad she's coming. Out of everyone in my family, I talk to my sister the least, so it'll be good to see her.

"Good. So, you ready to lose tonight?" He grins and I flip him off.

It isn't us who lose tonight either. Derek manages to score a goal in the middle of the first period and it pisses me off when he makes sure to grin at me as he skates past me after his celebration. What an asshole. But it fuels me as much as it does whenever Jackson tells me I'll score a goal because of his good luck.

Every time my line is on the ice, we swipe the puck if we don't have it and charge toward their net. Shot after shot after shot, the puck flies toward the goalie. He makes a glove save and then one with the tip of his toe, but I do manage to send a puck soaring high. It clangs against the bar.

But it goes in!

"Fuck yeah!" Scotty rubs my helmet.

Tommy shouts something and hugs me like I just gifted him a brand new car on Christmas morning.

Hockey hugs are the best as the defensemen on our line crash into us as well. I don't bother grinning at Derek. Not just yet. I save that for right before the end of the first period. We're on the ice with four seconds left. I shoot a one-timer.

The goalie doesn't stand a chance.

Then I skate by Derek with a big fat grin on my face.

We end up winning the game two to one.

Henry looks uncomfortable as fuck as he sticks one foot onto the ice. For one blissful second, I relish in his unease. Then, I banish that because I don't need to have those kinds of feelings toward Jackson's father. I'm almost surprised he's here. He even got off work early, so we wouldn't have to come later than we originally planned.

"Do you want Mr. EJ to hold your hand and help you?" Jackson asks him.

Holding back my grin is nearly impossible.

"I'm okay, kiddo."

Jackson frowns, and he surprises me when he says, "I don't like that."

Henry is now on the ice and holding on to the boards. He glances over at Jackson with surprise. "What?"

"Kiddo," Jackson spits the name like it tastes disgusting. "My name is Jackson." He pauses and then adds, "Well, Momma calls me baby sometimes and Mr. EJ calls me J-man. But I don't like kiddo." His nose wrinkles.

"Okay," Henry says with a nod. "I won't call you that anymore."

Jackson nods curtly in satisfaction. He holds out his hand to Henry, which he takes. I listen as Jackson repeats the instructions I gave him when I first brought him. Pride swells my chest that he remembered so clearly. At the end of the day, though, I hope this will make him more comfortable around Henry. I've noticed Jackson has yet to refer to Henry as dad, Henry, Mr. Henry, or any sort of name. Raelynn and I always refer to him as 'your dad' when we talk to Jackson, but he's not calling Henry anything yet.

We slowly skate around the rink, Henry more wobbly than Jackson. Henry talks to Jackson about school, learning about his teacher and the things he likes and dislikes. I worry my plan is going to shit when Jackson very obviously pulls his hand away from Henry's. He looks up at me.

"Can I try skating on my own like last time?" he asks.

"Sure thing, J-man." I move in front of him and crouch. He holds both his arms out in front of him and my hands hover under his so I can grab them if needed. He moves his feet, but he's more hesitant this time. I wonder if Henry makes him nervous. "Be confident, Jackson," I tell him. "You can do it."

"Yep," he says more to himself than to anyone else. Jackson pumps his legs, wanting to go faster. I don't think he's ready for that. I skate backward to give him room and the moment I do, he loses his concentration and his balance. My hands clasp around his before he can think about falling.

"Why are you frowning?" I ask him.

"I almost fell. That didn't happen last time."

"You're still learning, J-man. And falling is okay. It means you're trying. Plus, you know what?"

"What?" He looks at me with big hopeful eyes.

"You went further this time."

His eyes light up. "Really?"

I nod and release one of his hands so he can fist bump me. He turns to Henry. "Did you hear that? I went further this time!"

Henry smiles, but I can't tell if it's forced or not. "I heard. That's awesome, Jackson."

The rink begins to crowd and I have to crush Jackson's spirits. "Time to go, J-man."

"Already?" He frowns. "When can we come back?"

"Maybe next week. I'll have to look at my schedule."

Jackson nods and I help the both of them off the ice. Outside, I get Jackson into his booster seat and close the door once Henry has said his goodbye.

"How old do you have to be to start lessons?"

My heart stutters. *No.* Skating gear and lessons is supposed to be my gift to Jackson for Christmas. Henry can't usurp me. "He's old enough, if that's what you're asking."

He nods. "Do you think Raelynn would let him?"

No. Not from you. Damn it. This is killing me more than I thought it would. I decide to be honest with him. "I don't know. I'm planning to surprise him with skates and lessons for Christmas." Henry's shoulders fall with defeat. "But maybe we can split it? One of us gets him the skates, the other pays for the lessons."

"You'd do that?"

"Yeah." It was my idea first, but Henry is Jackson's father and he needs to build a relationship with him more than I do. This might help.

"You get the skates then. Do we need to ask Raelynn?"

"Are you willing to help her take him to the lessons?" I ask. If he isn't, then I'm about to rethink this.

He nods. "Of course."

"I wasn't planning to ask her, but that's because I thought she might say it's too much from me and say no. If you're halving it with me, then she probably won't protest too much. Plus, Jackson's going to love this. I'll test the waters with her and if she doesn't object too much, then don't worry about it."

"Okay. Thanks for letting me do this."

"No problem." I start to turn away from him and even

open my door, but I stop. "Hey, do you know who Raelynn plans to spend Christmas with? She said she's going to see an old friend, but if you're seeing Jackson on Christmas..." My voice trails off. Raelynn never said she wasn't going to see her friend, so she still isn't supposed to be at the house over Christmas.

Henry frowns. "Raelynn doesn't have old friends anymore. She would never go back home either. She told me she would come to my house on Christmas Day for me to see Jackson."

What? "Maybe she changed her mind then. See you later, Henry."

Raelynn is keeping something from me. If there's one thing I learned from my relationship with Vicky, it's that I didn't really know her. Not only that, but while I was with her, I was okay with not pushing to learn more about her. If I had, I'd have known about the drugs. Had I cared enough, I would've paid attention, period. Going forward, I worry about not knowing as much as possible about the person I'm with. About secrets and being blindsided like I was with Vicky, both with the drugs and with Bree. I don't want the person I'm in a relationship with keeping things from me.

And it sounds like Raelynn is.

My gut tells me she is.

Damn it!

Just when I think I'm making progress on the woman and getting her to open up to me more, something like this happens. But why would she lie about this?

"Mr. EJ?"

"Yeah, Jackson?"

"Why are we sitting in the garage?"

I realize we've made it home and we're now in the garage, car off, but the door to the garage still open. "Sorry." We get out and head inside. Raelynn has the table set and she's feeding Bree.

"DaDa! Ja-Ja!" she shouts with a grin. A few more words tumble out, but I can't make sense of those. My heart bursts with love every time I see her. Now that she's talking a little, it's just getting worse, in the best possible way.

"Hey, princess." I walk over and kiss her forehead.

"Did you have fun, baby?" Raelynn asks Jackson.

Jackson launches into his recap while I take us over to the sink to wash our hands. My mind lingers on the fact that Raelynn has made two different plans for Christmas, but I don't know which one is the real plan, or why she's making secret plans to start with. I can't ask outright because then she'll know I mentioned it to Henry, and whatever happens, it can't look like I'm going behind her back or taking Henry's side in any way.

"You're quiet."

My eyes flit to Raelynn. We're at the table now, eating, and I've been lost in my thoughts. "Thinking about Christmas." That's partially honest.

Raelynn stiffens slightly. "Has something happened? Everyone is still coming, aren't they?"

"Yes. I was thinking of what presents I have left to buy."

Her shoulders relax. "You better get on that before it's too late."

What I better to do is find out what she's hiding. That is the one thing I can't do. That I don't want to do. Not again.

I crouch in front of Jackson where he sits on the couch. "J-man, I need you to listen to me for a second." His eyes slide away from the TV to focus on me. He didn't seem bothered that Deanna and Brayden showed up, but now, I have to tell them why they're here. I would let Raelynn handle this, but she hasn't come downstairs yet and after I tell him, we have to go or we'll be late for our reservations. I don't want her to get hung up with Jackson. "Ms. Deanna and Mr. Brayden are staying with you and Bree while your mom and I go to dinner."

His gaze flits to my friends. "Who's tucking me in?"

"We'll be back in time for your mom to tuck you in," I promise. It's one reason why I made early reservations. Jackson didn't like the switch to me last time and I had a feeling he wouldn't like Deanna or Brayden being the ones to do it this time. I'd rather eat early and come home in time to tuck him in than worry the kid.

"I can't go?" His inhale is shaky, and fuck, I don't want him nervous. I thought he'd be fine. He went to a game with Deanna not too long ago, but maybe it's different with his mom leaving him instead.

"Not this time," I reluctantly tell him.

"EJ says you know how to build a fort," Brayden says from behind me, causing Jackson's eyes to widen in shock. "I've never built one before, so I was hoping you'd show me. Think you can do that while they go to dinner?"

"Are girls allowed in your forts, Jackson?" Deanna asks him.

Jackson nods. "Bree likes them a lot. I'll show you."

He looks back at me. "Momma will tuck me in?"

"I promise she will."

"Okay."

"Good man, Jackson." I hold out my fist and he fist bumps me. With that, I stand and take the stairs two at a time. She's been in her room for hours. Okay, so maybe only two. Either way, it's time to go. I rap my knuckles on her door.

"One second!" she squeaks.

"Raelynn, we have to go. I just promised Jackson you'd be back in time to tuck him in and if we don't leave right now, you'll make me break—" The door swings open. My gaze travels up and down her body at least five times in a second. Her black dress hugs her frame and shows off a little cleavage. No. That's not right. That dress takes her breasts, pushes them together, and places them on clear display, yet somehow doesn't reveal too much.

"You're supposed to look me in the eyes," Raelynn teases.

But I can't. Because fuck. She's wearing heels. She's at least three inches taller now. I step aside, confusing her, but she steps out of her room and walks past me. Holy hell, her ass looks sweet in that dress, too.

Raelynn glances back at me as I clear my throat.

"I have words, but they're curses," I say, causing her to grin. "You're beautiful."

"Thank you," she whispers. She holds out her hand, but then it falls to her side at the sound of Jackson's laughter. Just because we're going out to dinner doesn't mean we can have any PDA going on. The times I have touched Raelynn around Jackson before I kissed her, they were more subtle. I doubt he saw them.

I take her hand anyway. Before she can tug it away, I say, "You hold Jackson's hand. I can hold yours. Maybe I'm making sure you don't fall in those heels."

She laughs. "I wouldn't wear them if I couldn't walk in them."

And she can walk in them too. Fuck me.

After a quick goodbye to Jackson, Bree, and our babysitters for the night, I whisk her to the garage and to my car. As I drive, I rest our interlocked hands on my thigh. I'm itching to bring up Christmas, but I don't want to ruin tonight by making Raelynn uncomfortable, especially when I already know she's hiding something. The ride to the restaurant is silent.

"Nervous?" I finally ask once we're seated in a small booth at a fancy restaurant. It's one of the most upscale ones I've ever been in. I wanted to treat Raelynn more than anything, and I thought maybe she'd like this.

"Not with you." When I arch an eyebrow, she adds, "Not usually."

"Then what was taking you so long?"

She laughs. "I said not usually." She glances down at herself. "I'm not used to this. Any of it." She looks around the restaurant again. "It's a little nerve-wracking."

"You just said you weren't nervous."

"To be on a date with you, I'm not. To be in this dress in this restaurant, I am."

That makes no sense. "Would you rather go elsewhere?"

Horror fills her eyes, much like they would Jackson's if he made a mistake and he thought he was in big trouble. "No, not at all. Just because I'm a little nervous doesn't mean I'm not excited."

I nod in acceptance and we take a few minutes to look over the menu. My plan tonight is to learn more about Raelynn. To learn as much as she'll let me. And then, we'll go home. Tuck Jackson in, read him a book, and I'll hold my princess for a bit. After that, Raelynn is coming to my room where that dress is coming off. That's my plan and it's time to get started.

13

Raelynn

EVERY FEW SECONDS, I peer up from my menu to gaze at Elias. He looks freaking delicious in his simple suit. I still can't believe we're in a place this nice. It makes me feel self-conscious, but at the same time, I'm relaxed because I'm with Elias. Then again, I can't believe I'm here with him. On a date. How crazy is that? I haven't thought about dating or relationships in so long. That part of life has been sitting in the very back of a closet in the dark recesses of my mind ever since Henry left me.

Yet here I am.

With a handsome, hunky hockey player who is sweet,

fantastic in bed, and a wonderful father.

"Do you know what you want yet?" Elias asks me as the waitress walks up to our table.

My cheeks heat for a moment. "I haven't really looked," I admit with a touch of embarrassment.

"Want a steak like me? Just pick your sides if you do." He places his order while I quickly look over the sides, so I can get the same meal. When the waitress walks away, he asks, "When do you graduate?"

"In the spring, actually. I can't believe I only have one semester left. It would've been next fall, but working with you, I've been able to add a few extra classes next semester so I can finish. I'm pretty sure I can manage Jackson, Bree, and a completely full course load."

The corners of Elias's mouth dip. "Will you hunt for a job or stay on as Bree's nanny for a while?"

Oh. I hadn't thought about what comes after graduation. "I don't know what to do with my degree yet, so unless something miraculously comes to mind, I'm all yours for the foreseeable future," he begins to smile, "unless you get rid of me." His smile disappears.

"I don't plan to get rid of you. You're perfect with my princess."

I smile. "She's an amazing little girl."

"You really don't know what you want to do? You didn't have any dreams before Jackson came along and changed things up?"

"I didn't know before then, no." I laugh a little. "The future wasn't something I thought about that much back in high school. I was completely living in the here and now. And when Jackson was born, my life became all about him and making sure I could take care of him." I frown. "I almost feel like I chose the wrong degree, but I didn't know what else to do and I knew I needed a degree to make good money one day."

Elias rests his elbows on the table and leans forward. "What are you passionate about? Curious about?"

I shrug, almost wishing he'd change the topic. "I love my son. That pretty much covers it. Maybe I'll work for you forever," I joke, but secretly serious. I'm not sure what kind of role model that makes me for Jackson, but I *do* love what I do for Elias and considering I have no clue what else I'd want to do, it sounds like a mostly solid plan.

Elias smiles. "I have no problem with that."

"What about you? What will you do when your playing career is over?"

"I want to become a coach, but for kids. I knew I wanted to still be in the sport somehow, and maybe in the coaching aspect, but since having Bree and especially since taking Jackson, I know that's exactly what I want to do when I'm done playing. Plus, I learned something from all of my coaches growing up. They were some of my biggest influences and role models, aside from my parents, and I think it would be awesome to be in that position for other kids."

Jealousy rises within me. He has a plan. He has his life figured out. I couldn't figure my life out if my next breath depended on it.

"Would you ever consider reconciling things with your parents?"

"No." The harsh answer snaps out of my mouth before I can think twice about it. "I don't think they could change, or would. I'd have to see serious change. It's been five years and I haven't heard a peep from them. You couldn't pay me to go back home."

Confusion scrunches Elias's face. "Then where exactly are you spending Christmas?"

Oh, shit. I did say I was going to see an old friend, so it makes sense that he'd think I'd go back home for that.

Before I can offer a response, he adds, "You know you are more than welcome to stay with us still. Jackson can stay in Bree's room. You can stay in mine." My heart catapults out of my chest and lands somewhere across the room. "Is Jackson seeing Henry? Don't you want him to? Wouldn't it make more sense to spend Christmas at my house then?"

"Elias, stop," I blurt out. "I'm not spending Christmas at your house. My friend no longer lives back home. She's close enough that we'll be able to stop by Henry's on Christmas Day."

He eyes me for a moment as if he knows I'm lying, but he can't pinpoint what the exact lie is. It takes everything I have not to squirm in my seat under his stare. "When do you want to exchange gifts then? Before you leave or once you get back?" When I shrug, not really sure it matters, he makes the executive decision, "After."

"Tell me more about your family." Any change of topic is good. Elias tells me more about his parents, his sister, and even his friend, Derek, who is supposed to come down for Christmas. It's almost like he's hoping they'll appeal to me enough that I'll change my mind about staying away over the holidays.

Not happening.

"Enough about me," he says after awhile. "What was one of the hardest days of your life?"

I frown. "I thought dates were supposed to be all

positive and whatnot?"

"They're supposed to allow each person to get to know the other person better. That's what I'm doing."

I sigh. The hardest day of my life? Which day takes that title? The day my high school boyfriend abandoned me when I told him I was pregnant? Was it the day I saw the absolutely horrified and then disgusted expressions on my parents' faces, which eventually hardened as they let me know that I would have to leave? Was it the day I had to pick up and leave for North Carolina? Or maybe it was that brief period of time when I was worried I wouldn't have a job to support Jackson or a home for him to live in before Elias hired me?

A heaviness rests on my chest. A rock clogs my throat. "There are a few too many to pick just one. How about I tell you the best days were the day Jackson was born and when I came to North Carolina? Nothing else matters."

Elias nods in understanding. "My only regret with Bree is that I wasn't there throughout the pregnancy and for the birth. I feel like I've missed out on part of her life somehow."

"Would you ever consider retiring early so you could be around her more, especially since you're her only parent?"

He frowns. "I don't know. I haven't thought about it."

The waitress finally arrives with our food, which smells as good as it looks. Elias doesn't probe me with any more questions. He still seems pretty bothered by my last question. There's a (hopefully) temporary frown on his face as he cuts into his steak. I didn't mean to upset him, or insinuate that he should quit his job to be home more with his daughter. I was simply curious if he had thought about that possibility.

"I'm sorry," I blurt out, unable to stand the silence between us any longer.

Elias glances up at me. "For what?"

"You're still thinking about what I asked, aren't you?"

"Oh. Yeah, but don't be sorry for that. I'm just wondering if it was something I should've considered before or not. And whether it's something I *should* consider now. I love my job, but definitely not more than I love my daughter, but my job also provides a very good life for the both of us right now and will in the future, even though it requires me to travel so much." Elias pauses and shakes his head. "I just can't imagine switching careers yet. I feel like what I'm doing works."

"It does; that was also why I was apologizing. I didn't mean to make you think you were doing something wrong. I—"

"You meant well, Raelynn, I know," he interrupts.

Conversation flows easily after that. Elias has always been easy to talk to, though I don't always talk to him about everything. Too soon, Elias's phone vibrates repeatedly. He grins.

"Alarm to remind me when we have to leave, so we'll be home in time to tuck Jackson in." He waves down our waitress, pays, and holds out his hand once he stands. Butterflies flutter in my stomach as my hand slips into his. "How did I do for your first real date since Jackson was born?" he asks as he pulls out of the parking garage.

"I don't know yet," I tease. "The date isn't officially over until I'm home. Plus, I'm curious if you kiss on the first date."

Elias laughs. "With you, absolutely."

"That'll earn you some points then as long as it's a good one."

He laughs a little harder and glances at me real quick. "You think I could ever kiss badly?"

"Everything is possible, Elias."

"Not that," he mutters.

A smile rests easily on my lips for the rest of the way home. He parks in the garage like usual, but grabs my hand and pulls me flush against him before I can step inside.

"We step through that door and the date is over, right?" I nod, but my brain stopped functioning properly the moment my chest touched his and his mouth was two inches from mine. "You want a kiss at the end of the date, don't you, Raelynn?"

"Yes," I breathe.

His grin is quick, leaving me breathless from the sight of it a second before he kisses me. A deep, tongue twisting, soul searching, let's-get-naked kiss. I don't know whose hands touch whose body first, but it sends us into a crazy frenzy. Goosebumps prickle over my chilled skin as Elias's fingers curl and bunch to lift the fabric of my dress. My leg wants to lift up and wrap around his waist so badly, but my back bumps into the door behind me.

We break apart.

Elias drops his head to my shoulder, which must be uncomfortable for him until I realize he lifted me off the floor at some point, so I'm a little higher up. He takes three deep breaths, kisses me hard one more time, and then sets me back on my feet. He even readjusts my dress. Do we really have to go inside? Unfortunately, yes. Elias is the one who reaches around me to open the door.

A small sigh manages to escape me, causing him to chuckle.

"Momma?" Jackson shouts from the living room.

"Yep, it's us, baby. We're back," I answer as he comes running into the kitchen. He throws his arms around my waist. He's already in his pjs, ready for bed. "Are you ready to be tucked in?"

"Yeah. Will you read to me?"

"Yep." I kiss the top of his head. "You have to let me go so I can walk, though." He releases me after a second and Elias and I walk into the living room.

"Everything go well?" Elias asks.

"Are they alive, EJ?" Brayden replies, earning a glare from Elias.

Deanna rolls her eyes and bounces a still-awake Bree. I go over to take her, thank them, and lead Jackson upstairs. I'll read to them and get them both asleep. Elias can usher our babysitters out. The only problem is deciding where to do this. Bree falls asleep best in the recliner, but I obviously can't carry Jackson to his room. I haven't tried starting out in Jackson's room either. With Bree on my hip, I enter Jackson's room after changing her diaper, where he's waiting with a book for me to read to him. I always read the bedtime stories.

"Why is Bree in my room?" he demands to know with a frown that's partly a pout and his arms folded over his chest.

"She wants to hear a story too. Mr. EJ read a story to you in her room the other day, remember?" I remind him.

He sighs a little, but doesn't comment as I sit next to

him and situate her in my lap. Her head is already on my shoulder. It won't take her long after all. Jackson leans his head against my ribs since he's mostly lying down. What isn't fun is figuring out how to hold the book with both of them on me like this, but I manage.

"Momma?" Jackson asks before I start.

"What, baby?"

"How come you and Mr. EJ couldn't have dinner with me and Bree? Was I in trouble?" He looks up at me.

My heart beats ten thousand times faster. I don't want to explain a date to him, or anything like that. What can I tell him?

"There was a place I wanted to show your momma," my head whips around at the sound of Elias's voice, "and we couldn't take kids." He walks into the room and sits on the other side of Jackson. "That's all. We'll all go out to dinner soon, okay?"

Jackson nods, completely satisfied with that answer. "Read, Momma."

So, I read.

The weekend passes with me having to spend more time with Henry. My favorite thing to do. We're still hanging out at the house for now. It hasn't been too bad because Elias had a game both Friday and Saturday, which they lost. Jackson had no choice but to give Henry his full attention. He still got distracted by Bree here and there, though. I'm surprised by how much he loves to interact with her, compared to how he was in the beginning. Ever since she called him Ja-Ja, he's been a bit in love with her, I think. He wants to see her walk next. He likes to help me help her walk around the house and to play with her. He'll be an awesome big brother one day.

Elias has the day off and so far, I haven't heard from Henry about coming over to see Jackson, but I'm sure he'll be here at some point. Elias left a bit ago to pick Jackson up from school. We already told Jackson that he might, so he won't be surprised, but he should be back by now.

My gut churns because something is nagging me today and I don't know what it is. I told Elias earlier that I felt like him. Like my gut is telling me something, but hell if I know what it is.

My phone rings and anxiety cripples my heart when I see it's Elias. Why is he calling me? Maybe he wants to change their plans?

"Hey," I answer.

"Hey. You're at home with Bree, right?"

"Yes, of course. You left us here, Elias," I remind him of the obvious.

"And you didn't leave after I did to pick Jackson up yourself?"

"Why would I do that if that's where you were going? Why are you asking me this?" I pick Bree up off the floor where we're playing and begin to pace. "Where's Jackson, Elias? Let me talk to him."

"Hold on a second, Raelynn. There's a teacher here."

"Don't tell me that!" He doesn't have him? Complete silence is all that comes from the other end of the phone and I have to quadruple check that we're still connected. "Elias? Elias, tell me you have Jackson!" My head possibly floats in the air, separate from my body and I have to sit before I faint. "Elias?" I whisper.

"Have you talked to Henry today?" he asks, suddenly back. "The teacher said he was picked up by another man and Jackson said it was his dad and that they were going to the movies. Did you forget he was picking him up?"

"*Forget?*" I screech. "No! I...He...Elias, he took him!" Dots cloud my vision and I hold tighter to Bree who squirms in my arms. "We have to call the cops, Elias. I didn't tell Henry he could do that, and he certainly never told me." Bree puts her hands on my cheeks and tries to press them together. I start to cry because...what else am I supposed to do right this very second? Bree gently pats my cheeks.

"Raelynn, I'm sure he didn't kidnap him. He's probably being a fucking idiot and just took him to the movies like Jackson said. I'll come and pick you up. Call Henry. We'll go to every damn movie theater in the city to see if we can find them. If we don't, then we'll worry."

"Are you crazy? My son is missing!"

"Call Henry and keep calling him until he answers," Elias orders calmly. "I'm on my way back to the house." He hangs up and I'm frozen for all of two seconds before I do what he says. Maybe *his* gut thinks everything is fucking cheery, but *my* gut thinks the world just exploded and ended.

I call and call and call until Elias returns, but Henry's phone rings and rings until it goes to voicemail. And I leave a voicemail every damn time. I can't help it. I plead. I get angry. I demand he answer and bring my son back. I threaten him more times than I can count. What the hell was he thinking? Why wouldn't he ask me first?

"He's not answering," I blubber to Elias as he kneels

146

in front of me.

"That doesn't mean anything. He and Jackson could be in the movie theater."

"Or on their way out of the country," I retort.

"Raelynn," Elias says softly.

"No! Why aren't we calling the cops? This is insane!" I yell at him. It startles Bree enough that she cries and I feel terrible. Elias goes to take her, but I pull her closer to me, soothing her. "Please don't," I whisper. "I don't know where Jackson is; please let me hold her. She's probably the only thing holding me somewhat together right now." I don't think I could handle it if he took her from me right now. It sounds completely crazy, but he'd probably have to pry her away from me. I can't let her go. Not until I get Jackson back.

Elias nods. "Let's go."

"You're sure we don't need to report this, Elias? Because your plan feels wrong." His plan makes me want to throw up.

"I'm sure."

That isn't reassuring at all. The only thing that will reassure me will be to have Jackson back.

RAELYNN ALMOST CRAWLED into the backseat with Bree, but I made her get into the front with me. My excuse is that I need her to help me search the parking lots for Henry's vehicle. It worked. However, my hand is completely numb from how tightly she holds it. Her other hand has been calling Henry relentlessly. Still no answer. The first two theaters are a bust, but we find his car at the third. If it isn't for getting out and actually seeing Jackson's book bag in the backseat, Raelynn wouldn't have believed it's his.

She nearly faints with relief right then and there. She sags in my arms and kisses Bree's cheek, who she let me hold when we got out of the car.

"Let's go." She takes two steps, but I grab her hand and pull her back.

"No. We'll wait here for them."

"What? How many times do I have to call you insane today, Elias? He took my son without my permission. I don't care if he was planning to bring him back. I'm going in there and bringing him home."

"Take a deep breath." I rub my thumb over her knuckles and absorb her glare as she does it reluctantly. "Think about what you want to do and think about what Jackson thinks right now. He thinks his dad simply picked him up from school and took him out. He doesn't know Henry shouldn't have or anything. You don't want to fuck up their relationship or make Jackson scared to leave with him again. We should wait, take Jackson home, and then deal with Henry separately without ever letting Jackson know something didn't happen the way it should have. Right?"

She doesn't seem so sure, so I add, "If you go in there hot, guns blazing, and drag him out of there, you're going to terrify Jackson. Think about it, Raelynn."

Her shoulders slowly sag in defeat and she hides her face in my chest. "I hate this. I just want him back with me where he belongs."

"Patience, grasshopper."

She laughs and wraps her arms around my waist. "I'm glad you're here. I'm obviously not as calm or clear-headed in a crisis as I should be."

My knuckles drag up and down her back. I kiss the top of her head. "Don't worry about it, Raelynn. I probably wouldn't be either if I was in your shoes. And honestly, I think the only reason I am calm is because you're not and my gut told me not to worry."

"I have a love/hate relationship with your gut."

"Me too."

I hold her for about thirty more minutes until I see Henry. I gently nudge her away, knowing she doesn't want either one of them to see us like that. We step toward the trunk to be in view. Henry sees us first and he frowns in confusion. Raelynn is going to rip his ass a new one when she does finally get ahold of him. Hell, I might before we leave. Jackson sees us a few seconds later. He's confused, but he looks happy to see us. The moment Henry gives him the okay to run over to us, he does.

Raelynn cries before he reaches us and drops to her knees to bear hug him.

"Why are you crying, Momma?" Jackson asks, wiping her tears instead of hugging her back.

"I've had a bad day, baby, but it's better now that you're here." With that, he throws his arms around her and squeezes with all of his might.

"What are y'all doing here?" Henry asks.

"We're here for Jackson," I answer, causing him to frown. He definitely doesn't like when I'm around, but I can't help it. Well, I probably could, but I'm not today.

"We were going to get ice cream next," Jackson says with mild protest. Raelynn still has her arms around him.

"Maybe another day, J-man. Your momma wants us to go home."

"But—" Henry objects.

"No," I cut him off. "He's going home with us." I touch Raelynn's shoulder. "Why don't you take Jackson and Bree and go ahead to the car?" She nods and takes the keys from me. "Jackson, tell your dad bye."

Raelynn almost doesn't let go of his hand for him to hug him bye. That's right; Jackson has starting hugging Henry. And calling him Dad, apparently. Raelynn glares at Henry. "Expect a call from me later."

"I don't understand what just happened," he says to me once they're out of earshot.

"I'm not here to argue on behalf of Raelynn, but are you really that much of a fucking idiot that you didn't think you should ask Raelynn if you could pick him up first?"

"I did ask."

"And she answered?" I ask. "Because she says you never asked her."

"I did," he insists. He pulls out his phone. "Jesus," he mutters. "There's over a hundred missed calls and a shit ton of voicemails from her."

"Because you took her son without asking and she didn't know where he was or if you even planned to bring him back."

His face had already paled a bit, but he looks as white as a sheet when he turns his phone to me. "My text never went through to her."

There is a text to her, asking if he could pick Jackson up and take him to the movies, but it failed to send.

"I fucked up, didn't I?"

"Big time." I hand his phone back to him.

"Do you think she'll keep him from me now?"

"I want to say no, but she was scared. Listen to those voicemails. You'll hear how completely and utterly terri-fied she was." The look in her eyes and the sound of her voice will haunt me for weeks, if not longer. "I need his bag."

Henry nods. Once I get into the car, Raelynn looks at me expectantly, but I shake my head. We'll talk about it once Jackson is asleep. He hears everything and this isn't something he needs to hear. While it's good that Henry *did* ask, he didn't think he needed an answer, which is just as bad as not asking. And really, the text he would've sent wasn't phrased as a question. It said, *If you don't mind, I would like to pick Jackson up from school today. We'll go to the movies, maybe out to ice cream, and then I'll bring him straight home.*

There's a tension in the air back home as I cook dinner for us, giving Raelynn time to snuggle with Jackson. Bree is on my hip. She's talking her little heart out and trying to rip my necklace off.

"When is my princess walking for me? Hmm?" I ask her. She's close; I can feel it. I just hope it doesn't happen while I'm not here. Dinner is ready, so over Bree's ramblings, I call for Raelynn and Jackson. Bree wiggles against me, wanting to get down and go to Jackson if her shout of Ja-Ja means anything.

"Help her walk to me, Mr. EJ."

I set her down on her feet, hold her hands, and help her walk to Jackson.

"Good job, Bree!" he congratulates her. I let go of her hands since she can stand fairly well on her own and I swear to you, they awkwardly fist bump. That's something Jackson has surely taught her. Bree claps as Jackson praises her some more. It's not only sweet to see him with her, but it's great to see her interact with another kid, even if he is older than her.

With Raelynn right next to Jackson, I take a step

away to grab my bottle of water from next to the stove. "Try walking over here now, Bree," I hear Jackson say.

I glance down to see that Raelynn now crouches behind Bree and Jackson stands next to me. Bree looks between us and then back at Raelynn.

"Come on, Bree. Walk to DaDa and Ja-Ja," Jackson encourages her.

I crouch down and hold my arms out to her. "Come here, princess."

Are we really doing this? Trying to get her to walk on her own, especially after the day we've had? My heart pounds in my chest like this is an important game and my ass is on the line. Bree takes one step forward. Holy shit. She takes another, giggles, and then with Raelynn on her heels, she wobbles with heavy steps right into my arms.

"You did it!" Jackson shouts, his voice bubbly with excitement. "You did it, Bree! Good job!"

I pick her up and hug her. "Good job indeed, princess." I kiss her forehead. This is overwhelming. My little girl just walked! My gaze shifts to Raelynn who, I swear to it, looks just as much like a proud mom as I feel like a proud dad. Before she can protest and before I can change my mind, I pull her into my arms and hug her with Bree between us.

"Elias," she whispers after a few moments.

I release her and bend to scoop up Jackson in my other arm. He hugs Bree and me both, but my eyes are on Raelynn. She's uneasy in this moment. I can tell. She may think it's because this is another milestone of Bree's I'm sharing with them, but I disagree. Raelynn still isn't used to her world expanding and every big moment she spends with Bree and me solidifies her place in our world. *That* is what makes her uneasy.

What I want is to figure out her deal with Christmas, place myself in her and Jackson's world as much as they're in ours, and live happily ever after. Sounds simple to me. Well, maybe not simple, but completely possible. I don't want to be a single dad forever. I want Bree to have a good female role model in her life as she grows up. I want someone who'll watch movies with me and when they're having a bad day, I want to be the one who cheers them up.

Hell, I want a true relationship with someone. The kind where I can count on my woman for support just as surely as she knows she can count on me. The kind where I'll always love her, even during the struggles. I want to settle down and be happy, sad, angry, excited, scared, and all the other emotions we feel with someone else.

And I'm pretty damn certain I can do all of those things with Raelynn.

"Tell me what you said to him before I call him," she says to me later once the kids are in bed for the night.

She sits next to me on the couch, which isn't good enough. I grab her hips, lift, and place her in my lap, which does nothing but cause her to frown at me over her shoulder. That quickly disappears when I begin massaging her shoulders.

"Relax, Raelynn."

"This isn't a situation that calls for being relaxed," she points out.

"I know. I also don't care." That earns me a glare, but she sighs as I knead her muscles some more. I wait until she's resting her back against my chest, completely re-laxed, before I spill any details. "He texted you, but it failed to send. He knows he fucked up and he's worried you'll try to keep Jackson from him."

Raelynn tries to sit up, but my arms are now around her waist and chest, so I keep her against me. "I would never do that to Jackson so long as Henry's trying and he's being a decent human being. And he still should've waited for an answer. Let me go so I can call him."

"What are you going to say to him?" She's all tense again, my hard work for nothing.

"That he's a pain in my ass."

I laugh, totally not expecting that. "Okay, Little Grizzly, maybe you shouldn't start with that."

She twists in my arms. "Little Grizzly?" she questions with a hint of a smile.

"You're a momma bear, Raelynn, but you're small." I squeeze her hips to prove my point. "Hence, Little Grizzly. It makes perfect sense to me."

I don't know what it is about what I said, but Raelynn wraps her arms around my neck and kisses me like I just professed my love for her and proposed marriage. My entire body reacts to this kiss. I pull her closer, though surely she can hear the rapid acceleration of my heart, and then I lay us down on the couch. Her fingertips trail lightly up my arms as if she's tracing over my tattoos. That shit drives me crazy, especially since she can't see them. The moment my hand sneaks underneath her shirt, her phone rings.

Henry.

Fucking Henry!

Guess he doesn't want to wait for Raelynn to call him. I sigh, my breath hitting Raelynn's cheek. She smiles. I don't know why. She kisses my cheek before pushing me away and grabbing her phone as we sit up. She surprises me again because I'd think this is a conversation she'd want to have in private, but she leans into my side, tucking her feet up next to her thighs.

"Yes, Henry, but..."

Guess he wants to make sure he fully apologizes and makes his promises before she can lay into him for what he did.

"You want to do what?" Raelynn asks quietly, her body solidifying next to me. "Well, of course that makes sense, but..." She reaches up and begins twirling her hair around her finger. "I don't know, Henry. It sounds like a long, complicated, and expensive process." Her shoulders slump a fraction. "I *know* that, and I swear if you imply I'm not doing what's best for Jackson one more time, I'll hurt you. You have to give me time on this. Unlike you, I don't have a lawyer on standby." She's quiet for a moment. "I don't think you're in a position to be asking more of me right now. Thursday won't work for us; sorry. I'll talk to you this weekend." She hangs up the moment the last word is out of her mouth.

"What happened?" I ask.

"He apologized, but then came at me with a list of demands. I swear, he's his daddy through and through. He might be down here, trying to be in Jackson's life and to get away from his parents, but he's still just like his daddy." Raelynn huffs. "He thinks it'll make me feel better if we just go ahead and make 'custody arrangements.'" She does the air-quotes with her fingers. "Which means I need to get a lawyer, which will cost god only knows how much, and I doubt my lawyer will be as good as his. He can say this will be smooth as much as he wants, but if he thinks he's getting anything other than visitation, he's lost his fucking mind.

"Then, he said he wanted Jackson to go to his house Thursday since he hasn't been there yet. I feel relieved I could legit say no since you'll be away and I'll have Bree. I don't know if you'd be okay with her going over there with us, but either way, I'm not taking her right now, even if you are okay with it. It feels like he's stealing my power and I don't like that."

I pull her back in my lap, but make her straddle me this time. My hands cup her face and I rest my forehead against hers. "Repeat after me."

"Elias," she starts, thinking I'm not being serious.

"Repeat after me," I say more firmly. "Jackson isn't going anywhere except for visits because I'm Little Grizzly and the best parent he could possibly have."

Raelynn rolls her eyes, but it's with a smile on her face.

"Say it, Raelynn."

"Jackson isn't going anywhere except for visits because I'm Little Grizzly and the best parent he could possibly have."

"And I'm going to let EJ help me find the best lawyer to ensure everything happens the way I want."

She frowns. "Elias..."

"Say it."

"And I will unhappily and reluctantly let Elias help me find the best lawyer to ensure everything happens the way I want, but only because it's ultimately for Jackson. Anything else?"

"No, but I'll let you know if I change my mind."

Raelynn shakes her head. "Let's watch a movie while

you give me another massage."

Sounds like the perfect idea to me.

15

Raelynn

"**D**ADA!" BREE GRINS and reaches for the phone where Elias's face appears on the screen. He's been talking to her for ten minutes already and that's probably the thirtieth time she's said his name.

"Yes, princess, it's me," he says to her with a smile before focusing on me. "Raelynn, would you do something for me?"

"Sure; what is it?"

Elias grins. "You agree to things without knowing what it is?"

I shrug. "I trust you."

That makes his smile brighten even more. "You re-member Sylvia, right?" I nod. "She's been on bedrest for a little while and will be until the baby comes. I was talking to Scotty and she's extra restless today. Maybe you can take the kids over there and give her a fresh face to see." He takes a deep breath. "You'd make her really happy if you'd give her some gossip," he adds with a pointed look.

"You mean..." Surely, he doesn't.

But he nods. "You don't have to; you could tell her about Henry, but anything would cheer her up. Will you go see her?"

The idea of hanging out with a woman I don't know all that well *and* spilling my guts doesn't sit well with me. However, she is stuck on bedrest and this is the first time Elias has asked a favor of me. I can do this for them both.

"Of course. Text me her address and her phone num-ber; I want to let her know I'm coming over."

"We're going to see Mrs. Sylvia?" Jackson butts in. "Does that mean Stella and Stephanie will be there?"

Elias laughs. "They live there with her, so I'm pretty sure you'll run into them, J-man."

Jackson sighs, but I think it's for show. He likes those girls, but he likes to act as if he doesn't. He hops off the couch and runs up stairs as if he's on a mission.

"I miss you guys," Elias admits when my gaze returns to the screen.

"We miss you too. Good luck tonight."

"Thanks, Raelynn."

"Wey!" Bree giggles and my jaw drops as I look at her. That almost sounded like Rae. "No!" She actually started saying no earlier this week. She loves it almost as much as DaDa and Ja-Ja. But I can't believe she just said my name! My eyes water before I can control my emotions.

"Oh, Bree," Elias starts in a teasing tone. "You're in trouble now. She doesn't like to be called Rae," he says with a little laugh.

"Bree can call me whatever she wants."

That makes him grin. "Wait up for me?" he asks. His mouth parts wider and he adds, "Oh! My family is coming in today! I forgot to tell you that. You don't have to worry about picking them up. They're getting a cab ride to the house."

"They're coming today?" My heart pounds in overtime. We can't check into the hotel until tomorrow.

"Yeah, that's okay, isn't it?" Confusion clouds his face.

"Yes, of course." Bree starts to squirm a little and I use that as my excuse to get off the phone with him, never promising one way or the other to wait up for him.

I get the kids together, text Sylvia, and then we're on our way to her house. But only after I finish packing and loading the car. I can't stay here tonight, whether Elias thinks I'm leaving tomorrow or not. The idea of spending Christmas with Elias and his family still scares the hell out of me. I'll figure out another plan somehow.

First, I have to spend some time with Sylvia Boyd.

A woman I presume is her mother answers the door. "Sylvia said she was expecting guests," she says with a smile. "Come on in. I'll show you to her room."

We follow her to Sylvia's bedroom and the moment she sees us, she shouts, "Raelynn! I'm so happy you're here!" She pats the bed. "Jackson, you can play with the girls in their room, if you'd like. My mom can show you where their room is."

Jackson looks up at me. "Play nice, remember your manners, and don't break anything," I tell him. He nods and runs off without waiting for Sylvia's mom to tell him where to go. I walk over to sit next to Sylvia, feeling slightly awkward to be in the same bed that Scott Boyd sleeps in.

"Come here, Bree. Let me see this beautiful face," she coos, holding out her arms as Bree unsteadily walks on the bed with my help toward Sylvia. "Please tell me something interesting is happening in your life," Sylvia says to me.

"My life definitely isn't boring."

Her eyes light up as Bree plops down next to her and Sylvia rubs her stomach. "Tell me," she demands.

I decide to start small, get a feel for how it would be to spill my guts to her. "Well, as you can see, Bree is walking a little." I hand Bree one of her toys before she can start crawling around. "She's fluent in DaDa, Ja-Ja, no, and she said Wey today. Some other words slip here and there, too. Jackson seems to be coming out of his shell more and more each day."

Sylvia reaches over and puts her hand over mine. "If I wanted to know about the kids, I'd ask EJ myself," she interrupts.

"Oh, well..." Am I really about to divulge more? For her? For Elias?

"Don't feel pressured by me either, Raelynn. Make something up, if you'd rather, I don't care. Just give me something."

For some reason, that's what relaxes me. Bree makes her crying face and I realize she's missing her nap right now. I pick her up, rest her on my chest, and rub her back. "Jackson's father is in the picture for the first time. He moved down here once he tracked us down because he's decided he wants to be in Jackson's life now."

Sylvia's eyes widen. "How is that going?"

"Not so great. We're probably about to go through the court system, which will reassure me but terrify me at the same time. I have quite a few irrational fears." I explain more about the situation. Sylvia acts like she's about to get up, but when I ask, "What are you doing?" she stops and huffs.

"Right. Bedrest." She looks down at her stomach. "I really love you, baby boy," she whispers. With a sigh, she looks at me. "Before you leave, you need to get my wallet out of my purse. There's a business card in there for a lawyer. He's the best, I promise. Once the holidays are over, call and set up an appointment; mention that Scott and I referred you. He'll look after you and Jackson."

"Thanks. How are you doing?" The only piece of gossip I have left for her is Elias and me.

Sylvia rubs her belly once again. "I'm losing my mind, but it's totally worth it. This is likely a once in a lifetime opportunity here and in a way, I'm cherishing bedrest, even though it's driving me crazy. I'm ready to have this baby, so I can get back to taking care of my girls and my household instead of just sitting here and watching someone else do my job." She sighs again, tears trailing down her cheeks. "I'm sorry, Raelynn. I'm a mess lately. This baby boy is determined to make me cry at least twice a day until he comes, which means I cry every time I talk to Scott. I'm worrying my husband to death." Before I can attempt to cheer her up, she takes a deep breath. "Tell me

163

some more gossip."

I give her the one thing I know that will for sure brighten her day. "I'm dating Elias; no one really knows." No need to tell her that Deanna knows, but other than that, no one knows.

Her bright eyes widen and her jaw drops. "No way."

"Yep."

She pushes and prods for details, most of which I give her. The kids eventually run into the room as I get a call from Elias's mother, Alice. The family has arrived.

"I have to go, Sylvia." She makes sure I get that lawyer's business card before I leave. "Text me if you ever want me to visit again."

"Thanks for coming over, Raelynn."

"Any time."

It actually wasn't that bad. I don't know yet if she'll be a friend like Deanna, but it was nice to cheer her up, especially with Christmas right around the corner.

Alice is the first one we run into when we get home. She scoops Bree from my arms the moment she sees us. "Oh, look at my precious little granddaughter. I've missed you so much!" She kisses her on each cheek. "How have you been, Raelynn?"

"Good. Thank you. I hope your flight went well."

Alice shrugs. "James! Nicole! Get in here and meet Elias James's nanny and her son." A moment later, a man and a girl younger than I am walk into the kitchen. "Raelynn, this is my husband, James, and my daughter, Nicole. This is Elias James's nanny, Raelynn, and her son, Jackson."

"Nice to meet you." At the arrival of new people, Jackson wraps his arms around my thighs, but doesn't hide behind them. He even offers his own hello that makes my heart proud. There's a brief moment of silence as we all stand slightly awkwardly in the kitchen. My heart begins to pound in my chest. Elias won't be back until late tonight. I can't stay here with his family. My throat already closes with the awkwardness I feel. "Are you all settled in? Is there anything I need to help you with?"

"We're fine, Raelynn. We've made ourselves at home."

"Good. I don't know if Elias told you, but I have other plans for Christmas. If you're good with keeping Bree until Elias gets back..."

Alice raises one thin eyebrow at me. "I'm perfectly capable of taking care of my granddaughter."

"Right. I didn't mean..." She doesn't seem like she cares what I meant. "Do you mind if we say goodbye to her?"

"Of course not." She hands her back to me.

"We'll see you in a few days, sweet Bree." I kiss her cheek and crouch. "Do you want to hug Bree bye?" I ask Jackson. He knows we're leaving, but he doesn't exactly know where we're going.

He carefully hugs her. "Don't do anything new while I'm gone," he says, echoing what he's heard Elias say to her. "I'll miss you." He kisses her cheek. "Love you, Bree."

My heart combusts at his declaration. The only person Jackson has ever said he loved was me and now, he's telling it to Bree. Jackson releases his hug and I stand, giving Bree back to Alice. Doing my best not to shed tears, I tell her when she last ate, napped, and was last changed, and any other pertinent information.

And then we leave.

It takes me a minute to figure out where to go since there's no chance we can check into the hotel a day early. I called and checked already. I despise the decision I've made, but somehow convince myself it's for Jackson. That's why I find myself knocking on Henry's door, fulfilling his wish that we'd come over anyway.

Surprise widens his eyes when he opens the door. "Rae, what are you doing here?"

"Can we come in?"

"Yeah, of course." He steps aside and we come in. His house is nice, clearly a simple bachelor's pad, but what surprises me the most is that in the corner of the living room are toys. "Those toys are here for you to play with, Jackson," Henry says, noticing that Jackson's focus is also on the toys. "You can play with them if it's okay with your mom."

Jackson looks up at me.

"Go ahead, baby. I need to talk to your dad for a minute anyway. We'll be right in there." I point to the archway leading to the kitchen, visible from where we are. Once Jackson is diving through the toys, we step into the kitchen. "I'm sorry to show up unannounced, Henry."

"It's no problem. Do you want anything to drink?"

I shake my head.

"Not that I'm not thrilled to see Jackson, but what are you doing here, Rae?" he asks.

I don't even flinch anymore. Calling me Rae is too ingrained in him and he hasn't been able to kick the habit yet. Maybe I can pretend it's Bree calling me that, or that Bree is the one who originally gave me the nickname, and all the hurt and history that the nickname holds will begin to fade away. I take a deep breath and try to figure out how to answer his question before settling on the truth.

"I'm not used to having people in my life, okay? Elias and Bree are in my life, which is great. But right now, his entire family, plus a friend, is spending the Christmas holiday at his house and I don't think I can stay there with them. I didn't realize they were coming today, and I can't check into the hotel until tomorrow, so..." I stare into his eyes, hoping he'll understand.

"You want to stay here tonight?" There's surprise and something else in his voice.

"Please? We'll still come back on Christmas Day."

"Raelynn, you and Jackson shouldn't have spend Christmas in a hotel room."

I hold up my hand. "Do not question my decisions, Henry."

"I'm not," he swears. "I'm just saying if you'd prefer, you can stay here. I have an extra room. I made sure to find a house with an extra room in case Jackson ever spent the night. Wouldn't you rather be in a house instead of a hotel room?"

For Jackson's sake, yes. But do I want it to be *Henry's* house? I don't know.

"And this is my first Christmas with him, so I'd be extremely grateful to have the extra time with him."

"I'd lose the money I paid on the hotel." And I definitely don't want to waste money.

"I can pay you back for that," he offers. "Please, Raelynn. I've made too many mistakes. Let me give you somewhere to go other than a hotel room. Let me spend Christmas with Jackson, even though I don't deserve it."

His admission that he doesn't deserve it might just be

what does it for me. I hand him my car keys. "Our bags are in the trunk."

He smiles and stands. I walk into the living room and sit on the floor with Jackson, who plays with some toy cars.

"Hey, Jackson." He looks up at me. "We're spending Christmas here with your dad. What do you think about that?"

Jackson frowns. "What about Mr. EJ and Bree?"

"They're spending Christmas with his family. We'll see them in a few days."

He nods, glances down at his toy, and then looks at me. "But there's no tree here."

"I brought ours." There was no way my boy would be spending Christmas without us carrying out our usual traditions. "It'll be Christmas as usual, but here and with your dad."

"Okay."

Once Henry brings our things in, we get our tiny tree set up and decorated. Jackson frowns once it's done. Apparently, it's not as pretty as the one we did with Mr. EJ. Being here in Henry's house and with Henry is just as awkward and uncomfortable as I imagine it would be back at Elias's house.

What's worse is around three thirty in the morning, I'm still awake and lying in his spare bedroom next to Jackson. My phone vibrates on the nightstand just like I was hoping it wouldn't.

Elias: *I thought you weren't leaving until tomorrow? Mom said you bolted the second you got back from Sylvia's.*

Me: *Change of plans, sorry. We made it here safe and sound. Enjoy the time with your family. We'll see you soon.*

Elias: *I was hoping to see you before you left. It actually feels weird for you and Jackson not to be here.*

Elias: *Have fun with your friend and let me know how it goes with Henry.*

Me: *I will.*

I hate texting him. Over video or calling is so much easier. I feel like we actually *talk* that way. It's worse now when I'm lying to him over something I'm sure he'd hate that I'm lying about. This is not how I expand my world. But maybe it's working out since Jackson will spend more time with his father? Jackson allows for his world to expand far faster than I will. If anything will be my downfall in life, it'll be my inability to do this.

EJ

"RAELYNN SAID SHE was going to stay with a friend?" Mom questions for the fifth time today.

"Ma, why do you keep asking me that?" She's really irritating me, especially since I don't think that's where Raelynn is.

"Follow me." She stands and I have no choice but to follow her up to Raelynn's room, which is where my parents are currently staying. She picks up a piece of paper from the dresser and hands it to me. "I found it on the floor when we were going to bed last night."

It's an email confirming hotel reservations. What the

fuck? Why would Raelynn need a hotel if she's staying with a friend? I *knew* something was up. The paper crinkles in my hand. "Can you watch Bree for me?"

"Yes, of course."

I swivel on my heels and leave for the hotel. This isn't right. Raelynn shouldn't be spending Christmas in a hotel room when she could be staying here. I need to talk to her. But when I get to the hotel, they eventually tell me that those reservations were canceled this morning.

This morning!

So where the fuck is Raelynn?

Where would she go?

My stomach sinks. There's only one other person in Raleigh. With my gut in knots, I put Henry's address into my phone's GPS and drive over there. When Raelynn got Henry's address, she gave it to me, just in case I ever needed it, and boy is today one of those days. The nausea causes my knuckles to whiten as I grip the steering wheel when I see Raelynn's car in his driveway. Sure, she could be here to let Jackson see Henry, but my gut tells me that's not the only reason she's here.

With a deep breath, I make my way to his front door. I knock and I wait. Henry answers the door.

"I need to speak to Raelynn," I say before he can utter a word.

Jackson sees me first. "Mr. EJ!" he shouts, running toward me. "Are we going home?"

"Hey, J-man." I pick him up and allow his tight hug around my neck to relax me a bit. "I'm just here to talk to your mom for a few minutes."

"Elias."

My gaze meets hers, which is surprised, but also very

171

worried. "Can I talk to you?"

"Yeah, of course."

I set Jackson down on his feet.

"Come back inside, Jackson," Henry tells him as Raelynn walks past them.

Looks like we're having this conversation outside. As soon as the door closes behind her, I take her hand and lead her to my car. We get in and I crank the car, turning on the heat.

"How'd you know where I was?" she whispers.

"Mom found a copy of your hotel reservations on the floor of your bedroom, but they told me you canceled this morning. Who else do you know here?" She nods. "Why are you here, Raelynn? Why were you going to stay at a hotel? Why aren't you at home with Bree and me?"

"Did your mom tell you that Jackson told Bree he loved her yesterday?" she asks with her gaze on the front door.

Her question stuns me. Because it's not an answer, I didn't know that, and I'm not sure what that has to do with her not spending Christmas with us. "Is that a bad thing?" I ask since I can't read how she feels about it.

"Of course not." She turns her head to look at me, showing her sincerity.

"Why did Jackson ask if he was going home when he saw me?" Maybe we need to start small.

She sighs. "He misses you and Bree. He wants to go home."

I want to smile because that means Jackson is finally truly comfortable in my house, but if she's here because she wants Jackson to spend time with his father, smiling seems wrong. "So why aren't you there, Raelynn? Just explain it to me and I'll go home."

Her gaze slides away again until she's staring out of her window. "It's too much," she whispers. "For five years, every Christmas I've spent only with Jackson. If it was only you and Bree, then that would be okay, I think. But the idea of being there with your entire family, especially after I pissed your mom off? And she only thinks I'm your nanny, so sleeping in your bed isn't going to work, Elias. It would've been off the charts awkward." She glances at me. "I've expanded my world enough, don't you think?"

Shit. This is partly my fault. "How did you piss her off?" Let me get that out of the way first.

"I asked her if she was okay with keeping Bree until you got home and she let me know she was capable of watching her granddaughter." Her face winces as she recounts that tidbit.

"Don't worry about that, Raelynn." I take her hand in between mine and rub my hands over them as if she could still be cold. "I planned to tell my family about us while they are here, so it would've worked out. Derek already knows, actually." Her eyes widen in surprise at this. I release her hand to grab the lever and push my seat even further back. Not much further it can go, but I want a bit more room. I take her hand and tug. "Come here for a second. It feels like there's an ocean between us."

She's small enough that she has no trouble crawling over the center console and straddles my lap, her hands resting on my chest. "You're disappointed in me, aren't you? I mean, my five-year-old has been able to let more people in than I have. I don't know what it is about this holiday, but the thought makes me uncomfortable, Elias."

173

I cup her cheeks. "I'm not disappointed, Raelynn. I only want to understand, so I can help. Staying here with Henry can't be more fun than staying with me, can it?" I kiss her cheek, then the other, her forehead, and finally her mouth.

"It hasn't been too bad so far," she mumbles against my lips. "He practically begged me to stay so he can spend this time with Jackson. He's been behaving."

"Are you really kissing me and talking about Henry?"

She laughs, but her mood quickly sobers. "I'm sorry for lying to you, but it seemed easier than telling you I couldn't stand the thought of spending Christmas with your family."

I smile. "Does this mean you're not coming home with me?"

She rests her forehead on my shoulder. "I don't know."

"I really want you to meet Derek." She remains silent, so I add, "How can I convince you?"

"I already told Jackson we were staying here," she says.

"And he told you he wants to go home."

She shakes her head a little. "It's a little mind-blowing that your house is our home," she whispers.

"Only way to overcome your fear is to conquer it." Her silence isn't encouraging, so I try one last time. I kiss her softly. "I feel like Little Grizzly would come home with me."

Raelynn laughs and finally lifts her head. "How exactly does that apply here?"

"Because Little Grizzly is fierce. She tackles what she perceives as threats, or fears, head-on. She is more than just a momma bear. Little Grizzly encompasses her entire being and all the things she fights for. I think this is something she'd fight to overcome." Raelynn's eyes water. "I promise to make it a good Christmas for you both. Please, Raelynn."

She nods. "Okay. We'll come home."

"You won't regret it." I turn off the car, open the door, and as we're both climbing out of the driver's side, we see Henry at the door with his jaw hanging. "Shit."

Raelynn walks to him as if we both didn't obviously get out of the driver's seat.

"You're..." Henry can't seem to form words.

"Might want to watch what you say," I tell him. "You have a bad habit of sticking your foot in your mouth."

His eyes harden.

"All you need to know, Henry, is that this is new. Jackson doesn't know right now, and he's good to us both. Now, move, so I can go inside to my son."

Henry moves out of the way as she asked and this time, I don't wait to be invited in.

"Are we going home?" Jackson asks hopefully once again. His eyes flit to Henry. "I miss Bree and my house."

"It's okay, baby, and yes, we're going home. Let's get our things together." She takes Jackson's hand and leaves the room before Henry can open his mouth.

But never fear, Henry still speaks.

"You're taking my son from me on Christmas Eve?" Anger laces his voice. "You're a real prick, you know that?"

"It wasn't my intention. I came to talk to Raelynn, and Jackson clearly wants to go home. Raelynn made the decision."

"On her own?" he asks skeptically.

"Don't start shit with me, Henry. I'm not an enemy you want. Raelynn and Jackson never should've been here, and she'll be back tomorrow like she originally promised."

He glares at me, but doesn't say another word. His glare hardens when Jackson and Raelynn return and Jackson asks if he can ride with me back home. He takes my hand and we walk out while Raelynn stays behind for a moment to talk to Henry. By the time Jackson is buckled in, Raelynn walks out. The look on her face makes me want to storm back into that house and remind Henry of what I just said.

I walk over to her, but she waves her hand in dismissal.

"It's nothing. He's upset." She tosses her bags into the trunk and then slides into the driver's seat. She attempts to crank her car, but nothing happens. "Shit. No, sweet car. You can't die on me now."

"Die on you?"

She looks at me. "It's been trying to die for a year. Let me just leave it here for now. Will you bring me back tomorrow? Or Henry can come get us?"

"Yeah, of course."

Once she grabs her bag and puts it in my car, we're on our way home. Right where we all should've been from the start. This better go well because if this blows up in our faces, I don't know what it'll do to Raelynn. I also have to figure how out to tell them I'm dating Raelynn without spilling the truth in front of Jackson.

"Can you stay in here for a minute?" I ask Raelynn when I park in the garage. "I'll come get you when I'm finished." This seems to be the best and easiest way to break the news. It also ensures that it'll happen quickly. Raelynn nods. I escape into the house and find everyone in the living room, watching a movie. I steal my kid from my sister and clear my throat.

"I need to tell you guys something real quick before Raelynn and Jackson come inside." All eyes finally land on me. "I'm dating Raelynn. Don't mention this in front of Jackson. Got it? Great." I ignore their surprise and start to walk away, but Mom's voice stops me.

"You're *what*?"

"Ma." She heard me; there's no need to repeat myself. "Trust me."

She frowns, but nods. Good enough for me. I leave to get Raelynn and Jackson.

"Did anything new happen while we were gone?" Jackson asks, reaching up to tickle Bree's foot. "We didn't miss anything, did we?"

"No, Jackson. She's saving whatever she does next for when you're here," I reassure him, causing him to grin. I can't believe he cares that much. "Come on. Let's get inside." Raelynn takes Bree while I get their things.

Bree is ecstatic to see Raelynn and Jackson. She reaches for Jackson, but he's only held her when he's sitting down. He doesn't look like he wants to make an attempt at something different right now either. I think me and him are on the same page. After I drop their things off in my room, I find Raelynn, Jackson, and Bree sitting on the floor. Bree stands in front of Jackson and fist bumps him.

"You can sit here, Raelynn." I motion to the only empty seat left, but she shakes her head.

"I'm fine down here."

Bree takes a step closer to Jackson, but stumbles. She falls on her bottom, tears well in her eyes, and Jackson takes her hand. "Falling is okay, Bree," he tells her. "It means you're trying."

My chest tightens at him repeating words I've said to him to my own daughter. Bree grabs his hands and between the two of them, she manages to stand again. This time, she walks to him and plops into his lap, laughing.

"Good job, Bree," he tells her, offering another fist bump. She slaps his hand this time, giggling. Jackson suddenly hugs her and kisses her cheek before releasing his hold on her, except for a hand on her back in case she starts leaning backward.

"Ja-Ja!" Bree shouts, adding in some other words.

Jackson nods like he completely understands her. "I missed you too, Bree." He looks at Raelynn. "Are we making cookies, Momma? Can Bree help?"

"She's too little." Raelynn stands, picks up Bree, hands her to me, and then holds out a hand to Jackson. "Let's bake cookies." They leave the room without a second glance.

I don't even know if I have the ingredients to make cookies. I stand, give Bree to my mom since she holds out her arms for her, and walk to the kitchen. When I see the ingredients for cookies on the counter, even cookie cutters, I tilt my head. "How do I have all of this stuff?"

Raelynn jumps, not realizing I came into the room. "I buy your groceries." She shrugs and then adds, "You'd want to leave cookies out for Santa, too, even if we weren't here. I made sure you were stocked on the necessary ingredients."

Derek walks in as I pick Jackson up to sit on the

counter. I'm not sure how she lets him help, but he'll need to reach the counter at some point, I'm sure.

"So you're the famous Raelynn," he says.

Raelynn glances at me. "I guess so." She hands a measuring cup to Jackson to dump into a mixing bowl.

"Do you play hockey like Mr. EJ?" Jackson asks him.

"Yeah. I play on a different team, though. He played against us around Thanksgiving."

Jackson looks at me. "Did you beat him?" I love how he formed this question. Not did the Rebels beat his team or did the Rebels win, but did I beat Derek?

"Yep." I grin and that causes Jackson to smile. He even sticks his tongue out at Derek.

"Don't tell me that EJ is your favorite player?" Derek asks with a horrified gasp. When Jackson nods, Derek shakes his head. "Oh, Jackson. Buddy, we have to teach you more about hockey and introduce you to more players. Like me."

Jackson basically ignores that comment. "I like Mr. Brayden too. He gave me a puck one time. He threwed it right over the glass!"

Derek sighs. "Well, what do I have to do to make your list of favorites?"

Jackson shrugs.

"What about your mom? Does she have a favorite player?" Derek asks with a quick glance at me. I glare at him. What is he trying to do?

Jackson focuses on his mom. "Maybe Mr. EJ or Mr. Collin."

I frown. Collin? Why the hell would he think her favorite player is Collin Kessy?

"I don't have a favorite player, Jackson," Raelynn

corrects him. "Although, Mr. EJ and Mr. Collin are good choices. Help me stir." She hands him a spatula to help her stir the mixture they've concocted.

"What's your favorite thing about living here, Jackson?" Derek asks. Why is he grilling the kid? I expected him to ask Raelynn questions, not Jackson. There doesn't seem to be any harm in them, but I almost want to kick his ass and tell him to go away for being so nosy in this way.

"Bree, even if she is a baby." He glances at me. "And Mr. EJ," he adds as an afterthought. I smile at him, my heart almost unable to take the fact that we're his favorite things about living here.

"You're one of my favorite things about living here, too, J-man."

Jackson grins, thrilled to hear this.

Raelynn begins getting the dough ready for them to cut out shapes. I think she's making sugar cookies. To keep Derek from asking another question, I ask Jackson how it was to see Stella and Stephanie yesterday. He talks about playing with them until the cookies are in the oven.

"Okay, Jackson, let's get you in the bath while they bake."

"When are we making the fort?" he asks.

"Uh, I don't know if we are. Derek or Nicole is sleeping in your room and Elias's parents are sleeping in my room. So, we're camping out in Mr. EJ's room tonight. He may not want a fort in his room."

Jackson turns to me with big, hopeful eyes. "Momma says we always have a Christmas fort. Please, Mr. EJ?" Before I can answer, he looks at Raelynn. "Why can't we sleep in the living room instead? Santa won't wake me up."

"What's a Christmas fort, Raelynn?"

"A regular fort but with Christmas lights inside. I did my entire living room last year, but I can do a small one this time."

"Why don't I help Jackson with his bath while you build the fort? You can have free rein in my room."

"I'll help you, Raelynn," Derek offers.

She looks like she wants to say no, but she nods. We walk upstairs and head our separate ways. I wish I knew what was being said between them in my room. Derek better not make Raelynn uncomfortable or make her wish she was still at Henry's. I've never kicked anyone out of my house before, but that might make me do it.

"Mr. EJ? Do we have to move?" Jackson asks. He stands before me with his towel wrapped around him and a frown planted firmly on his face.

My first instinct is to frown, but I manage to keep my face passive. "Why would you ask me that?"

"People are sleeping in our rooms." His eyes well with big fat tears. "I don't want to move again. I like it here. Why did you give our rooms away? And why doesn't my dad like you?"

Fuck, this kid is killing me. Where's Raelynn? Jackson wipes away a tear that betrayed him by falling and I grab his shoulders.

"You aren't moving, Jackson. Unless your mom decides it's best for you two to move, you are staying right here with Bree and me. You'll have your room back soon. My family is only here for Christmas and then they are going home. You are not moving," I repeat so he believes me. Jackson nods. "Now," on to the topic I really don't want to address without Raelynn, "why do you think your dad doesn't like me?"

Jackson drops his head, staring down at his feet where one slightly rests on top of the other. His voice is barely above a whisper. "Sometimes, he looks mad when you're around, and today, he called you and Momma names." Jackson looks up at me. "I don't like him anymore. I don't want to go there tomorrow. I want to stay here with you and Bree."

My heart both breaks for him and fills with rage that he feels this way. "What did he say?"

His eyes widen in horror. "I can't say those words, Mr. EJ! I'll get in trouble!"

"You can just this once."

He seems conflicted for a moment before he leans forward and whispers, "While you were outside talking to Momma, he said, 'He's a prick and she's a liar.'" Jackson steps away, his eyes all watery again. "I don't want to go tomorrow. He's mean!" He wraps his arms around my neck and cries.

That is when Raelynn walks in.

Raelynn

WHAT IN THE world? Jackson is still only in his towel from his shower, but that isn't what has my heart in a panic attack. My son is in Elias's arms, crying. What happened?

"What's wrong?" I ask. "Jackson, baby, what's the matter?" I crouch down just in time for him to barrel into me, leaving Elias in a second.

"Dad's mean! I don't like him anymore!"

Huh? I don't understand.

"I don't want to see him tomorrow," he adds, hiccuping with his tears.

"What? Why? What happened?" He was only supposed to get clean; what could've happened with Henry when he isn't even here?

"Jackson overheard Henry call us both some names and he's upset," Elias tells me. Damn it, Henry. I squeeze my eyes closed and bear hug Jackson. "He was also momentarily worried about having to move because someone else is staying in your rooms, but I told him not to worry about that."

"Thanks," I say to him. I pull away from Jackson and wipe his tears. "Jackson, baby, listen to me. I'll talk to your dad. In the meantime, we need to decorate those cookies before you go to bed, okay?"

"Do we have to go tomorrow?"

"Let me think about it, okay?" He'll hate me tomorrow when we see Henry anyway. I don't know yet what Henry called us, but if we don't do anything else while we're over there tomorrow, he will be apologizing to my son.

Jackson nods. I hand him his clothes, item by item, so he can dress himself in his pajamas. Jackson's mood lightens bit by bit as we head downstairs and decorate cookies; this time it's only Elias, Jackson, and me.

"Shoo, Elias." I hold up a butterknife with icing on it as if I might fling the icing at him. It's maybe the third time I've said something in efforts to get him out of the kitchen.

He raises an eyebrow, as if daring me to follow through on my idle threat. "Why are you trying to get rid of me, Raelynn?"

"Because your family is here and ever since we've been home, you've been with us." That was another reason why I didn't want to spend Christmas here. As an afterthought, I whisper, "And it's past Bree's bedtime."

He glances at the clock on the oven and frowns. "Okay, you have a point. J-man, I need you to finish this one for me." He slides the cookie he was working on over to Jackson and a moment later, it's just the two of us in the kitchen.

Soon, Jackson and I leave out a plate of cookies for Santa, say goodnight to everyone in the living room, and then head upstairs to bed. Elias's bed was made to be a fort, especially a Christmas fort. Derek helped me wrap and string lights on the headboard and footboard as well as the tall bedposts. While his questions to Jackson irked me because I felt like he was spying on me in a way, the questions he directed at me while we hung the lights and draped blankets and sheets over Elias's bed were almost casual and friendly.

He also tried to tell me that I was Elias's perfect type, but failed to elaborate. Derek thinks his friend is head over heels in love with me already and he said I better not hurt him. I'm not so sure about that, but I do know things are definitely serious. Far more serious than it may be if kids weren't involved.

And maybe it's risky, but I decide to slide into the middle of the bed with Jackson to my left. This way I get to sleep next to Elias, too, instead of only Jackson. Jackson cuddles against my side and whispers about how he loves Christmas forts the best. Also part of our tradition is me reading a few Christmas books. I love these moments with him.

Each year, he gets bigger, older, and soon, he'll start complaining about these traditions, I'm sure. I cherish every year he eagerly cuddles with me and waits for me to read him a book. Or when he wants to build a blanket fort and play underneath it for hours rather than watching TV. Practically any moment where he needs me or wants to spend time with me because one day, he'll grow up and those moments will come less frequently.

I'm lightly dozing off when the bed dips and a kiss is pressed to my cheek. Elias sits up next to me with a smile.

"This is magical," he whispers.

"That's why it's a Christmas fort."

"Santa is here. Where are...?" He nods toward Jackson.

"That heavy bag you carried in?"

"Got it. You stay. I'll take care of it. Don't want to wake him if you move."

"Thanks."

Elias kisses me one more time before disappearing to place Jackson's gifts from Santa underneath the tree. Jackson rolls away from me while he's gone. After a little while, Elias returns and scoots as close to me as possible, taking my hand in his.

"Do you know what Henry said?" I whisper.

"I'm a prick and you're a liar. He said it while we were outside and Jackson heard him."

I sigh. So far, Henry has done more harm than good. If he can't get his act together, he can just go away. Henry still has some growing up to do. He needs to *think*. He's making stupid mistakes and he's not thinking about how his choices affect Jackson.

Elias pulls me into his arms.

"Elias," I say, about to argue.

"Don't even think about it. It's been a rough day. You need the comfort I can give you. Jackson will be okay."

I don't really want to argue either. I chose to sleep in the middle of the bed for a reason, didn't I? With a deep breath, I relax against him.

"I have a request," Elias whispers a few minutes later.

"What is it?"

"If it's okay with you, I'd like to be just EJ to Jackson. No more mister. Think about it."

Oh, wow. Elias is asking a lot of me tonight. Taking away the mister, the formality, is a big deal. He's getting even closer to my son by taking that away. He's removing another one of our layers, damn it.

"I'm okay with it," I whisper. How can I say no? I'm currently in his bed, in his arms, with my son on the other side and it's all on Christmas Eve. Elias doesn't ask for much; he can have this. "I know it probably doesn't seem like it all the time, but I am glad I'm here and with you."

"Does this mean I get a good night kiss?"

Smiling, I lift my head and press a chaste kiss to his lips. Elias pulls me even closer and soon, I'm drifting to sleep.

When I wake up in the morning, Jackson's head is on my chest and his little body is turned sideways, his feet hanging off the side of the bed. But what I notice is how hot his forehead feels against my chest and the fact that Elias's arm is around my waist. I move his arm with one hand and with my other, feel Jackson's forehead.

Oh, no.

He's burning up. Jackson moans as he wakes up. "Momma," he whines. He shifts and crawls over my body, hugging me and burying his face in my neck.

"Do you feel bad?" I ask and he nods into my neck.

"What's the matter?" Elias grumbles as he rouses

187

awake.

"Jackson's sick. Pretty sure he has a fever. You might want to get away while you can."

Elias rubs Jackson's back. "What's wrong, J-man?"

"My throat hurts," he mumbles.

Great. He probably has strep. I nudge Elias with my elbow. "Go. He's likely contagious. You don't need it and you don't need to spread it. We'll hang in here today."

Elias frowns. "It's Christmas."

"And he's sick."

Although he doesn't look like he wants to, he gets out of bed and leaves us to get ready for the day. I'm tempted to check on Bree, but her baby monitor is quiet; she might still be asleep. Plus, I need to follow my own advice and keep Jackson's germs to myself.

Jackson falls back asleep in my arms. I rub his back and run my fingers through his hair, hoping it soothes him. But then, I hear sounds from Bree's baby monitor. At first, it sounds like Elias's mom, Alice, talking to Bree. There's nothing wrong with that. If she's in there, then Derek must already be awake and downstairs.

"What do you think about our son dating his nanny, James?" Alice says. "I don't like it."

My body stiffens. There's a brief pause and James says, "It's none of our business."

"It will be when they break up and I have to move down here again because he's without a nanny. This is a disaster waiting to happen, James. I like her, I do, but this blurs the lines, and if something goes wrong, I have to come back. Not that I don't love my granddaughter and wouldn't do it, but it's not the ideal situation. And we both know Elias James doesn't always do well with picking a good woman. Just look at what happened with Bree's mom."

"It's none of our business," James repeats. "EJ is happy. She does her job well. That's all we need to worry about."

It's decided. I like James better than Alice, although I worry about the same things she does. I hear Elias step out of his bathroom at the same time we hear Alice's voice again. "I'm not so sure I like them together is all."

Elias peeks into the fort. For a moment, I'm completely distracted by his body because he only has a towel wrapped around his waist. "Is she talking about us?"

I nod. "Has been for the past few minutes."

Without another word, he storms out of his bedroom and his voice filters through the baby monitor. "Ma. We can hear you."

"Oh, I'm so sorry," she replies. "But you can understand why we're worried—"

"Yeah. I'm sure for the same reasons we've already thought of, but it's not stopping us, so keep it to yourself. The last thing I need is for you to get into Raelynn's head and cause her to change her mind."

Silence emits and a few seconds later, I hear Elias step back into his room. He doesn't acknowledge me as he finds something to wear. I feel like I should say something to him, but I'm not sure what. Awkwardness settles into the air. It's probably all one-sided, too. I don't think Elias ever feels awkwardness.

"Do you want me to bring breakfast up to you?" he asks as he sits on the edge of the bed, now fully dressed and ready to face the day.

"No. I'll wait until he's ready to eat. Thank you,

though."

He nods. "You okay?"

"I'm fine." That might be one of the first times I've said that and meant it. All because Elias is right. We have thought about what Alice is worried about. I wouldn't leave him hanging either. Although it's odd to say, I'm okay with his mother being upset about this because it's totally understandable and she's on the same page as we are with the exception of being upset and wishing we wouldn't see each other because of it.

Elias glances down at Jackson and pushes some of his hair away from his eyes. The action is so endearing and sweet, I nearly burst into tears. "Are you sure you want to stay in here all day?"

"I don't want anyone else to get sick, and look at him. He's sleeping on me. I can't exactly get around like this."

He smiles a little. "Good point. I'll check in on you, but text me if you need anything." He leans forward, kisses me softly, and then it's only Jackson and me in the Christmas blanket fort.

A buzzing on the nightstand catches my attention about an hour later. It's a task to lean over, push the blankets aside and grab it, all the while Jackson sleeps with deadweight on my chest. All for a text from Henry, asking what time we're coming over. I might as well deal with that now.

I call him and he answers quickly.

"Do you want the bad news or the worst news?" I ask him.

"You're not coming," he states.

"Jackson is running a fever and his throat hurts, so no. We're not coming." He begins to curse, and I talk over him. "We're spending the day in bed, but you are more than welcome to drive over here and see him."

Henry is quiet for a moment. "Is that the bad or worst news? Is he okay? Do we need to take him to the doctor?"

"He's asleep right now. I'll take him to the doctor tomorrow. That was the bad news. The worst news is that he heard you call Elias a prick and me a liar. He doesn't want to see you today. You really upset him, Henry. You made him cry."

Henry sighs. "I didn't even think about it."

"Do you ever think?" I can't help but to bite out. "You have to always think about how your choices, your words, and your actions will affect him."

"I know; I didn't think anything of it, I guess, because..." His voice trails off. "You know what it was like for me growing up."

"Yes, I do," I reply softly. "Don't let history repeat itself with our son, Henry. You don't have to turn into your parents. You can do better for Jackson. I need you to do better for Jackson."

His voice is deeper, more tortured. "You're right. God. I'm sorry. I'll apologize to all of you when I come. I'll do better. I promise. I don't want Jackson to grow up and have nothing to do with me because of my actions."

"I don't want that either." Despite my feelings toward Henry, I would love it if Jackson could have a happy and healthy relationship with his father like every child deserves.

Henry clears his throat. "Okay. I'll stop by later. Oh, I called around and found a guy willing to look at your car yesterday." My stomach is in knots by the time Henry finishes telling me about the problem with my transmission.

"So, basically, it will cost more to fix it than what your car is worth. Do with that what you will."

"Thanks for doing that for me." Henry can be nice, even when he thinks I'm a liar.

"No problem. I'll text you when I'm on my way."

We hang up and my bladder demands I get out of bed. Jackson whines a little when I move him off of me, but he doesn't wake up. Within five minutes of my return, he wakes up enough to crawl right back onto my chest. Poor baby. Is it terrible of me that I almost cherish this? He's sick and he still wants me. What if when he gets older, he no longer wants the comfort of his momma when he gets sick? I cherish *all* the moments.

Henry texts me around one in the afternoon and the moment I hear the doorbell, I manage to get out of bed with Jackson in my arms. He's been sleeping on and off all day. Right now? He's asleep and nothing but deadweight in my arms. I don't know if I can make it; he's so heavy and my arms feel like they might yank out of their sockets at any moment, but I'll try. I won't drop my son, if only from sheer determination alone.

"Raelynn, what are you doing?" Elias asks, changing his route from walking toward the front door to jogging to me as he sees me walking down the stairs.

"Answering the door. It's Henry."

Elias takes Jackson from me. "I meant why are you carrying him down the stairs?" He glares at me. "What if you dropped him or if you both fell?"

"I was fine." Dying from his weight, but I was managing.

"You couldn't have left him in bed?" he asks as we walk to the door.

"He was latched onto me." I open the door to Henry, who has a bag full of presents. "Hey. Come on in. I was about to find something to eat. You can take those upstairs to the second bedroom on the right."

"Is he feeling any better?" Henry asks.

"Not really. Just meet me in the kitchen." Henry nods and heads upstairs. I turn to Elias. "Give me my son. You're supposed to be avoiding the germs."

Elias opens his mouth to object, but Jackson rouses awake and guess who he wants? His momma!

"Please don't be smug and sit down. I'll heat up leftovers for you." His voice turns all soft and sweet as he speaks to Jackson. "J-man, you want something to eat?"

Jackson shakes his head, but he hasn't had anything to eat today. "Fix him some soup, please."

Henry walks in and says hey to Jackson, who turns to hide his face in my neck. Henry looks helpless for a moment as he sits down next to me.

"Baby, your dad has something he wants to say, and I need you to listen. Okay?"

Henry shouldn't feel too special. Jackson ignores me too. Henry apologizes to Jackson, for saying what he did and for Jackson hearing him, and then he apologizes to Elias and me. I make sure to tell him he's forgiven. I don't want Jackson to think I'm mad at him or that we should hold a grudge.

Elias sets a bowl of soup and a plate of leftovers in front of me. He looks like he wants to stay and be supportive, or maybe to supervise, but I flick my gaze to the living room. He's not about to spend the majority of his time with us again.

"Don't let her carry him anywhere, Henry," he says.

"He's too heavy for her."

I roll my eyes. "Go away, Elias *James*."

Elias glares, but leaves us alone. Getting Jackson to eat is a task at first, but eventually, we both eat and head back upstairs. Henry carries him as requested. We sit on the bench in front of Elias's bed.

"This isn't your room," Henry states.

"No. We're staying in here while his family visits." I wait for him to make some kind of comment on that, considering he brought it up, but he doesn't. "Your dad brought presents. Do you want to open them?" I ask Jackson.

He nods against Henry's shoulder. I'm surprised he doesn't want to sit with me again. I grab the bag Henry brought and reclaim my seat.

"Has EJ given him his presents yet?" Henry asks.

"No. He hasn't even had presents from Santa." Why does it matter if EJ gave him his presents already? "Does it matter which he opens first?"

Henry shakes his head, so I begin to hand presents to Jackson. He gets new books, a few toys, some clothes, and then there's an envelope. I open the envelope for him and pull out the piece of paper. Confused, I read what it says to Jackson.

"Congratulations. In three weeks, you start skating lessons!" I inject some excitement for Jackson as I realize what Henry's done. Jackson's eyes are wide and for the first time all day, he looks like himself.

"I'm gonna learn how to skate? Like Mr. EJ?"

"Yep," Henry answers for him. To me, he says, "I'll help you get him to the lessons, don't worry."

I'm excited for Jackson, I am, because he will *love*

this. It's already written all over his face. But why would Henry do something like this without asking me first? He *needs* to consult me. And what if Jackson gets hooked on this? Sports can be expensive and money is not something I've always had. The last thing I want is to tell Jackson he can no longer do something he loves because I can't afford it, if something happens one day and I no longer have this job.

But this kind of fear doesn't help me or Jackson. It doesn't help my mission of expanding our worlds. I'll let the fear go, but I still wish he'd asked.

EJ

IT DOESN'T FEEL right to carry Jackson's presents upstairs and to leave Bree downstairs, but she's the very last person who needs to be around him. Seeing the three of them sitting on the bench in front of my bed sends a ridiculous spout of jealousy through me. They are a family. We're sort of a family. Altogether, we're some kind of a family. It's weird, but it's what's happening.

"Hey, J-man. You feeling better?"

"Mr. EJ! I'm gonna skate like you! Dad got me lessons!" he says instead of answering.

"He did? That's awesome. Now you don't have to wait around on me." I hold out my fist and he bumps it. "I thought you might want the rest of your presents. Some are from Bree and me, some are from your mom, and some are from Santa." I look at Raelynn. "I left yours downstairs, but I can get them if you want."

"No, that's okay," she answers.

I kneel in the floor in front of them. "What do you want first?"

And so, Jackson opens his presents. He's absolutely thrilled when he gets to his skates. He wants to put them on right then, but Raelynn tells him no.

"We have to make sure they fit, though. Right, Jackson?" I say with a grin.

"Right," he agrees, extending his feet out to me.

"But then we're taking them off because your mom doesn't want you wearing them right now, okay?"

"Okay, Mr. EJ."

"Hey, you can call me EJ from now on, okay?"

Jackson's eyes widen and he looks at Raelynn. "If he says it's okay, then it's okay," she tells him.

"Time to stand up." I help him stand. "How do they feel?"

"Like we need to go skating," he answers, causing the three of us to laugh.

"We'll break them in once you're feeling better." I take his skates off and he crawls onto Raelynn's lap.

"Am I missing out on the party?"

Everyone looks to see Derek walk into my room.

"We're just giving Jackson his presents. Derek, this is Henry, Jackson's dad. Henry, this is one of my best friends, Derek." They say hello. "Hey, help me take the fort down," I say to Derek. While I don't like the idea of Henry anywhere near my bed, especially if Raelynn is in it, why deal with the hassle of getting in and out of the fort? And Christmas is basically over. Plus, if they want to watch a movie, they wouldn't be able to because of the fort.

Henry, Derek, and I get the fort taken down. As Derek and I are about to leave them to their family time, Jackson stops me.

"EJ?"

"Yeah, J-man?"

He looks to be on the verge of falling back asleep. "When do I get my room back?"

I laugh. "Tomorrow, but if you really want to sleep in your room tonight, I can see about rearranging some things."

He nods and even says please while Raelynn shakes her head. The kid is sick. If he wants to be in his own room, then who am I to stand in his way? Nicole can move to Bree's room and sleep on the twin bed and Derek can sleep on the couch. It's everyone's last night. I doubt they'll be that upset by the change.

I pluck Bree from Nicole's hold, feeling like I haven't had any time with my own kid since they've been here, and sit in one of the chairs. "Nicole, don't you want to take Derek's place in Bree's room and Derek, don't you want to sleep on the couch?"

"Why?" Nicole asks.

"Jackson wants his room back." I shrug. "He's sick, so I kinda want to give him what he wants."

Derek, who sits next to Nicole, throws an arm around her shoulders and pulls her into him. "You mean you want to kick your baby sister out for the preference of a five-year-old?" He looks at Nicole, who's already laughing.

"We don't have to deal with this, Nicole! Your brother should treat you better. Let's get a room at a hotel instead."

"Take my daughter to a hotel and I'll kill you myself." My dad says pretty much the exact thing I was thinking.

"You hear that, Nic? They think I'd go to jail for you." Derek shakes his head in disbelief at us. My sister, though? She's still smiling and laughing a little, which I think is a bit weird.

I grab a pillow and throw it at him. "Get away from my sister, Novak."

He rolls his eyes as he removes his arm from her shoulders. "I don't mind letting your sister take over my bed."

I groan at his choice of words, though Nicole thinks it's funny once again.

"If Derek's okay with it, then so am I," she says.

"You two need to separate." Not that I think there's anything going on between them. Derek is my age and he's my best friend. He likes to joke around and Nicole? Well, she just likes that Derek annoys me sometimes.

It's nice to spend time with my family, but really? I can't wait for them to leave. I don't like my house full of people who don't live here. People who like to take my kid and hog her. It's my time off, and I don't feel like I've spent any more time than usual with her. I love that they came and that they're here for Bree's first Christmas, but I can't wait until it's just the four of us again.

Well, and the occasional visits from Henry.

Speaking of, he leaves around eight. Bree is knocked out in my arms and I really want to check on Raelynn and

Jackson. I keep hearing Raelynn's voice in my head about how I was spending more time with her and Jackson than my own family.

Fuck it. It's my house. My time off. I'll do whatever I want.

I get up with Bree in my arms and march upstairs. Jackson is in the bathroom, brushing his teeth.

"Hey, J-man. Your room is all yours again."

"Thanks, Mr. I mean, EJ."

I grin and leave him to pop into my room, but I find Raelynn in hers instead.

"Hey. I'm hopping into the shower once he's asleep," she says, holding up her clothes.

"Can I come too?" I whisper.

Her eyes widen. "No!" she whisper-shouts. "Are you crazy?"

"About you? Absolutely. Please? I miss you. I'll even behave." Maybe. I might be lying about that last part.

"Your family—"

"Yeah, I know. They're here. I don't care. I want this, so let me have it."

"Momma, I'm ready for bed," Jackson says, suddenly appearing between us.

Raelynn closes a dresser drawer and walks past me without another word. I walk to Bree's room and lay her in her crib. Raelynn and I leave their rooms at the same time. I hold out my hand. If she takes it, then we go to my bathroom. If she doesn't, then that's a very loud and clear no.

"I've had a sick kid laying on me all day," she tries. My hand still hovers in the air. Three, two... She sighs and takes my hand. "We need to talk anyway."

With any other woman, this would raise a red flag

that something bad is coming. With Raelynn, she probably just needs to get something off her chest. Not to mention, I highly doubt she's about to break up with me while we're taking a shower together.

"It looks like you and Henry coordinated that gift for Jackson," she says as I turn the water on.

"I was going to get him both the lessons and the skates, but then he thought about it, too, so we decided to split it."

"Why didn't either of you ask me first before essentially signing my son up for a sport?"

I raise an eyebrow at her. "Because I figured you'd say no because of the expense."

Raelynn frowns as we undress. "I wouldn't have."

Okay. I'm confused. "Then why did you want us to ask you first?" It sounds like she's okay with what we did, so what's the problem? Raelynn steps into the shower and I follow after her.

"Because he's my son and I should be consulted. It should be my decision if he does something. I should know first, not last."

I rest my hands on her shoulders and massage. She's working herself up and that's the last thing I want. "Noted," is all I say.

She turns to face me, interrupting the massage as she tilts her head back to wet her hair. "And you were in cahoots with Henry. I thought you were only supposed to do things with me?" There's the slightest hint of a smirk on her face to let me know she's teasing.

"That was an exception because it was for Jackson."

Raelynn nods. "Will you miss your family when they leave tomorrow?"

"Do I look like I want to talk about my family?" I glide my fingers over her body as she washes herself. Suds move either around my fingers or over them.

"No, you look like you want to eat me up and have sex with me, which is why I asked about your family."

I grin. "You can read me pretty well. I'm ready for them to leave if only so I can have my house back to normal and you to myself."

She lifts her arms to wash her hair and my gaze naturally drops to her breasts, which rise a bit at the action. "I need to ask you a favor."

"Yes," I answer immediately. My hands move to her breasts as if magnetically drawn there. Raelynn laughs and I half listen as she recounts what's apparently wrong with her car. Before she can get to what her favor may be, I offer a solution. "Do you want us to go look for another car then? We can go Monday. I can buy it and you can drive it as long as you live here."

My hands are swatted away, which causes my eyes to lift to hers. She doesn't look too happy with me.

"No. I don't need you to ride in on your white horse, Elias," she says with a huff. "I know you do these things because you care, but I still need to make decisions on my own and for myself. I still need to pay for things on my own. Otherwise, even though you don't intend it, you take my power and make me feel helpless. What I was going to ask you is if you'll help me look for a car. I can afford car payments; you are not buying me a car."

I understand what she's saying, I guess, but... "Are you sure? I don't mind, and you do use your car to do a lot of things for me."

"I'm sure, Elias. I would just like for you to help me

find a car and make sure I'm not taken advantage of." She adds a little smile.

"If that's what you want me to do, then consider it done."

Her arms are suddenly around my neck as she lifts as high as she can on her tiptoes and she kisses me. "Thank you. We should get out of here."

I frown. "Without having any fun? You're wet and naked against my wet and naked body. Why would we miss out on that opportunity, Raelynn?"

"Elias," she says with a sigh. That's all I need to hear to know absolutely nothing is happening in this shower. Her sigh says it all.

That's perfectly okay, but I need one thing at least. I dip my head and allow my lips to caress hers, slowly and lightly at first and then harder and deeper as my tongue slips inside her mouth. A kiss is all I want. One simple kiss. She's tense at first, possibly thinking that I'm ignoring what my sighed name obviously meant, but I keep my hands on her waist and my body as still as possible to show I don't want to move things further. Raelynn slowly relaxes as she grips my arms and begins to lean into to me.

That's when I pull away. "We need to open our own presents anyway."

She sighs again, but there's the tiniest of smiles on her face. Her arms fall from around my neck, she swivels to turn off the water, and then we're stepping out of the shower. Soon, after a quick trip downstairs, saying good-night to my family, and peeking in on Bree to find her awake, I carry presents into my room and place them on my bed before going back for Bree.

She reaches for Raelynn, who now sits on the bed and

shakes her head. "What if I still have Jackson's germs on me?"

I roll my eyes. "Then you need to learn how to shower better. You should be fine, and she wants you."

Bree sits in her lap a moment later. "I missed you too, ladybug," Raelynn whispers to her.

"Okay, stop the love fest. We have presents to exchange. Do you want to go first?"

"You first."

For a moment, I watch her. Bree leans back against her chest, her tiny fingers clutching Raelynn's, her little feet crossed at the ankles, and Raelynn has her head bent, smiling down at my princess who smiles up at her. The two of them together are too much.

I grab a random present addressed to me from both Raelynn and Jackson. I open the assortment of gifts, all of which I love, and thank her for them. Bree has fallen asleep with her head tilted off to the side when it's Raelynn's turn. My presents for her are all centered around ways she can treat herself. That's something she doesn't do nearly enough, so I'm helping her out.

"A present from Jackson?" she questions, her throat clogging immediately.

"Yeah. Maybe we should wait until morning, so he can be here for this."

She hasn't even opened it yet and she's already crying. "So he can see me be a mess?"

"Yep."

"When did he get me this?"

"We took advantage of our time together while you were on your date with Collin. He did everything all on his own, too."

Raelynn shakes her head as she stares at the wrapped present in wonder. "I'm going to ugly cry, aren't I?"

"Maybe." She will. If she cried just seeing that he got her a present, she's definitely going to cry when she opens his gifts. I take the present and place it on my nightstand for now. "We should lay her back down."

"I'll do it." Raelynn leaves the room with my daughter and returns a minute later to crawl directly on top of my body. "Thank you for my gifts. You've spoiled me, Elias."

"You deserve it as my nanny, my friend, *and* my girlfriend."

She grins. "You're being handsy, Elias." Just a little. My hands glide from her shoulders, down her back, along the curve of her ass, down the back of her thighs, and back up again. "I don't mind, though, because guess what?"

"What?"

She leans down, kisses my jaw, my neck, and then whispers in my ear, "I locked the door when I came back from Bree's room."

My hands freeze where they currently are on the back of her thighs. "You did?"

Raelynn nods, her hands slipping underneath my shirt and roaming over my chest and stomach. She kisses me with such need, all thoughts collapse and I match her feeling for feeling, movement for movement. It's moments like these when I know Raelynn is perfect for me just as much as I'm perfect for her. When words don't have to be said. When together, we react seamlessly without thought to pleasure one another, exacerbate our already heightened senses, and to use this sensual manner to tell one another how we feel.

Afterward, she places a sweet kiss on my cheek and curls into my side. Raelynn hides her face in my shoulder, her lips brushing against my skin as she whispers, "I think my gut is finally trusting and believing in everything here with you."

"About time," I whisper back, causing her to laugh a little. I can officially go to sleep with a smile on my face.

In the morning, I hold Bree in my arms and lean against the doorframe while Raelynn crawls into bed with a grouchy Jackson. He's feeling worse today; good thing she's taking him to the doctor as soon as Henry gets here. In the meantime, she opens her presents from him. My family is downstairs cooking breakfast, but no way am I missing this.

"What if you don't like it?" Jackson asks with fear just as Raelynn reaches to tear the wrapping paper.

"I will love it because the best son in the world gave it to me." She kisses the top of his head and tears into the present.

The gift box holds a homemade picture frame that was an absolute bitch to make, but Jackson had fun making it. Jackson also wanted to give his mom a necklace and we were able to order one online. It is the typical heart with "mom" inside, but it's what he wanted to get her. Lastly, Jackson painted her a picture, but there's also a "painting" from Bree. She had an absolute blast getting messy with finger paints, but it was not fun cleaning up or making sure she kept the paint only on her hands and away from her face.

Raelynn's tears are steady and her smile is huge. "I love it, Jackson. Thank you so much." She sets the items aside to bear hug him.

Asking him if he wanted to give his mom a present that day we were tree shopping was one of the best decisions I've ever made. Her smile proves it.

Raelynn

JACKSON DID HAVE strep. Elias's family went home. I trusted Henry to take care of Jackson while Elias and I went car shopping, where we did find a new vehicle for me. Elias left for a game, returned, and now, today, I have an appointment with that lawyer Sylvia recommended. It's Friday and there's a game tonight. Jackson feels better and he's excited because not only are we going, but Henry is coming as well. But first, I have to meet with the lawyer.

And I do. Not with his assistant. Not with someone else in the firm, but with the head honcho. Color me impressed. Not only impressed, but I really liked him. He's everything I could want in a lawyer. He seems ready to fight, if needed, for what I want in this situation, what's best for Jackson, and while lawyers may not have the greatest rep in the world, he has an almost honest air about him. I want him.

Too bad it won't happen.

"How did it go?" Elias asks the moment I walk into the living room. I feel bad for leaving the kids with him when he's supposed to be having his pre-game nap, but he didn't mind.

"It won't work out."

"Why?"

I sit next to him, smile a little as Bree crawls into my lap, and kiss Jackson on the top of his head since he's on the other side of me. "He's great and I really liked him."

Elias frowns. "Then what's the problem, Raelynn?"

"You pay me well, Mr. Bertuzzi, but you do not pay me anywhere near enough for me to afford him." Elias stares at me for a moment, so I look at Bree, who grins. She talks her baby talk and a Wey slips out.

"Call him and tell him he's hired, Raelynn," Elias says, garnering my attention once more.

"But—"

"Call him," he repeats.

"You aren't—"

"Call him," he says for a third time. "I'll help you. You can accept it as a gift or figure out a way to pay me back, I don't care, but if you like him and you want him, then *call him*."

My heart rams into my ribcage like a bull trying to escape its pen as I stare at him. I know that Elias cares for me, but for him to do this for me? My blood feels light as it flows through my veins. "We can find someone else," I say because I have to try one more time.

"Call. Him."

"You'd let me pay you back?" Hope swells in my chest.

"You can do whatever you want as long as I can help you," he says with a nod of his head. "And you said that you'd let me help you," he reminds me.

"Even if it takes me until I'm eighty?"

Elias laughs. "Yeah, Raelynn. Even if it takes you until you're eighty."

I don't know what it is about this moment. What's so special about him helping me with this? About him letting me paying him back on my own time? But it's those things and the fact that he's helping me assure the custody and visitation papers with Henry are exactly the way I want them, which is what will be best for Jackson. And that means more to me than anything else.

Overcome with emotion, I lean over and kiss him right on the mouth. Elias is surprised, but why doesn't register to me until I pull away and hear Jackson gasp, "Momma! Why are you kissing EJ?"

My cheeks burn with the intensity of hell from embarrassment as I face him. I say the first thing that comes to mind because I have to say something to him. I need to be the one to answer him first, not Elias. "He decided to help me with something really important. I'm grateful and it made me like him even more, so I decided to kiss him real quick."

Jackson only stares at me like I've grown two extra heads.

"She gave me cooties, J-man," Elias says as he wrinkles his face and looks a little grossed out, breaking the odd tension-like feeling between us.

"My momma doesn't have cooties!" Jackson defends. He suddenly wraps his arms around my neck and pulls me away from Elias. "You do!" Jackson laughs and says, "Stay away from my momma with your cooties!"

Bree, the poor girl, doesn't know what's going on, but she pushes herself up just enough to hug me around the neck too and giggle as she joins in on the fun.

"If I have them, and she just kissed me, then she has them now," Elias points out.

Jackson seems to think about this for a second before releasing one arm. Next thing I know, he rubs my lips. "Now, they're gone!" Jackson sticks his tongue out at him. "I wiped them away."

I laugh. "Okay, baby. Let me go. You're both pulling on my hair." Leaning over like this isn't that fun either.

"What if she wants my cooties?" Elias asks and I toss a glare his way as Jackson releases me and I pull Bree away. Elias ignores me.

"Do you want to kiss EJ and get his cooties, Momma?" Jackson asks, tapping my arm to get my attention back on him.

See? This is why he shouldn't have asked. This is why I shouldn't have kissed him to begin with. Elias discreetly pokes my side. All I have to do is answer in a positive way and we don't have to be so sneaky. There can be some PDA. But is it too soon to introduce something like that to Jackson?

I squeeze my eyes closed and decide to stop thinking. Stop worrying. Stop trying to figure out the present and the future and all the variables in between. I follow in Elias's footsteps and go with my gut.

With a deep breath, I look at Jackson. "If EJ decides he wants to be my boyfriend, then maybe." He's already my boyfriend, but Jackson doesn't know that yet.

My little boy looks at Elias as if he's waiting for an answer from him. Bree crawls into Elias's lap, but I can't muster the courage to look at him. I see him shift in my peripheral vision, lean closer, and then he kisses my temple.

"I definitely want to be her boyfriend, J-man. Is that okay with you?" Elias's fingers interlock with mine and I almost cry with him asking Jackson if he's okay with it.

Jackson nods, though he looks a little unsure. He crawls onto my lap. This feels like a huge moment.

"Do you know what it means for someone to be her boyfriend?" Elias asks. Jackson shakes his head. "There are things your mom's boyfriend is supposed to do. He's supposed to be good to her and to you." Oh lordy. He's definitely going to make me cry now. "He's supposed to treat her like she's one of the most important people in his life and the same goes for you. He's supposed to try his hardest to never make her cry and if he does, he apologizes, fixes his mistake, and doesn't let it happen again. Your momma's boyfriend is supposed to make her even happier than she was. That's what it all comes down to. He's supposed to make her really happy, Jackson."

"You make Momma happy."

Elias smiles. "I'm doing my best."

I inhale a shaky breath. I'm two seconds away from a breakdown because I can't handle all the love and sweetness in this room. Elias squeezes my hand before getting up to try to put Bree down for her afternoon nap before he leaves.

My heart slows, but it feels fuller than ever. Elias eventually leaves and Henry comes over. We eat at home because I don't want to go out somewhere. It's too cold and when I leave, I want to go straight to the arena for the game. I wait with bated breath for Jackson to mention his knowledge of my relationship status to Henry, but he hasn't so far.

We make it to the arena and to the suite. The only familiar faces are Meredith's, Sydney's, and Deanna's. I knew Deanna would be here, as I asked her if she would come tonight if she could and would. I know her the best and I don't want to be up here without an ally. Henry and I take a seat next to Deanna with Bree in my lap and Jackson walks straight to Deanna.

"Ms. Deanna! Can I sit with you?"

"You sure can!" She lifts him into her lap.

They start talking while I wave and say hello to Meredith and Sydney and introduce Henry. Meredith wiggles her fingers with her arms outstretched in a silent question and I hand Bree over to her.

"How have you been?" Deanna asks me.

"Good. Busy. You?"

She grins. "Good. I'm living with Brayden now."

"What? That's awesome!"

"It does feel good." She leans forward a little to look at Henry. "Who are you again? I missed the introduction talking to this little guy." She tickles Jackson's sides, making him giggle.

"Henry, Jackson's dad."

Before she can say anything, Jackson looks at Henry. "Dad, she has this *big* dog." He holds his arms out as far as he can. "His name is Otis." Jackson faces Deanna. "When can Otis come over to my house? Can my dad meet him? Mr. Brayden can come over too."

We laugh at that. I don't think Brayden would willingly stay behind. Deanna promises to figure out when they all can come over. Soon, the game starts and Jackson moves to my lap to sit between Deanna and Henry. Henry seems to relax when he does that because his whole reason for being here is Jackson and now, Jackson will talk to him some more.

And he talks.

I, however, focus on the ice and the game I only somewhat understand. I smile when I catch sight of Collin Kessy, who oddly feels like a bit of a friend to me now, but I grin when I find the number twenty jersey of my boyfriend. For the most part, the players remind me of the little people on a foosball table. They all kinda look alike. They all move around the ice in this odd and chaotic sort of synchronization, obviously having more leeway than those on the foosball table, but it reminds me of them nonetheless.

"EJ will score, Dad. Watch," Jackson tells Henry. "I bring him good luck."

I try to find Elias, but the Rebels charge down the ice toward us to defend their net. They aren't going to score right now, that's for sure. Liam Irving makes a save that has the crowd in the lower level standing. My eyes flick to the big screen since I obviously missed it. The puck was sailing through the air, looked like it was going in, and at the last second, his glove moves up to where it needs to be, the puck slams into it, and he captures the little black object.

A minute later, Jackson repeatedly hits Henry on the leg as the Rebels on the ice set up to make a play. Elias is on the ice. One of his teammates passes the puck to him. His stick rears up seemingly so high in the air, swoops down, and thwacks the puck to send it flying. My eyes don't know whether to watch Jackson or the ice. Jackson holds his breath. The goalie looks briefly defeated the moment the horn sounds, signaling a goal. His arms shoot up in the air with wild enthusiasm.

"See? I told you! Yeah! Go EJ!"

I check Henry over for his reaction to not only my son's obvious love of the game but his affection for Elias. Henry smiles and he fist bumps Jackson when he holds up his fist to celebrate the goal. Bree cries, taking my attention away from them, and Meredith reluctantly gives her back to me. I step away for a diaper change and while I'm gone, I miss another Rebels goal.

But I get some looks from a few of the women I don't know as well. Maybe it's because I've brought another man in here with me? As long as Meredith, Deanna, and Sydney treat me well, I guess that's all that matters.

Jackson brims with excitement from the second goal. He crawls over into my lap, causing me to shift how I hold Bree, who really wants to sleep. Bree takes Jackson's hand and he lets her hold it. These two are adorable.

It's now intermission, so I ask Henry, "Having fun?"

"Yeah. Do y'all come often?"

"We try to come to the weekend games and watch those during the week at home since he's in school and has a bedtime."

Henry nods. Things with Henry have improved in the past week. I think what snapped him out of it was comparing him to his parents. As long as they are better, that's all I care about. I'm almost surprised the girls aren't grilling him like they did me, but then, Sylvia isn't here.

"How are Sylvia and Lizzy?" I ask them.

"Ready to have those babies," Meredith answers. "Everything is still going well, though." Meredith leans in and speaks quietly so the other women don't hear her. "Sylvia demands a get-together. She wants us all over for lunch." Meredith rolls her eyes with a smile. "She wants the latest gossip."

"And you're invited," Sydney tells me.

"She was thinking about one day next week," Deanna adds.

"Just let me know when and I'll be there."

"Here they come!" Jackson shouts with excitement as the guys return for the next period.

Bree falls asleep, totally missing the action on the ice. Sydney's husband, Ian, gets into a fight that adds a whole new level of intensity to the raucous crowd. The Kessy twins break away and fly down the ice with only one of their opponents in their way as he skates backward about midway between them. He doesn't seem like he knows what they will do, but one of them, I can't tell which, ends up with the puck and crashes the net, the puck trickling past the goalie and over the line.

Thankfully, Jackson slipped off my lap in anticipation, so his celebration doesn't wake Bree. The score is now three to zero. The Rebels hold that score until the time runs out. Jackson can't stop smiling over the victory. The guys are leaving tonight for Tampa Bay, so we head on home. Henry drove separately to the game, so it's just us.

I walk into the house, but I frown when I see the alarm panel blinking. Looks like I wasn't paying enough attention when we left and I set the silent alarm instead. All of a sudden, two things happen.

Footsteps bound from upstairs, rushing toward the front door, and police sirens wail nearby.

I scream at the sight of the three intruders, pulling Jackson closer to me by his shirt. They yank open the front door and keep running. My feet cement into place, even as Jackson looks up to me and asks me a question I don't quite comprehend. Even when two officers come in, I can't seem to move.

"Ma'am, do you live here?" one of them asks.

I nod.

"Is anyone else in the house?"

"I...I don't know. Three guys just ran downstairs and out the front door."

One of the officers talks into the walkie talkie on his shoulder and the other heads upstairs, presumably to make sure we're alone in the house. The guy that stays asks me what happened but my nerves are so shot to hell, my hands tremble, and my legs feel weak. I walk over to the table and sit down with Jackson balancing on one thigh and Bree on the other, my arms firmly around them both.

"Can I call someone first?" I ask. Elias isn't here, I can't stay in this house alone tonight, and I need some support. There's only one person I can think to call.

Henry.

EJ

THERE ARE VOICEMAILS on my phone when we land, and assuming they are from Raelynn, I attempt to videochat with her the moment I'm in the hotel room. It's late. Late enough that I'm thrown off and surprised when Jackson's face appears on my screen instead of hers.

"Hey, J-man. What are you still doing up?"

"Momma hasn't told me to go to bed yet."

Okay, that's weird. "Where is your mom? I want to talk to her."

Jackson stands, the view changing to his feet as he walks, and it seems as if he lifts the phone because I'm

218

suddenly hit with another view. Of Raelynn and Henry hugging. Henry looks as if he's holding on as tightly as possible because Raelynn might slip through his fingertips at any moment. What the hell is he doing at my house at this hour? And why are they hugging? Even though I can't see Raelynn's face, I can see some of her arms and she looks to be holding onto him just as tightly.

"Momma, it's EJ."

Raelynn whirls around. "Oh, thank goodness!" Why does she look so relieved? Doesn't she realize I caught her red-handed? I'm not sure what exactly I caught her doing, but it feels like I caught her. She takes the phone from Jackson. "Someone broke into the house, Elias. They were here when we got home."

Her lips move, but my entire world stops. They were in danger? "Is Bree okay?" I blurt out, interrupting her.

"Yes. We're all fine." She repeats what happened, that they ran soon after she walked into the kitchen door from the garage. That the police arrived right after. They found the guys before they could escape in their car. Nothing was taken from the house, but some repairs need to be made to my front door. "I didn't want to stay alone, so I asked Henry to come over," she further explains. "He's sleeping in my room, so I'll be taking over yours." She gives me a little smile.

"That's fine." But a new uneasiness settles over me. I'm glad Henry is there, especially if it makes her feel safer, but I should be the one there with her. And there's something about them being together now that bothers me. I can't put my finger on it just yet. "Can I see Bree?" I ask because I honestly want to see for myself that my princess is unharmed and asleep in her crib, but I also want her away from Henry for a few minutes.

"Of course." To Jackson, she says, "Come on, baby. It's way past your bedtime too. Your dad will tuck you in while EJ checks in on Bree." Nothing else is said to me until she's in Bree's room. "I wish you were here, Elias," she whispers as she adjusts the phone so I can see my little princess peacefully sleeping.

"Me too," I whisper back.

"Is it okay if Henry stays until you get back?" She switches the phone back to herself and slips out of the room and into my bedroom. "I don't want to face being by myself at night just yet, especially until the door is fully fixed. But if you don't want him here..." Her voice trails off. "I could call Deanna, maybe? I didn't think about her." She frowns. "Or any of the other girls."

"It's fine, Raelynn." Damn it, why does that feel like a lie?

Her shoulders relax. "I'm glad you called me back. My heart has finally decided to calm down. You—"

"Rae?"

Her eyes lift above the screen. "Yeah?"

What happened to her demanding he stop calling her that? She just gave up.

"Jackson is scared to sleep alone and," Raelynn's face softens, "he doesn't want me," Henry finishes quietly.

"Okay. Bring him in here." Her eyes fall to mine. "I should go. It's been a long night and we really need the sleep. Jackson will be exhausted tomorrow as it is. Call me when you can?"

"I will."

She smiles and says goodbye. I listen to my voice-mails before going to bed myself. Two were from the alarm company, alerting me of the alarm going off at my house; I should probably also give them Raelynn's number. The last one is from Raelynn, her voice trembling with fear as she tells me a group of men broke into the house, they are okay, that Henry was on his way, and the police were there with her, and to please call her back.

How is it that my house was broken into and what wars my mind for attention is the image of Raelynn and Henry hugging?

Brayden: *Want to go running with Collin and me?*

We have the morning off after the game last night and our late flight in, but apparently, those two want to go for a run. I didn't even know they ran together. Or that Brayden chose to spend his time with anyone. I always thought I sort of forced him to hang with me and he tolerated it because he liked me decently enough.

I text back that I'm willing and soon meet up with them in front of the hotel. Nothing is said. Brayden looks at me, nods, and takes off in a jog with Collin right behind him. We run in silence. Normally, that would be fine. It would be what I prefer. I dislike it so much today. My thoughts run rampant, swirling and crashing together in my mind.

Did Raelynn ever get closure with Henry?

Does she have any feelings at all for him?

Should she have the chance to make it work with Jackson's father?

221

That stupid image of their hug sears into my mind, plastering itself front and center. Henry didn't concern me before, but now, I wonder what his feelings may be for Raelynn. She could've called anyone. Deanna, Sydney, Meredith, or any number of the women, but her only thought was to call Henry.

"What the fuck is the matter with you?"

I look at Brayden. "Nothing. Why?"

"Nothing? You keep huffing. What's the fucking problem, EJ?" We slow to a stop and he stares at me with his hands on his hips.

My eyes flick to Collin for a moment and then I lie about the problem. "My house was broken into last night."

The irritation slides off of Brayden's face immediately. "Damn. Raelynn and the kids weren't home, were they?"

I nod. "Seems like they broke in right before they got home and they ran out soon after they came in the door." I skip over the details with the police and jump to the next important part. "Raelynn called her ex to come over and spend the night so she wouldn't be alone."

"So what?" Collin asks. "She was probably scared."

"He's jealous," Brayden tells him with a bit of a laugh.

Collin frowns. "Of Henry? That's her ex, right?"

"I'm not jealous of Henry," I snap, but my response comes too late for them to believe me, though it's true. "I just..." My voice trails off as I try to figure out what I want to say. "We got together before she got on semi-good terms with Henry; what if one or both of them wants to try to make it work as a family for Jackson?"

That's not an outrageous idea. People stay in relationships all the time because they want to repair and improve it to keep the family together for the children. The family as a single unit is important enough that they want to deal with the bad until they hopefully reach the good. They prefer the usual family unit compared to other versions. What if Raelynn is like that? She hasn't mentioned it, but that doesn't necessarily mean anything. Raelynn keeps things to herself sometimes.

"You don't think she'd tell you?" Collin asks.

"I don't know."

Brayden watches me for a moment and then shakes his head. "You need to keep running, and this time, don't think about your woman. You can do that when you get home and see her after she's spent all this time with her ex."

I groan again, but follow after him since he's running again. This is just what I need, to think about Raelynn spending all her free time with Henry until I come home. But I follow my captain's advice and shut it down. Compartmentalization is easy for me. What I need to focus on is the game ahead and that's just what I do.

Later that night, I focus on pumping my legs as I skate down the ice to chase the puck and a player on a breakaway. He's about three seconds ahead of me. I reach out with my stick as he takes a shot, but it's useless. Savage is ready for him, though. He squares him up, but constantly adjusts, always watchful, and when that puck sails in the air, he lifts his body to block it. The puck deflects off his shoulder and lands on the ice behind the net.

I get to the puck first and send it along the boards to Bruiser before getting off the ice as my shift ends and a new guy, Luukas Lathi, takes my place. Aaron Peters was traded and Luukas Lathi came in his place. He's nice enough so far. He seems to easily fit in right off the bat on the ice. How do I know this?

Because I watch him make a pass to Tommy Boy without even looking and the puck hits his stick like there's some magnetic force snapping it to the blade. With the puck now in his possession, Tommy makes a U-turn to haul ass down the ice, weaving around the traffic of people in his way. The goalie skates out to the top of the blue paint, but he ends up falling to his knees during Tommy's quick approach and Tommy shoots high to score the first goal of the game.

"Yeah, Tommy Boy!" someone shouts from next to me.

Everyone stands to fist bump him and the other guys on the line as they skate by the bench. The rest of the game is a constant battle for possession, of skating from zone to zone, or absorbing hits and dishing out just as much contact. Savage stands on his head, making save after save, but their goalie does the same thing, not letting another mistake happen to allow the puck to get past him.

Tommy Boy's goal ends up being the lone goal of the game.

When we make it back to the hotel for the night, I think about calling home, but something stops me. I know they're okay because Raelynn texted pictures of Bree throughout the day, up until two hours ago. I stare at her name on the screen before putting the screen to sleep and setting it aside. I'll see her tomorrow.

When I park in the garage, I sit in my car for just a moment before forcing myself to get out and walk to the door that will open into the kitchen. Nerves knot my stomach and I hate it. I feel like a wuss. I open the door and sitting at the kitchen table is Raelynn. She quickly closes her laptop, picks Bree up from her highchair, and walks toward me with my princess on her hip and a big smile on her face.

"You're home," she breathes.

I drop my bags and her arm is around my neck a second later. I hold her close, smiling as Bree says, "DaDa!"

"Where's Jackson?" I ask as we both pull away to look at one another.

"With Henry. They went out for lunch and to buy Jackson a new jacket. I wanted to be here when you came home, so I stayed behind," she explains. She lifts onto her tiptoes to kiss me. "I'm glad you're back, Elias," she adds as I take Bree from her.

"Me too," I half-lie. She shows me the damage to the front door, but before we can sit down, I blurt out, "Can we talk?"

Her smile disappears and her body tenses, but she nods. We move into the living room and sit on the couch. I haven't been able to stop thinking about her and Henry, and I'm not entirely sure what I'll say, but my gut says this needs to come off my chest sooner rather than later. Raelynn watches me expectantly, waiting for me to start the conversation I obviously wanted to have.

"Did you ever get closure with Henry?" is the question that glides out of my mouth. "When he came back and you talked?"

Raelynn frowns with confusion. "You want to talk

about Henry?"

"Sort of. So, did you?"

Her mouth opens, but no sound comes out at first. "I guess," she says weakly. "I'm not hung up on him, if that's what you're after. We parted ways when I left home. Did I think about him some? Sure, while I was still pregnant and for maybe two months after Jackson was born. I knew Henry wouldn't be a part of my future, so I left all of my past behind."

Okay, but... "Then he came back. He is in your life when you didn't think he would be," I point out. Bree leans against my chest, content with simply being held.

"I don't understand why we're talking about this, Elias."

"I've been wondering if maybe you would want to talk with Henry more."

"About what?" she interrupts.

"About what happened. About any possible feelings." Raelynn stands and stares down at me with her hands propped on her hips as I continue, "About whether you'd want to make it work as family."

"Is this your way of breaking up with me?" Before I can answer, her outrage doubles and she points at me. "You! Who had to go and tell my son we were dating! Are you kidding me, Elias? Where is this even coming from?"

"I'm not breaking up with you," I cut in before she can continue on her rant.

"It sure sounds like it!" She throws her hands up. "You're pushing me on *Henry*, Elias." For a moment, she looks completely baffled. "What the hell?"

The front door opens and Jackson runs into the living room. "Momma! Look! I have a Carolina Rebels hoodie!"

He tugs on the new hoodie he wears.

"Awesome, Jackson." He turns to show me and she says to Henry, "Did you get him an actual jacket too?"

"Yeah. He really wanted the hoodie, though, so we splurged."

To me, she says, "Can I have the rest of the day off?"

"Um, yeah. Sure."

She walks off, up the stairs, and a moment later, returns. "Come on, Jackson. Henry, I'll walk you out. See you later, Elias." They walk out of the house.

Immediately, and for the first time, I feel like my gut was wrong and it betrayed me.

Raelynn

"RAE, IS EVERYTHING okay?" Henry asks as we walk into the garage.

"Fine." This world expanding business is not for me. What kind of boyfriend asks me out of the blue if I want to get with my ex? That's basically what just happened. And not just any ex, but Henry!

He gently grabs my elbow as I open the back door of my car for Jackson. "Rae." I thought that word lost its meaning for me since he's been around, but hearing it right now causes all the hurt from the past to resurface on top of my confusion caused by my conversation with Elias and I want to curl up in my bed and cry.

Instead, I motion for Jackson to get in since he's watching us closely. "I just want us to get out of the house, Henry," I say as I lean in to buckle Jackson in.

"What are y'all going to do?"

"I don't know," I say with a huff and annoyance bleeding through my tone as I stand upright and close Jackson's door. All I want right now is to get far, far away from this house. I wish I'd grabbed my laptop, but no way am I walking back in there now.

"You're upset," he whispers. My shoulders sag. If Henry can tell, then Jackson can too. "Can I come with you? Drive y'all wherever you want to go?"

I don't have it in me to argue with him, so I hand over my keys. Soon, he's backing out of the driveway and driving to an unknown destination, if he even has one in mind. Henry takes us to a fast food restaurant.

"What are we doing here?" I ask. They had lunch not too long ago.

"Milkshakes," he answers simply.

So, we order milkshakes and take a seat at a booth. Jackson wants to play in their playhouse, of course, but Henry tells him he has to finish his milkshake first. We have small talk, about their day together, about Jackson returning to school soon with Christmas break ending, and about his upcoming skating lessons because Jackson talks about that at least once a day. Jackson seems to finish his milkshake in record time and escapes to the playroom.

"Want to talk about it?" Henry asks as I eye my son. Luckily, it's not too busy in there right now.

"About what?"

"Whatever caused so much tension to be in the house when Jackson and I got there."

Maybe if I handle this now with Henry, I can go home and tell Elias that he is in fact crazy and can stop whatever nonsense he started. "Do you have feelings for me?" I glance over at Henry to find his mouth parted slightly. He stares at me without answering until I nudge him with a, "Well?"

"I never stopped loving you, Rae," he answers quietly. My heart stops beating and my lungs still in my chest. I certainly never expected him to say that. "But when I came down here, you could've sent me to hell on the spot with the look in your eyes. And I didn't come here for you. I came for Jackson. I can't undo what I did, Rae, and I don't think we'll ever have a second chance. That's okay, as long as I get to be a father to Jackson." His eyes drift away from me to where Jackson plays.

I don't know what to say. Elias put me in this position and I don't know why. Where am I supposed to go from here? What else am I supposed to discuss with Henry in order to satisfy Elias? I don't even understand what Elias is after with this.

"You've moved on, right, Rae?" Confusion colors Henry's voice.

"Yes. Even if I wasn't with Elias," my head shakes, "I couldn't." My eyes find Jackson who waves at me before he jumps into the ball pit. "Between your parents and mine, what happened between us, and everything else, it's too much to get over. Co-parenting is much easier. It's all I want." I'm not so sure I'm *still* with Elias. He said he wasn't breaking up with me, but it certainly didn't sound like it.

"That's what I figured. Have I somehow messed things up between you and EJ?"

I shake my head. "No." Should I tell him more? Maybe he could tell me what the hell is going on. That doesn't seem wise, all things considered, so I stay quiet.

"But something has happened?" he presses.

"Stay out of it, Henry," I warn as Jackson runs out of the playroom and climbs into my lap.

"Don't you want to play with me, Momma?"

I laugh. "You know I'm too big and too old to be in there."

"You're not too big," he argues. "Dad and EJ are too big. You could play in there with me."

I smile. My son innocently points out my height disadvantage because it means I can still fit into all the nooks and crannies of the playhouse.

"Please, Momma?" He then adds in a whisper, "No one will notice you're not a kid."

Henry can't hold in his laughter anymore and I shake my head with a smile. "Okay, but only for a few minutes." He slides off my lap, takes my hand, and drags me into the playroom. I kick off my shoes and follow after him. While I may be short and small, the tube we crawl through still feels like a tight fit. For a moment, I panic about how embarrassing it would be if I was to get stuck in here.

Jackson cannonballs into the ball pit. I simply step into it.

"Let's play hide and seek, Momma!"

"Okay. You're on."

He dives under the balls and I grin before coming after him. He can move easier than I can in here. I blame the fact that he's more experienced and even smaller than I am. I eventually capture him, tickling his stomach and sending him into a fit of giggles.

"Okay, Momma! Stop!" he shouts in between his laughs.

"Tell me something I want to hear."

"I love you! Best momma ever! Please!"

I stop and he takes a couple of deep breaths with a wide smile on his face. "Maybe we should stop and go hang out with your dad. He looks lonely."

Jackson swivels to look at Henry. He nods solemnly. We climb out of the playhouse, put our shoes back on, and walk to Henry.

"All done?"

"We didn't want to leave you out of our fun," I say. "Let's go to your house for a bit, if that's okay?"

"Yeah, sure."

At Henry's, we play with the toys Jackson has quickly accumulated here and play board games. We even watch a movie. I ignore a few texts from Elias, who attempts to check in and start conversations with me. I replay the conversation with Elias in my mind over and over. What possible good did he think would come out of it? That's what I don't understand.

Maybe this is Elias's way of deciding he doesn't want this with me anymore. He thinks if I talk about unresolved issues with Henry, then I'll leave him for Henry? Is that what he wants? He said he didn't, but then why mention it? I don't freaking know. All I know is that it's time for Jackson and me to go home, a home that isn't really mine, and the thought makes me want to vomit.

I drive us home. Henry says goodbye, wishes me luck, and returns to his house in his car. With a deep breath, we walk inside.

Elias is in the kitchen and he turns after grabbing a

bottle of water from the fridge. "Hey."

"Hey. We're going upstairs so Jackson can shower before bed." I grab my laptop from the table, exactly where I left it.

He nods. I worry he might follow us, but he doesn't. My stomach aches at the thought that this might be awkward. I don't want that, especially since I love my job, and the last thing I need is for this to interfere. My heart hurts and bursts with pain over the idea that Elias and I might be over. Even worse is that little voice in the back of my mind that wishes for it. The one that wants my world to revert back to the way it was when it was just Jackson and me. The only person I had to worry about was Jackson. Now, I'm concerned with Elias, Bree, and me. It's too much!

What was I thinking anyway? Getting involved with someone I work for? In allowing my son to know so soon, only for his heart to be broken right alongside mine when things inevitably go wrong? This is only the first sign. It's the start of my new life going downhill. I was stupid for thinking I could have anything good in my life other than Jackson.

My world has finally expanded, but it hinged upon my meeting Elias. Will my new, wide world collapse if we fall apart? It feels as if it already is.

When Jackson finishes up, I tuck him into bed and manage to change into my own pajamas before there's a soft knock on my locked door. I tiptoe over. I could keep ignoring him, right?

"Raelynn?" he softly calls. "Can we talk?"

My forehead lightly bangs against the door. He's not even in the room and tension wraps around my heart like a vise. "Can we do it tomorrow?"

Silence answers me at first. "I'd rather handle this now."

"Well, I'm tired and I'd rather not." At least there's some truth in that.

"Okay. Tomorrow then."

Not if I have anything to say about it.

Tomorrow comes and after I drop Jackson off at school, I find myself driving to Deanna's quilt shop. All I've been able to think about while avoiding Elias and giving him the silent treatment as much as possible is my last relationship. Not only did it end, but it ended so terribly that I eventually left the state to get away from him and everyone else there. I can't run in this situation. Not only is North Carolina now Jackson's home, but Henry is here, Jackson's friends are here, and despite how hard it would be to live in the same house as Elias, I couldn't leave him hanging and without a nanny in the middle of the season.

Getting over Henry was hard. Picking up those pieces while my parents disowned me, while my body changed as a baby grew inside of me, it was incredibly difficult to do. My hurt transformed into anger, where it lived a healthy life in the back of my mind in the event Henry ever did show up one day.

And Elias has seen my reactions to Henry. Why in the world would he ever think there would be any positive feelings left over? That I would want to be a family with Henry? Maybe we don't know each other that well after all. Maybe we're rushing into things. Maybe we shouldn't have started anything at all.

I don't have to think about things for a bit because it's time to see Deanna. She smiles when I walk in with Bree on my hip.

"Hey! What are you doing here?" She walks around the counter to hug me and steal Bree away.

"We came to visit."

"I'm honored," she says with a smile. She and Bree take baby steps around the store as Deanna allows Bree to walk. "Is everything okay, Raelynn?" Deanna asks, cutting a look at me as she and Bree walk around the corner of a table and head toward me.

I shrug. Nothing is okay. Everything is falling apart.

"Detour, little lady." Deanna takes Bree's hands and leads her away from the front. "Come on. We'll go to my office where we can talk." I follow after her. She soon scoops Bree up to hold her and sits with her in her lap once she sits in the chair behind her desk. She takes a quick picture of them on her phone and appears to send off a message, probably to Brayden. The moment I sit in the chair across from her, she asks, "What's going on?"

I love that she asks and leaves it at that. There aren't any follow-up questions about whether it's Elias and me or Henry or Jackson. She simply asks and doesn't try to fill in the very big blanks at this point. With a sigh, I tell her everything that's happened, from the break-in to Elias coming home to me avoiding him right this very second and feeling like we never should've started dating in the first place.

"First, what you need to understand is that men are idiots," she says, causing me to laugh. "We don't understand them just as much as they don't understand us. But you aren't going to figure it out by avoiding him every second you get, Raelynn. Don't make that mistake."

"I know. It's just..." My voice trails off as I glance down where my hands rest in my lap.

"What?" Deanna pushes softly.

"I liked my life before. It wasn't easy, but I had Jackson and he was all I needed. I was happy." I tilt my head back and blink, emotions welling and rolling around inside of me like a tidal wave at the thought of things potentially changing. Of everything I've been thinking about coming true. "And now, I *really* like my life and I'm even happier. I'm terrified Elias wants to change that. I don't want to lose him."

"You won't know unless you talk to him and figure out why Henry all of a sudden concerns him."

"I know." That's the unfortunate part. I have to talk to him and give him the opportunity to break my heart. But it's also the same opportunity to explain things and keep us together.

"Secondly," Deanna says, apparently not done with her lecture, "the world isn't ending, Raelynn. I don't know your past, I do know this is your first relationship in a long time, but just because this is a bump in the road doesn't mean it'll crash and total the car. This is something that y'all can overcome if you want to make it work."

"You're right."

She gives me a small smile. "So, maybe you should head home soon?" She glances down at Bree. "After I've had plenty of baby time, I mean."

So, we hang out in her office some. We do spend time out front as well. Around lunch, I finally head back home. Elias isn't there, but he could have meetings or whatnot to do. Our morning adventures must tire Bree out because after she gets some food in her, she dozes off. But any time I lay her in her crib, she wakes up and whines. To fix this, I let her rest against my chest, her head on my shoulder, while I sit at the table with my laptop in front of me. I can type while she sleeps.

When Elias walks in the door, I quickly close my laptop, not wanting him to see what's on it. I must look like he caught me because he asks, "What are you doing?"

I don't want to tell him the truth, not right now at least. I hesitate as I think of a good answer and then it hits me. "Schoolwork."

His eyes flick to the otherwise empty table. "Where are your textbooks?"

"Oh, um, well, I don't need them yet."

He doesn't believe me. That much is clear. Elias lets it slide, though. "We need to talk and get this shit over with."

"Oh, you mean the shit you started?"

His expression hardens. "This started when I saw you hugging Henry like your life depended on it."

What?

"The night of the break-in," he adds.

"You're kidding me. You're jealous I leaned on the only person around when I was terrified?"

"I'm not jealous," he snaps.

"Certainly sounds like it," I retort as I stand. "And of someone I only tolerate because he's my son's father. You should know better, Elias."

"How?" He throws his arms out. "You barely let me in, Raelynn. How am I supposed to know you would never consider getting back with Henry?"

How could he not know, even without me verbally saying so? I shake my head and walk away to put a still-sleeping Bree in her crib. I don't want to argue with her in my arms.

EJ

MY GAZE RETURNS to her laptop over and over. She closed that thing so fast when I walked in. Is she hiding something again? Why? Why must the women in my life torture me by being secretive? I can't handle it now. Not after Bree's mom, Vicky. My body seems to have a mind of its own as I move over to where Raelynn was just sitting. I hesitate for a few seconds, wait for my gut to tell me what to do, and then I open her laptop.

It's a document, the cursor blinking and waiting for something else to be typed. I scroll the long way to the top. That's when confusion sets in. The top of the document

239

simply starts with Chapter One. I can't help but continue down the path I've set myself on and begin reading.

Holy shit.

She's writing a book.

I'm so consumed in reading that I don't hear Raelynn walk down the stairs and back into the room.

"What are you doing?" she accuses, a tremble in her voice.

I stand and take a step away from the laptop as if that removes any contact I had with it. "You were acting weird." I wince at the lamest possible thing I could've possibly said, and it actually came out of my mouth. The only thing I should have said is that I shouldn't have done what I did, even though I knew that before I did it.

Raelynn stalks over to her laptop, closes it, and holds it against her chest. "And that gives you the right to snoop through my things? What is wrong with you? That is personal, Elias. If it was something I was ready to share, you would know about it. I... I can't believe you did that. I need to go."

I grab her elbow loosely enough that she can still walk away if she wants, but enough that it stops her from walking away. "Wait a second. You can't keep leaving, Raelynn."

She lifts her chin and stares at me. "Watch me." She doesn't move yet, though.

"Why wouldn't you tell me you write?"

"Are you serious?"

"Yes," I answer simply.

"I am not used to this, Elias!" she yells, waving between the two of us. "That much should be crystal fucking clear by now! I'm trying here, but that doesn't mean I'm cracking my chest open for you to see what's inside. It takes time for us to get to a point where you can see this." She waves her laptop around. "You're acting like this isn't a huge deal, what you just did. You invaded my privacy!"

"I know, and I'm sorry. It's just with the way things were with Bree's mom—"

"I'm not her!" she shouts.

"And I'm not Henry! You do the same thing to me, Raelynn." She frowns, but I push forward. "Don't tell me you don't compare your past to your present. That you don't worry about mistakes repeating themselves. For fuck's sake, that's not what any of this is about."

"You're right. It's not," she says with all the calmness she can muster. "It's about you opening my laptop and reading something you had no right to read." Raelynn sighs. "I have to pick up Jackson." She turns and walks out before I can think of something to say to stop her.

Why would she be writing a book? And why would she keep something like that to herself? How long has she been writing? I have so many questions and no answers. She would likely snap my head off if I attempt to ask her anytime soon, considering this is knowledge I shouldn't even have right now.

Part of me can't believe I looked, while the other half isn't that surprised at all. Regardless, I *know* I shouldn't have done it. That's what makes all of this worse. I knew before I opened the laptop, but it was like I couldn't help myself. Now what are we going to do? Why did I have to knock down what trust we managed to build?

I go upstairs to sit in Bree's room. It's the only place in the whole house that will give me comfort. I pick her up and hold her while she sleeps, gently rocking back and

241

forth in the recliner.

"What am I going to do, princess?" I whisper. "Daddy made a big mistake." I sigh. I almost wish she'd left her laptop, so I could've kept reading. What I had read so far seemed pretty good. Bree's arms jerk in her sleep and she grabs my thumb as she settles. She looks so peaceful and more perfect as she sleeps. Her eyelashes fan over the tops of her cheeks. Her lips purse.

Regret and remorse filter through me as I gaze at my little girl. "How will I make it up to her, hmm? Because I don't want her to leave us. We clearly have things to work on, though." I want to work things out. I want to fix things. I want Raelynn to trust me and I want to be able to trust her.

"EJ!" Jackson shouts as he runs into the room. His eyes widen and he clamps a hand over his mouth when he sees Bree sleeping. "Did I wake her up?" he whispers, climbing onto my lap and seeing for himself that she's still out like a light.

"No, you didn't," I answer anyway. "Did you want to tell me something?"

"Oh, yeah!" He continues to whisper, which makes me smile. "Can we build a blanket fort tonight?"

"Sure thing, J-man."

"Did I miss anything today?" He leans forward to carefully kiss her cheek.

He missed a lot, but that's not what he's asking and not something he needs to know. "No firsts today."

"Can we wake her up so I can play with her?"

I laugh. "You never wake a sleeping baby, Jackson. You'll be able to play with her later, I'm sure. Hop down and let me lay her down. I'll play with you."

Once Bree is back in her crib, we leave her room to cross the hall to his room. Raelynn steps out of her room and her quick glance at me ties my stomach in knots. This won't be a quick, easy fix between us. She nods a simple acceptance as Jackson tells her we're going to his room to play.

"Do you want to come with us?" I ask.

Her "No, thanks," breaks my heart. I'm able to distract myself for a while by building a blanket fort with Jackson and building things with Legos until Bree wakes up around dinner time. While we may eat together, all the talking comes from Jackson and Bree. Afterward, Raelynn takes the kids and clearly leaves me to clean up. It wouldn't bother me any other time if we weren't in the middle of this tension.

When I sit next to her after cleaning up the kitchen, she ignores me and even slightly scoots away from me. But she has my kid on her lap. I don't plan on being too far away in case I decide I want some time with her. The silence between us eats away at me so much that I nearly fall to my knees in relief when Raelynn speaks to me.

"Are you okay if Bree goes with me to the lawyer's office tomorrow?"

It's like a bucket of cold water splashes on me. It's not what she said, but the realization that I have a game tomorrow and a road trip later this week. I can't imagine going on the road with this distance and discord still raging on between us. I don't know if it'll help things, make them worse, or keep them the same.

"Elias?"

I glance over at her. "Yeah, sure." If I remember correctly, I'll be at the arena when it's time for her appoint-

243

ment. "If you'd rather get one of the women to keep her, I can ask around. Meredith, Deanna, or Sydney might be open to it. She might decide to be a bad baby."

Jackson glares at me. "Bree is never a bad baby," he says as if he's disappointed I'd say such a thing. "Can we go to the game tomorrow, Momma?" he asks Raelynn, dismissing me just like that.

"Not tomorrow, but maybe the game Sunday."

He nods in satisfaction and Raelynn gazes down at Bree. "I think she'll be fine with me," she says, referring back to my offer to let someone else keep her while she has her appointment. "I don't want to bother anyone."

"You wouldn't be," I reassure her. "Meredith would probably love the opportunity; she always bugs me about wanting to keep her."

"We are all meeting at Sylvia's tomorrow for lunch." She sighs. "Do you think I shouldn't take her with me, even though she's normally so good?"

Bree looks at me as if she knows I'm about to make a decision about her. "No, I wouldn't. You should be entirely focused on what you're doing and she might distract you." Her shoulders slump. "Want me to get it arranged?"

"Yeah, I guess so."

I pull my phone out of my back pocket and text Meredith. I've had her number ever since she watched Bree the day I found out about her and needed someone to watch her until my mom could fly in. Meredith's reply to me asking if she'd like to keep Bree while Raelynn has her meeting includes all caps letters and lots of exclamation points. I'd say she's excited.

"She said she'll be here to pick her up and if it's okay with you, she'll go ahead and take her over to Sylvia's."

Raelynn nods. "Yeah, that's fine."

It's nice to know that even with this mess going on, we can still talk, even if it's nothing too serious. Raelynn insists on putting Bree to bed, so while she's upstairs with Bree and Jackson, getting them to sleep, I'm downstairs, twiddling my thumbs. I want to go upstairs, see if she needs help, but it seems like she wants space.

After an hour of sitting on the couch, staring absent-mindedly at the cartoons still on the TV, I begin to think she's avoiding me. That's totally not cool. I stand and jog up the stairs. The door to her room is wide open and the light is off. Her soft voice flows from Bree's room. I peek inside to see her sitting in the recliner. Bree hasn't fallen asleep yet.

Raelynn glances up. "She's giving me a tough time tonight."

It's on the tip of my tongue to ask her if she wants help, but that feeds into the fact that things aren't right between us. Would it be so bad if I didn't do that? It could backfire, of course, but I'm willing to take the risk. I walk all the way into Bree's room, sit on the arm of the chair, and return the smile Bree gives me.

I take her from Raelynn, rest her on my chest, and keep the recliner rocking as I begin to hum to the tune of "Go to sleep. Go to sleep. Go to sleep, little Bree." Over and over, I hum over her baby babble until she grabs a fistful of my shirt sleeve and begins to relax. She still fights it a little, but she's asleep soon enough.

Raelynn tries to make her escape as we step out of Bree's room, but I grab her hand before she can get too far away from me.

"Elias," she sighs.

Her sigh isn't getting to me this time. "We need to talk."

"Fine." She pulls her hand out of mine and walks downstairs. She sits as far away from me as possible. "First, you try to push me away just in case I want to be with Henry. I still don't understand that. I don't want to be with him, and I thought that was clear. Even if he came back into my life as the nicest guy I've ever met and told me he loved me, I still wouldn't want to try and make it work. He's even told me that he still loves me, Elias, and guess what? It doesn't change anything! Because our priority is on Jackson."

She stares at me and waits for a reaction. I'm trying to process the fact that he has told her he loves her still.

"When did he tell you that?" I ask.

Raelynn sighs and shakes her head. "That's not the point, but if you must know, I flat-out asked him when I left here after we argued about it."

"I'm sorry about that, okay? It felt like something I needed to do, to mention, in case you didn't have closure yet. I know I mentioned that other stuff, but it's not like I wanted you to get back with him, but," I sigh, "I don't know. I'm an idiot."

"Yeah, you are," she grumbles. "And then you snoop through my laptop, Elias. It's not like you looked through my phone, which wouldn't work for me either, but this is much worse than that. At this point, it's as if you read my diary. It's *that* personal, Elias." Silence cloaks the air and just as I'm about to apologize, she stares down at her lap and says, "I don't think this will work between us."

"What?"

She settles her gaze on me. "You don't trust me," she

says simply. "You do with Bree, but not when it comes to you. And after what you did, I don't know that I can trust you with myself either."

"Raelynn," I begin because this can't be the end.

"No, Elias," she cuts me off before I can really get going. "You're not listening to me."

"Yes, I am," I interrupt her. "I know I did something I most definitely shouldn't have done, but surely it's not unforgivable, is it? We can recover from this. Don't give up so easily." That last sentence earns me a glare. "Aside from this, wouldn't you agree that what we have is fantastic?"

"I would agree that it's too soon to tell."

"Now, you're just being argumentative."

Raelynn stands, so I stand as well. "I don't want to talk about this anymore. I have a long day ahead of me tomorrow and we're getting nowhere. I need some space and some time."

My gut screams in protest. I almost want to ignore it since it's what got me into this mess, but I don't want to let her walk away. I don't want my last words to her be me telling her that she's argumentative, which really makes me sound like an asshole. She turns to walk around the couch and I say, "Raelynn, I..." My voice trails off, but I'm empowered by the fact that she's facing me once again.

What if this is the last chance I have to really talk to her? To convince her to stay with me? It's as if everything suddenly clicks into place, the issues fall away, and one big important thing remains.

So, I begin again. "Raelynn, I love you."

Tears form and spill over immediately. She holds up

her hand and shakes her head. I wait for her to say something, but she doesn't. Raelynn runs from the room.

Well, fuck.

23

Raelynn

HIS LAST WORDS to me last night haunt me. I can't believe he said that, and I can't line up what those words are supposed to mean with his actions prior to saying them. Hearing him say he loves me officially tore my nerves up and continues to do so today. I have no idea what to do with that kind of information. When Henry says it, I know to ignore it because I no longer have any sort of romantic feelings toward him. When Jackson says it, my heart is happy and I have no problem telling my little boy that I love him too.

But when Elias said it?

My first reaction was to cry and run away from him.

What the hell?

"What are you moping about?"

My head snaps up at Sylvia's question.

"Did the meeting with the lawyer not go well?" Meredith asks.

We're all sitting on or around Sylvia's bed. We being Sylvia, Meredith, Lizzy, Sydney, Theresa, Deanna, and Bree and Andrew, of course. The attention is all on me and I wish it would go away.

"The meeting went great."

"Then what's wrong?" Lizzy asks.

Sylvia pulls herself up into a sitting position and leans forward. "Is something going on with you and EJ? Do we need to send our husbands over there to beat some sense into him?"

"Or do we need to beat some sense into you?" Deanna asks, probably because she already knows part of the problem.

"He invited you to the charity event, did he?" Theresa asks.

I frown. "What event?"

"Oh, don't bring that up," Sylvia mutters. "I still can't believe that they're letting Peggy Potter be in charge this year. She only took over because I obviously can't do anything. I'm finding a way to go." She crosses her arms and rests them over her stomach and waits, as if she wants someone to object.

But I'm too distracted by the fact that they think Elias would have invited me to this thing. And the fact that he didn't. "Why would he invite me?" I ask.

"It's hosted by the wives and girlfriends. The players will be attending. We do a main event every year," Theresa tells me. "If you're dating EJ, then you can go."

"She didn't know anything about it." Deanna points out the obvious.

"And I wouldn't go anyway. Who would keep Bree? Or Jackson?"

Sylvia raises an eyebrow. "Is Henry not still in the picture? If you really wanted to go, we'd find someone to keep the kids. But none of this is the point. Why are you upset?"

They all stare at me and wait patiently for me to spill my guts. So, I do. I start from the break-in to last night and all the crazy emotions in between. "My instinct is to leave and I don't want to, but this is too much for me."

"But he's in love with you," Lizzy says.

"So he says," I agree.

"You don't believe him?" Deanna asks.

I shrug. If I could get the fear out of the way, then maybe I could decide. If I could get the anger out of the way, that would help too.

"So, what are you writing?" Sylvia asks, earning glares from all of the women. "What? She did tell us. She doesn't have to answer. She knows this."

"Can someone else talk about their issues?" I practically beg, re-situating Bree who has fallen asleep in my lap.

"As long as you make sure to talk to him when you go home," Deanna says.

I nod and conversation veers away from me. Everyone indulges Sylvia by sharing the latest in their lives. I learn just a little about some of the others, but a lot about some. Like Deanna is trying to better her relationship with her father. Lizzy talks about Marc going overboard getting everything ready for the arrival of their twins. Meredith admits she's beginning to get discouraged on her own journey to getting pregnant.

I listen and listen, but eventually people begin to clear out one by one until I'm the only one left. Scott comes home, checks in on Sylvia, and then leaves us alone in their bedroom. If he's home for his pre-game routine, then I should probably go. That also means that Elias is probably home.

"Do you know how Scott and I have lasted this long?" Sylvia suddenly asks me. My shoulders sag because I just know I'm in for a lecture. She doesn't wait for me to respond. "He still pisses me off or does something to upset me, but we *always* talk it through. We don't wait too long to do it either because then things stew and get worse. Go home. Talk to him. Find ways to trust each other. Scott!" I freeze at her yelling for her husband. She must do this often though because he calmly walks back into the room.

"What do you need, Sylvie?"

"Be kind enough to walk Raelynn out. Tell her how we've lasted this long. I'm exhausted." She looks at me. "I don't mean to push you out, but," her voice softens, "you need someone to push you, Raelynn."

"Thanks." I'm not sure if I should be thanking her or why, but it feels right. I hug her and gather my things, just in time for Bree to wake up as Scott leads me to the door.

"I don't know what's going on and I don't want to know," he starts. "But we've made it this far because I love my wife." Scott shrugs as he opens the front door for me. "I love her and I can't live without her. I do whatever I need to do to make it work because of that. It's that simple."

I smile. "Tell her I like your answer better than hers."

He grins. "I will. Good luck, Raelynn."

I pick Jackson up from school before heading home. Jackson and Bree talk to one another from the backseat. Jackson mentions how he'll have to change into his jersey once he gets home since there's a game tonight. The last thing I need to do is talk to Elias prior to a game. But I do need to talk to him. If I were to catalog my feelings and sort them all out, things become a little easier.

I can't imagine being without Elias.

He's fantastic with my son, and my son loves him.

I love taking care of Bree.

But...

There's always a but, isn't there? He doesn't trust me, and now, I don't trust him. Not as much as I once did, at least. When we get home, the first thing I notice is a big bouquet of flowers on the kitchen table. There's a card propped up against them.

"Are these yours, Momma?" Jackson asks.

I pick up the card and open it.

I'm prepared to grovel for the rest of my life.
I'm sorry, Raelynn. Please forgive me.
Love, EJ

"Yeah, they're for me," I confirm as he leans forward to press his face against the flowers.

"They smell good."

I pick them up and smell for myself. Bree tries to yank one out for herself, making me laugh. "Let's find EJ, but remember to be quiet. He might be napping."

Sure enough, he's asleep on the couch. I take the kids upstairs; it's the easiest way to make sure we won't wake him. But he's upstairs within thirty minutes. He smiles as Jackson holds Bree's hand and walks with her around the room.

"I'm about to leave," he says as he picks Bree up. "Did you see the flowers?"

"Yes. Thank you."

"Will you stay up for me tonight?"

I nod and I swear, he exhales in relief. He kisses Bree and tells his princess he loves her before setting her on her feet again. What throws me off guard, though, is that Jackson is there, waiting to give him a hug, wish him luck, and he sneaks in a "Bye, EJ. Love you."

Elias immediately looks at me since Jackson's head is turned away. My throat tightens and tears threaten to spill. Elias crouches and hugs Jackson back. "Love you too, J-man." Jackson slips away from him to play with Bree and Elias walks over to where I sit in the recliner. He leans down and simply presses his forehead to mine. "Thank you for still being here," he whispers.

My mouth parts, but the words are nowhere to be found, so I simply nod. A moment later, he leaves.

I'm still feeling a little uneasy about this entire thing, but another talk can't hurt things, right? Or maybe it can. Our last one didn't go too well. I worry about our impending talk of doom all afternoon, even once Henry arrives with dinner.

"Are things better?" he asks while we eat.

I shrug.

"I know I haven't been the best since I've been back,

my opinion might not mean much, and I don't know what's going on, but for what it's worth, I've decided I like him and I hope everything works out."

So, now my ex is telling me to stay with my boy-friend? What is the world coming to? I'm not so sure it's comforting to have Henry's support either. Maybe I'm not giving him enough credit. He's been better and hasn't made any flops recently.

"I want to ask you something, even though I'm fully expecting you to say no," Henry says later while we're watching the Rebels game.

"What is it?"

He motions for me to stand and I follow him into the kitchen. Bree crawls after us. "Can Jackson spend the night with me this weekend? I'll do whatever you want me to, Rae."

Bree slaps my leg and holds her arms up. I pick her up while having a mini heart attack. Jackson has never spent the night anywhere. He's been with me every night of his entire life. Hell, *I* haven't spent a full night without him in the same house as me since he was born. What am I supposed to do while he's with Henry if I say yes? Bree tugs on my hair and the action reminds me to answer him.

"I don't know if I'm ready for that, Henry."

He nods as if he expected that. "But maybe we can ask Jackson to see if he's ready?" he asks expectantly. "He might change his mind once he's there, but it's worth ask-ing, right? Once our lawyers set up an official schedule in the papers, he'll spend some weekends with me anyway."

Yes, because Henry wants every other weekend with Jackson at the very least. He wants an early start, it seems.

"I'll do whatever you want," he repeats. "Let's just

see if Jackson would be up for it."

"Okay." This is crazy! Yes, Henry would likely take care of him just fine. Yes, Jackson would probably have lots of fun. Yes, I'm only a phone call and a few minutes away. But my baby boy wouldn't be in the same house as me for the first time. The amount of anxiety pumping through my veins right now as we return to the living room is insane.

"Yeah!" Jackson shouts, jumping up and down in front of the TV. The Rebels scored, apparently.

"Who scored?" Henry asks.

"Mr. Brayden."

A commercial comes on, so Henry uses that as his opportunity to talk to Jackson without any distractions from the game.

"Hey, Jackson. I need to ask you a question." Jackson faces Henry and waits. "Would you want to have a sleepover at my house this weekend? Just you and me?"

Jackson glances at me before focusing on Henry. "Momma wouldn't come too?"

Henry shakes his head. "Just us. But you could call her as often as you'd like."

"But who will tuck me in if Momma and EJ isn't there?"

"I can tuck you in," Henry reassures. "I have books there to read to you, too."

Jackson seems to be analyzing what Henry has said so far. He comes over and crawls onto my lap, but looks at Henry.

"So, what do you say? Do you want to stay over?" Henry asks.

"Okay; yes."

Oh, my. He said yes. My baby wants to stay with his dad for a night. When is the appropriate time to cry? This is great. It's a big step for Jackson, and for me, too. But I am not ready. I'll never be ready. What am I going to do without Jackson here? Now I have something new to worry about.

To prepare Jackson for when he goes to Henry's, I let Henry help him with his nighttime routine while I try to get Bree settled in for the night. Just as she falls asleep, Henry steps into her room.

"He's down for the count," he says. "Thank you for this weekend."

"Don't thank me yet. I have to survive it first."

He smiles. "It'll be fine."

"I might call every five seconds," I warn. "He's never spent the night anywhere."

"I'll take care of him," he promises.

He better. Henry says goodbye, I lay Bree down, and then I pick up around the house and keep busy until Elias comes home. I don't want to think too much about the upcoming talk or Jackson's night away this weekend. Cleaning constantly helps with that. Maybe obsessively cleaning. I scrub the already clean at this point tub in the bathroom.

"What are you doing?"

I scream as I whirl around and throw the sponge at Elias. "Why would you sneak up on me like that?"

"I'm sorry." He bends to pick up the sponge. "Why are you cleaning this late?"

"Because."

He frowns. "Well, stop." He helps me stand and moves me out of the way to rinse the tub for me. "Why are you upset? Over us?"

"Sort of. There's also the fact that Jackson agreed to spend the night at Henry's this weekend."

Elias turns to face me with surprised eyes. "Can we table that until we've talked about us?" He holds out his hand and I take it with a nod. He leads me to the living room where we sit on the couch. He takes both my hands in his. "I'm sorry. I never should've done what I did. I'll do everything I need to do to make this work, for you to trust me, for me to work on my trust issues. And I won't ask about your writing because I shouldn't know about it to begin with; you can tell me whenever you're ready or not."

"Elias," I interrupt. "I'm eighty-five percent sure I'm still committed to making this work. For right now, can you just hold me? That's all I really want."

He doesn't say another word. He smiles a little and pulls me against him. Within seconds, I begin to relax. Today—hell, this past week—has been really stressful. Elias oozes comfort and that's exactly what I want and who I need it from. I need to return to my state of mind where I trust a little more and easier and I had more faith in Elias. That's how I'll make it through this.

And I want to make it through this with him.

24

EJ

THINGS HAVE IMPROVED slightly since that night with Raelynn. I've been making sure to grovel in all the right ways, hopefully. I've bought her chocolate. Made her get a massage before I left on this road trip. Cooked for her. Waited on her at the house. Got her car detailed. I even made her promise to take my credit card and go on a shopping spree for herself while I'm gone. She can buy new clothes, jewelry, shoes, purses, whatever she wants.

But I think I'll need to do something big to completely win her back over. Maybe Raelynn needs some grand gesture to show her exactly how completely invested I am to making this work. What worries me is that it may be too much for Raelynn, that it may overwhelm her. An overwhelmed Raelynn won't work in my favor.

What to do? That's the question. My end goal is for us to move on and a nice bonus would be hearing her tell me she loves me, too. She might not be there yet, though, so I probably shouldn't get my hopes up on that.

After our game, which we win, we're put on a plane to fly to our next stop. Some guys are smartly using this time to sleep. But then, there are guys like me, Brayden, Collin, Marc, and Noah that aren't. I shuffle a deck of cards, glancing at each of them with a raised eyebrow, silently asking if they want to play.

"We should be sleeping," Brayden says.

"But we aren't," I point out.

"Might as well entertain the poor sap," Marco says with a shrug of his shoulders. "And it's Uno. We'll be asleep in no time."

I ignore that and get the game set up as everyone agrees to play. I let us get into the rhythm of things before I drop my plea for help. "If I wanted to make a grand gesture, what should I do?"

Four pairs of eyes snap to attention and focus on me. There's a short stint of silence before Noah offers his advice first.

"Propose."

I shake my head. "Can't do that yet."

"Profess your love on the jumbotron?" Collin suggests.

Brayden rolls his eyes at that. "Tell her you no longer want her to be your nanny."

"Since when are you the relationship expert?" Marco

teases him.

"What do you mean?" I ask Brayden, ignoring Marc. "You want me to fire her? How will that help?"

"My girlfriend is your girlfriend's closest friend, which means whether I want to know what's going on or not, I know. If she's so important to you, eliminate that barrier. Make her family in whatever way you can right now, not part-family, part-employee. You're that serious about her, right? She's raising your daughter for fuck's sake, EJ. You want Bree to call her mom one day? For Jackson to be her stepbrother? Do you plan to keep them around for the rest of your life? Start there."

Well, damn. I knew I wanted her, but I hadn't thought that far ahead. I hadn't thought about it in that way, where we'd have a family together and could possibly even add on to our family later on down the road. No, I was too busy wondering if she wanted that with Henry when she hasn't shown me any inclination of that.

My mind whirls with all the different possibilities and ideas. A list forms in my mind of all the things I should do. Raelynn needs to see that I trust her. I need to do everything short of asking her to be my wife and Bree's mom. I feel like I'm on the right track, though I'm still not exactly sure what my grand gesture will be. And something tells me I need to call my mom and talk to her.

We play one game of Uno before putting the cards away. By that time, we've landed and it's time to switch from the airplane to the hotel for the night. I sleep restlessly and dream of various scenarios where I pour my heart out to Raelynn and she walks away every time. Before I bother to shower in the morning, I call my mom.

"Good morning, Elias James," she answers. "How's

my granddaughter?"

I laugh. "I'm assuming she's fine. I haven't called Raelynn yet." Mom tsks in disappointment, but I say, "I might've fucked up with Raelynn."

Mom sighs. "I knew this would happen."

"I don't need an *I told you so*, Ma. She didn't run and she doesn't plan to, so you weren't right anyway." I explain a little bit of what happened, that I invaded her privacy and didn't trust that she wanted to be with me, and tell her all I've been doing to make it up to her. "But I need to do more. Something bigger that says more because I want this to work and I want her to know that."

"It sounds like you've done a lot already," she says dryly.

"Why don't you like us together, Ma?"

"Because if she leaves, we're back to square one."

"Exactly my point!"

"I'm confused," she admits.

"Brayden thinks I should fire her."

"Are you insane? Didn't you hear me?"

"Yes, I did. But I need Raelynn to be a part of my family and the next time we get into an argument, I want her to stay primarily because she wants to keep working on us, not because she feels obligated to because it's her job to stay. If she really wanted to leave, I don't know if she would have, Ma, because she'd leave Bree without a nanny in the middle of the season."

Mom is quiet for a minute. "Okay. Say you fire her, then what? What happens with Bree? Is anything actually changing?"

"I'm thinking of a plan, but what happens with Bree partly depends on what Raelynn wants."

"I don't like the sound of that."

"My gut does."

I can practically see her rolling her eyes as she says, "Oh, great."

My gut has only steered me wrong once before, but the more I think about firing Raelynn, the more I relax. This will work. I just know it.

Luukas Lathi is a beast. A crazy, lucky beast. We've deemed him Lucky Luke, but just over twenty-four hours later, it's already shortened to Luck. Why? Well, I'd heard about how he gets bursts where he's a scoring madman. They appear out of nowhere. Last night, we experienced the start of a burst. Luukas not only got a hat trick, but had two assists. Almost everything he did turned into a magical moment.

And tonight in the second period? Luck throws his hands up to celebrate his *fourth* goal of the game. He looks smug at this point, too. It's crazy. We're definitely rolling with it, though. The crowd is a pissy silent because that puts us with six goals and their team only has two.

What's funny is I probably have something in common with some of their fans—the fans who have already deemed the game over, though there's still plenty of hockey to be played. Those fans might leave early, or some might be wishing the clock would hurry up and count down to the final second so the game could end already. I'm with those. I want this game to be over. I want to be home with my princess and my girlfriend. I'll be able to spend a little time with Jackson before he goes to Henry's too.

But first, this game must be tackled. Raelynn said she was letting Jackson stay up to watch this one since it's Friday night. If I don't score a goal or at least get an assist, Luukas will likely be his new favorite player because he'll forget all about me.

My opportunity comes when we earn a power play, thanks to a slashing penalty being called on the team in red. We're all crowding in front of the goalie, the puck going back and forth and being swatted away, but it lands on my stick and I poke, poke, poke until it slides underneath his leg and across the goal line.

I shout and throw my hands up with as much enthusiasm as I know Jackson would do if he saw the goal.

The game keeps up a fast pace, but ends with a seven-two score.

"Whatever you're doing, eating, drinking, I want to do it too," Cal declares as we dress after our showers, pointing a finger at Luukas, because yes, we're still talking about his seven goals the past two nights.

Luukas shrugs. "Sorry. You'd have to be me and you're not." Then, he grins with all the cockiness in the world and walks away.

"Okay, now I hate him a little bit," Cal admits with a laugh.

"There isn't two of him like there are of you," Sergey Orlovsky grunts. "We'd be in trouble then."

Cal makes a show of frowning and looks at Collin, who *is* frowning. Cal slings an arm around Collin's shoulders. "Do you hear that, my dear brother? It sounds like he doesn't like that there's a Thing One and Two. What the hell, Serge? The Kessy twins are everyone's favorite Rebels."

Noah groans and I laugh because on cue, Marc throws his towel at them. "*I'm* the favorite Rebel. Don't be delusional to think otherwise. Just ask Rams's wife."

"Leave my woman out of this," Noah snaps.

His comment is ignored and the twins, mainly Cal, argue for as long as Marc will banter back about who the favorite Rebel is. It's not until we're on the plane back home that Brayden stands and whistles to shut everyone up. He glares at each of them before saying, "*I'm* the fucking favorite because I wear the *C* and everyone loves the captain, now shut the fuck up and talk about something else. You're all annoying the hell out of me." He sits down before they can argue with him.

I wish I could laugh and make a joke, but he's across the aisle, sitting with Collin, who currently whispers something to him. I don't want to interrupt their conversation. I close my eyes since the plane is a lot quieter now and wait for us to land.

When I get home, I peek in on Jackson, then Bree, and my anxiety spikes when I find Raelynn's bed empty. Did she fall asleep on the couch? I walk into my room, turn on the light, and my breath catches when I see her asleep in my bed, the last place I expected to find her. I didn't think we'd made up to this point. I set my bag down, quickly change my clothes, and after turning off the light, I crawl in next to her.

"Elias?" she mumbles.

"The one and only," I reply. I wrap my arms around her and hold her as close as she'll let me. "I'm surprised to find you here," I admit quietly.

"I missed being here," she shares just as quietly. "And I wanted to be here when you got home."

"I'm glad you are."

She surprises me further by kissing me. It's not too long, not too intimate, but the perfect mixture of both. "Me too," she whispers. And then she settles in to fall asleep.

In the morning, I wake up first and sneak into Bree's room.

"DaDa!"

I smile at seeing her standing in her crib. "Hey, princess. Did you miss me as much as I missed you?"

"DaDa! No, no."

I laugh as I pick her up and sit in the recliner. "You didn't miss me? I don't believe you."

She smiles at me; what more could I ask for? After about ten minutes, Raelynn walks into her room. Would it be childish to pout when my daughter reaches for her, considering I've been gone for two days? Instead, I playfully turn away and say, "No." Bree giggles and reaches for Raelynn more eagerly every time I face her again. Eventually, I hand my little girl over and Bree claps as if she knows she won.

"Will you go with me to drop Jackson off?" Raelynn asks.

"Yeah, of course. Still nervous?"

"Just a little panicky."

I think she's lying, but I let it slide. Jackson runs into the room, and our morning officially starts. Jackson seems mostly excited about going to Henry's. Enough so, that when Raelynn mentioned he would have to pack a bag, they had to do it last night. After breakfast, Jackson runs upstairs to grab his bag.

"Let's go! I'm ready."

Raelynn tears up and I laugh at Jackson. "Hold up, J-man. We're all still in our pjs. Let's change and then we'll take you to your dad's."

We have to rush because Jackson is ready to go and since he's eager, we don't want to give him time to change his mind. On the ride there, Raelynn gives herself a pep talk by telling Jackson what he can expect.

"You can call me anytime you want, just ask your dad to call me."

"Okay, Momma."

"And he'll bring you home before dinner tomorrow, but if you want to come home sooner, baby, just tell him."

"Okay, Momma."

"If you feel bad, make sure you tell your dad."

"Okay, Momma."

I reach over and take her hand. "I think he's got this, Raelynn. So does Henry."

"Momma?"

She twists in her seat to look at him. "Yeah, baby?"

"What are you going to do while I'm with Dad? Do you want to stay with us too?" He gasps. "Can everyone stay?"

"There's not enough room for everyone, Jackson," she says. "Besides, you're staying so you can spend time with your dad. You know how we have mom and Jackson days when it's just us? You're having a *dad* and Jackson day."

"Okay. Are we there yet, EJ? Oh! There's Dad's house! We're here!"

His excitement matches Henry's as we head inside for a few minutes. Raelynn seems to inspect the place, even though she's been here before. I grab her hand before she can walk to the bedroom for further inspection.

"Don't delay the inevitable," I whisper. "He's okay." I nod to where Jackson has settled in on the floor with a toy he grabbed from the corner.

Raelynn sighs. "Come tell us bye, Jackson."

And *that's* when it really hits Jackson that he's spending a night away from his mom. His eyes water as he walks over to Raelynn and he's crying by the time he throws his arms around her neck.

"I changed my mind," he cries. "I don't want to."

I glance at Henry, who looks crushed.

"Oh, come on now, baby. Where's my brave Jackson? You've been excited about staying over here with your dad. We're not that far away, remember? And you have fun with your dad, don't you?"

"But you won't be here," he hiccups.

"Your dad will be," Raelynn says, hoping that will help. "And you can call me whenever you want, but I think you'll be having too much fun to want to call me until it's bedtime. Why don't you spend the day with your dad and try spending the night? If you still don't want to after you've tried, then I'll come back and pick you up, okay?"

Jackson nods, accepting this offer. He kisses Raelynn on the cheek, hugs her for about a minute longer, and then decides to do the same to me and Bree. Once we reassure him that he'll also be able to talk to Bree and me, he seems satisfied enough that we can leave.

Raelynn starts crying the moment we pull out of the driveway. "I'm fine," she insists. "Just need to let it out. God, this is too hard. I think he'll be able to make it through the night. Henry will be able to calm him down, which is great, but at the same time, this is too much. How is my baby not sleeping in the same house as me tonight?" Raelynn wipes her tears. "I hope he has a blast." She takes a deep breath. "Okay. My breakdown is over."

I laugh. "Good."

She uses the rest of the ride home to actually calm down and get herself together. When I park in the garage, she looks at me. "What are we supposed to do without him today?"

"I have a bit of an idea. Let's go inside."

Once we're inside and Bree is in her pack 'n play, I grab Raelynn's hand and we sit on the couch, facing one another. With a deep breath, I begin on the path that will hopefully lead us closer together.

"Raelynn, you're fired."

Her hand immediately yanks from mine.

Raelynn

IT'S OFFICIAL. MY worst nightmare has come true. Elias unexpectedly pulled the rug out from under me without any rhyme or reason. Stupid tears fall once again today before I can stop them. How could it be that he's just like Henry? It doesn't make sense. How could I be so stupid as to fall for someone who could destroy me once again? Only this time, it's so much worse.

"How could you do this to me?" I ask. "Why? I don't understand. I thought—"

As I stand, Elias grabs my hands and makes me sit back down. He cups my face and places his thumbs over my mouth to shut me up. "Trust me, Raelynn," he says.

"Let me finish. This is a good thing."

My eyes nearly jump out of their sockets. "Good? You just fired me!" I yell around his thumbs.

"Because I want you to be my family. I want you to be all family, Raelynn."

"Explain," I demand because this doesn't make any sense to me. He's jumping around all over the place. My heart slams in my chest and feeling it pulse and beat throughout my entire body from the panic attack he's giving me distracts me from what he's saying. I can't think clearly.

"This isn't going so well, so here." He pulls a folded piece of paper from his pocket and hands it to me. "Read it. It's a to-do list of sorts. Or maybe it's a list of goals. Either way, read."

My hands tremble so much it takes me a minute to unfold the paper and see his handwriting. The first thing is something he's already done. "Fire Raelynn." I shake my head, but keep going. "Regain her trust." Kind of hard to do when he's fired me! "Make her and Jackson my family. Move her into my room. Get her to fall in love with me. Help her discover her dream and make her go after it. Ask her to be my wife and Bree's mom." My voice cracks as I look up at him. "You want me to be a mom to her? And your wife?"

"One day, yes. But I already think you're a mom to her." He grabs my knee and squeezes. "I want you in my life and in Bree's life forever. I want her to call you mom, for Jackson to be her stepbrother, and for us to be a family. And the *only* relationship I want with you is a romantic one. That's why I fired you because I didn't want that to confuse things or get in the way or make you ever feel obligated to stay if you needed space."

That sounds really nice, but... "What about Bree? If I'm not working for you..." My voice trails off as I glance over at the little girl playing by herself.

"That's up to you."

"Me?" I squeak. He's giving me way too much power here. It's crazy. Why would he open his soul like this and then leave such an important decision as to what to do with his daughter up to me?

"Yes. You can let me support you and Jackson while you continue to help me raise my daughter. You can figure out what you want to do once you graduate and," he takes a deep breath, "Bree can go to daycare while you work. I'll still need you to help me, though, because I travel. Or," and he hesitates before finishing, "do something about that book you're writing. Either way, I'll support you entirely and in every way possible."

All I can do is stare at him, even when he says, "Well?"

"I don't know what to say." This is overwhelming. My mind is effectively blown. I didn't expect him to sit me down and have this kind of talk right after something as emotional as dropping Jackson off to spend the night somewhere else for the first time.

"Say you want to help me cross those things off my list. That you'll let me help you cross things off your own list. That we can have a list together. My daughter loves you. I love you. Just say that you'll be happy to keep me."

"You're serious?" I ask. I know it sounds like he is, but this can't be real life.

"The whole point of this is to show you I'm serious." He takes the paper out of my hands, throws it to the ground, and grabs my hand. "What more to do you need?" he asks desperately, misreading my question. "Do you want me to propose? I'll do it. We don't have to wait. Do you want—"

I cover his mouth with my hand. "That's not what I meant. It's just..." I remove my hand from his mouth and pinch my arm hard. Ouch! Yep. This is totally real life.

Elias laughs and frames my face with his hands. "Do you forgive me? Are you with me in this?"

The moment I start nodding, he leans forward and kisses me. I wish this kiss could last forever because it fills me with peace and a security I haven't felt in...well, never. Bree shouts a long, "Gah!" which causes us to separate. With a laugh, we glance over at her. She stands and bangs her hands against the sides, wanting our attention and wanting out of her pack 'n play.

Elias leaves me to get her. She crawls back and forth between our laps, not sure of where she wants to be, while pulling on my hair whenever she's close by. Elias smiles at her until I get his attention.

"You really want all of those things?" I ask quietly, still unable to believe it. "With me?"

"I really hate Henry."

I frown at his response. "Why?"

"And your parents and his parents," he adds as he grabs me by the hips and pulls me into his lap, causing Bree to giggle with the sudden movement. She loves that we both now sit in his lap too. "They are the reason why you're still struggling with believing me."

"I do believe you; I just can't believe it's real. That my family just grew by two."

Elias grins. "It's bigger than that. There's the rest of

my family and the Rebels."

"Quit overwhelming me. You've done enough of that today."

His grin widens. "I'm not done, Raelynn." He grabs his phone and sends a text. "We have a date tonight, but first, do you want to cross something else off my list?"

I swallow hard. "What do you want to do?"

He picks up the discarded paper and scans the list as if he isn't sure, but when he points it out, I know he knew beforehand which he wanted to do. He wants me to move into his room today. When I don't immediately agree, he says, "You said so yourself that you like my bed better. You miss sleeping there and you like being there, waiting for me when I get home." All true. "But we can wait, too."

I shake my head. This is a big step. Such a big step that I know I'll have to let Henry know things are more serious with Elias and me, so serious that he might as well know he'll definitely see Elias as much as he sees me. "We don't have to wait. I want to."

He kisses my temple and murmurs, "There's my Little Grizzly." He waits a moment. "Let's get started."

We walk upstairs and Bree crawls around Elias's room while he makes room for my things and I move them over. Whenever I thought of a future, even when I hoped Jackson had a sibling, I never saw myself in a relationship because I didn't think it would happen. That it could happen. And yet, here I am.

Once I'm all moved into Elias's room, we lay on his bed with Bree playing between us.

"Do you have a timeline for those things on your list?" I ask as Bree pats my chest and mumbles something along with Ja-Ja.

"First, tell me what's on your list."

"You already know those things." I told him once that I wanted to graduate, figure out my dream job, and give Jackson a sibling.

"I thought maybe it had changed."

"Well..." Has it? "I want you," I add. A big smile lights his face as Bree leaves me for him. "And if you're serious, which you are," I hurry to say based on the look he gives me, "you've given Jackson a sibling."

"Don't you want more?" he says before I can continue.

My eyes pop. "More?"

"More," he confirms. "One day." He picks Bree up and holds her up in the air, giggles coming from her as her legs dangle and her fists go to her mouth. "You had Jackson, I sort of had Bree," he brings her down to blow a raspberry on her stomach before lifting her up again and looking at me. "We need one together."

That almost means more to me than anything else he's said. I know what it means for Elias to say something like that. For him to choose me for a journey like that, where he'd want to make a baby with me. *That* proves he trusts me more than anything else does.

He brings Bree back down and rolls onto his side. "More tears?" he asks quietly, reaching out to wipe a few away as Bree comes over to rest her head on my stomach.

"I love you," I whisper.

He kisses me so suddenly, I'm stunned for a moment. I kiss him back with just as much passion and that security and peace I felt earlier is still there, even more present than before. Bree giggles and Elias pulls away, but rests his forehead against mine.

"I love you too."

"Da!"

Elias laughs and looks at Bree. "You're slacking, princess. Come say hi to your Ma."

Oh, goodness. He's really trying to keep me crying all day. "We'll have to tell her about Vicky one day."

He sighs. "I wish I had more to tell her. Or that she had grandparents who could tell her, but over the summer, I hired someone to track down any relatives of Vicky's. It looked like she was an only child and her parents had passed years ago. He couldn't find info on anyone else. We're the only family Bree has."

"Ah, da," Bree squeals.

"Ma," Elias repeats. "No more Rae. Ma. Ma. Ma."

Bree studies him and then looks at me. She crawls on-to my chest and sighs like she's tired. The only way this day could be more perfect is if Jackson were here.

Later, we're at Brayden's house to drop Bree off. They are babysitting while Elias takes me out on a date as promised. Bree wiggles to get down to their dog, Otis, so I set her down. The Rottweiler stands about a foot away next to Deanna, but Bree slams her hands on the floor and shouts, as if demanding he get his butt over here. Otis slowly closes the distance and plops down in front of Bree, his head in front of her feet. That excites her so much, a foot kicks out and hits his nose. Otis breathes heavy, but otherwise, watches her.

Bree crawls closer and tugs on his ear. I smile be-cause Otis simply lies there and lets her tug, pull, and crawl all over him.

"Look, Brayden! How cute!" Deanna says excitedly. "Maybe he won't be so jealous now."

"What do you mean?" I ask.

"Whenever I'm around kids, and even Brayden every now and then, he likes to be so close to me or wiggle between us. He's never shown any real interest in the kids, though."

"You two going to have kids?" Elias asks, earning a glare from Brayden. "What? Everyone else is popping them out."

"Do you want me to ask you?" Brayden snaps back.

"We have two already, so you can't," Elias replies with a grin.

"Get the fuck out of my house before I change my mind about keeping your kid." Brayden bends to swoop Bree up, pissing her off since she was having fun with Otis, and her upset makes Otis go on alert. He stands, looks up at her, and then braces his front paws on Brayden, so Bree can touch him as he nudges her with his nose.

I glance at Deanna to see she looks a little uneasy with this conversation. Maybe this is a sore subject for them. Elias opens his mouth to respond, but I grab his hand and squeeze.

"Thanks for watching for her," I say, stepping forward, next to Otis, to kiss Bree's cheek goodbye.

Brayden's voice barely softens as he addresses me. "No problem, Raelynn."

Once we're in the car, Elias says, "I must be missing something. Brayden can be an ass, but he was too quick to be defensive and an asshole. Deanna seemed relieved that we were leaving too. Didn't she?" He glances over at me and I nod. "Damn it," he mutters.

"What are we doing?" I ask to get his mind off of what happened with his friend.

"I love my movies and you love relaxing, so we're going to the movies."

I glance down at my dress. If I'd known we were only going to the movies, I would've worn something else. Sure enough, we arrive at a movie theater, buy drinks and snacks, and then head to our assigned room based on the movie Elias bought tickets for prior to us leaving the house. Not a single seat is occupied, and the seats? They are wide, roomy, comfy, and even recline as the the foot comes up like an actual recliner!

"Get over here, Raelynn. There's enough room, you can sit with me."

"No. Someone else will come in and see us."

Elias simply shakes his head and pats his leg. I'm not sitting in his lap through this movie. He can forget it.

"No one is coming in," he finally says. "I bought every ticket. It's only us. Now," he grabs my hand, "get over here."

"Why would you do that?"

"To ensure alone time with you."

"We could've watched a movie at home for that."

Elias shakes his head as if it wouldn't be the same. I settle on his lap as he presses a button so the foot rises and he reclines in the seat. His hand sneaks up underneath my dress and high up my thigh. When I tense, he chuckles and whispers in my ear, "Relax, Raelynn. Just want to touch you. I'll keep it PG."

"I think your hand under my dress automatically disqualifies you," I quip, but I relax at his words. We may be here and may be alone, but we're still in a public space. I grab the popcorn from the seat I vacated and begin munching on it while the ads run. "We need to keep an eye on the time. Jackson is supposed to call before he goes to bed."

Elias pulls his phone out, texts Henry to call his phone instead of mine when it's time, and sets it on the armrest. We'll see it light up when Jackson calls.

"Thank you."

"Whatever makes you happy, Raelynn."

EJ

"**Y**OU KNOW," I begin on our drive to Brayden's to pick up Bree, "my birthday is coming up."

Raelynn looks over at me. "When?"

"Friday."

She angles in her seat to face me more. "What do you want?"

"Babysitters," I answer immediately. We need more alone time. "Just not on Friday. I have a game." After a moment, I add, "Or Saturday. Same issue." I park in Brayden's driveway and look at her. "I just want to spend lots of time with you in my bed."

Raelynn's cheeks turn pink as she shakes her head at me. "I'll think about it."

I laugh, loving that's her answer. "Let's get our girl."

She looks away, but not before I see her grin. We get out of my car and walk up to Brayden's door. He answers pretty quickly, but without my princess.

"How was she?" Raelynn asks as we step inside.

"She's a tyrant," Brayden replies easily.

Raelynn smiles, but I don't. That's just mean to call my princess a tyrant. We step into his living room and there she is. Deanna lies asleep on the couch, Bree asleep on her chest, and Otis lies on her lower body with his head resting next to Bree's body. Her hand has a good grip on his ear, it looks like.

"She wore herself out playing with Otis. She was a pain anytime Otis had to go out and we separated them for those few minutes. Pretty sure you have to get her a dog, EJ," Brayden says.

I shake my head. I have enough on my plate, so unless Raelynn wants to conquer a dog, no way.

"Figured." He leaves the room and a moment later returns with a stuffed animal. It's a fake miniature Otis. "Deanna sent me shopping, just in case." He shoves the dog at my chest with a smile and walks over to Deanna. "Darlin'," he whispers. "The baby's going home," he says as he lifts Bree up. Raelynn walks over to help disengage Bree's fist from Otis's ear, the dog grumbling, and Deanna wakes up.

Brayden hands my baby off to Raelynn and Deanna looks a bit sheepish from having been asleep.

"Thanks," I tell them. "You're Bree's favorite babysitters."

Brayden laughs because he doesn't believe me, but Deanna smiles. "Any time, EJ," she says, earning a glare from her boyfriend. "Don't give me that look, Brayden. You have more fun than I do, and I have a *lot* of fun."

Brayden simply shakes his head. "Let me get her diaper bag for you."

A few minutes later, we're driving home. Raelynn holds my hand in her lap and stares out the window.

"I wonder if Jackson went on to sleep soon after we talked," she says quietly. Jackson called her right after our movie ended and he seemed uncertain once more, but admitted he had been having fun with Henry.

"Text Henry and ask," I suggest.

"Wouldn't that show I don't trust him?"

"No, it shows you want to check on your son. I mean, look at how often we've talked when I'm on my trips. Ease your mind and text him, Raelynn."

She releases my hand to grab her phone and do just that. By the time we're home, she sighs. "He was a little scared, but Henry says he calmed him down and he was asleep within twenty minutes. Instead of sleeping in the room Henry has for him, he decided Jackson might feel more comfortable sleeping in the living room with him under a blanket fort. I feel so much better now."

I knew she would. I'm also happy that Henry has everything under control over there and is communicating with Raelynn about it. We get Bree settled in for the night and then lay on the couch on our sides. The tips of my fingers walk from Raelynn's shoulder to as far as I can reach down her leg. I'm happy she's happy. I'm happy things are working out. That we took the risk and that it's been worth it. I think the best of us is yet to come.

"Elias?"

"Hmm?" I hum absentmindedly, wondering if she'll let me have her right here on the couch.

"I started writing after Henry left me," she says. My fingers pause at her hips and I look down at her since I'm propped up by my elbow. "I've always been good in school when it came to writing, but after I told him and my parents about Jackson and everything that happened..." Her voice trails off as she takes a few deep breaths. "I needed an outlet to stay sane."

Her inhale this time is shaky. "At first, I wrote like an alternate reality. A fictional version of my life that I wished would've happened instead of what did. Then, other stories started coming and I wrote those instead. But it was still an outlet, an escape when life got hard, and it was private. I was going to tell you about it eventually. Once I felt like I do now."

Out of all of that, there's one thing that interests me the most. "How do you feel now?"

"At peace and secure with who we are and where we're going, all of which I'm not sure I've ever felt before. But once it hit me, I realized this is what I was waiting for."

I smile. I can't help it. Raelynn has finally settled in with me and our relationship. She's finally truly comfortable and believes in us. "About time," I mumble, teasing her.

She rolls onto her back to show me she's rolling her eyes at me. She fists my shirt in my hand and a slow smile lights up her face. "Are you done?" She glances toward the TV. "I think we should celebrate the fact that I'm jobless and officially living with my boyfriend."

I laugh. I want to ask her if she's settled on what she wants to do about the jobless part, but not right now I don't. My hand slides back down to her legs and slips underneath the dress she still wears. "How do you want to celebrate?" I ask.

She grabs my neck and pulls me down for a kiss as her answer. I shift us so I'm on my back and she lies on top of me. Just as I'm pulling her dress up, she leans back.

"Quick question."

"What?"

"Why haven't you invited me to the charity event? Sylvia said you're supposed to."

I stare at her for a moment. "That's what you're thinking about right now. Really?"

"It just popped into my head," she says with a shrug.

"Hadn't thought about it much with everything going on." And that's almost a lie. I haven't thought about it at all, actually. "Do you want to go with me, Raelynn?"

She slides her hands from my neck to my shoulders, shifts her legs to straddle me, and sighs. "Do I have to? Seems kind of daunting."

I laugh. She wants to know why I haven't asked her to an event she isn't sure she wants to attend in the first place? I lift my head so my lips can meet hers. She's too cute to not quit talking and start back on the path we were on. A path where my hands lift and lift until she sits up to remove her dress. A path where she smiles as I flip over, her fingers curl into my hair as I kiss along her collarbone.

"Shirt, Elias," she whispers her demand.

I quickly pull it off and get back to enjoying her body with my hands and my mouth. Off comes her bra and soon after, her panties. I tease her with touches, licks, kisses, and sucking. She squirms and sighs and moans and pulls my hair until she eventually says, "Elias, I love you, but if you don't stop teasing me, you're sleeping on the couch tonight."

I laugh as I finish shedding my clothes so I can give her what she wants.

"Everything better?" Brayden asks as we change into our gear for the game today.

I nod. "Much better."

"Good." He frowns and I follow his gaze to see Collin Kessy sitting, hunched over, and half-dressed.

"What's wrong with him?" I ask.

Brayden's gaze snaps over to me. "Nothing."

He's lying. He looks concerned and Collin doesn't normally act like that, not that I've seen at least. The guy's chest is clearly laboring. His brother looks back and forth between him and everyone else in the room to see if someone notices Collin's odd behavior. I'd definitely say something is wrong.

Collin suddenly stands and walks as fast as he can out of the room. Cal gives Brayden a look before he follows after him.

"You sure nothing's wrong?" I ask.

"Yeah," he replies. "I'll be right back." And then he follows the same path as Collin and Cal.

Obviously, whatever is happening isn't any of my business. I hope it's nothing serious. And it must not be because he goes through our stretches, plays a game of soccer, and warms up with us. However, the usual Kessy chemistry doesn't exist today. Not at all. It's almost painful to watch those two on the ice.

Collin runs into Cal once. He makes one of their famous no-look passes, and it goes straight to the stick of our opponent, nowhere close to Cal. He gets more penalties than he normally does. Some for hooking, some for slashing, and one for tripping. Collin even scores on Savage. It's a terrible mishap. He stands in front of the net, tries to slap the puck away to the left of the net, but it goes straight past Savage's skate and into the net.

He's an absolute hazard out there. I've never seen the Kessy twins anything but composed out on the ice, but Collin falls apart. So much so that Coach Mike begins to double shift some of us to replace him so he can sit on the bench.

Collin looks absolutely distressed over his performance after the first. Cal seems disturbed by it. Like what I've seen at least once before, Brayden nods his head toward the door and he and Collin both stand and walk out. I don't know what they do out there or why they leave, but it seems Collin could definitely use some words of wisdom from the captain.

Coach Mike gives him an opportunity to redeem himself in the second, but he nearly scores on Savage *again* when trying to clear the puck. I don't know what's going on with him, but it's not good. We manage to play okay throughout the rest of the game, but we can't slip a puck past their goalie. Savage plays awesome, making sweet saves, too.

We lose two to zero, one of their guys scoring late in

the third. Not a fun day in the office, that's for sure.

Afterward, I walk up to the box to meet Raelynn, Bree, and Jackson. As soon as Jackson sees me, he runs over and I bend to catch him.

"Sorry you lost, EJ."

"It happens, J-man. We fought hard, that's all that matters."

I just hope whatever Collin's going through gets fixed and fast, for his sake and ours.

Monday, Henry, Raelynn, and I sit together in the very facility I practice in. Why? Because this place does more than let us practice here. This is where I brought Jackson to skate and today is his first lesson. Bree struggles in Raelynn's lap to get down, but every so often, she tries to navigate over to Henry. It seems she has developed a slight interest in him and she's beginning to get pissed that she isn't allowed to crawl on the floor or go to Henry.

Henry notices, though, and he glances to me after Bree pounds on Raelynn's shoulder in anger. "Can I?" he asks.

"Yeah, sure."

Raelynn gives Bree what she wants and she immediately claps both her hands on his cheeks and giggles.

"I can't believe y'all signed my son up for this," Raelynn whispers with a shake of her head. "That I approved." She looks at me. "What if he gets hurt?"

Henry is the one to answer her. "He's a boy. He'll get hurt at some point with or without this. Trust me."

Raelynn frowns, more so when I add, "He's right. This will be good for him. It'll expand his world." She can't say no to that. And this will most certainly do that. He'll make new friends, learn new skills, and so much more that he'll remember for the rest of this life.

"He's having so much fun already, too," she points out.

I've most certainly never seen a kid so invested and having an absolute blast at their first lesson. And it hits me then that this is my new life. Being with my girlfriend, my princess, J-man, and even with Henry, hanging out with this family of mine. A family. That's doubled in size, more if I keep counting Henry since he'll forever be around because of Jackson.

Even more surprising is that this feels fantastic. I'm happier than I've ever been.

"Raelynn."

She looks up at me with a slight smile. I dip my head and kiss her softly.

"What's that for?" she whispers.

"Because I love you."

At this time last year, Bree hadn't quite entered my life yet. And to think of how much my life has changed and with her turning one next month, it's insane. One thing is for sure, though, I can't wait to see what my life will look like in another year's time.

Acknowledgements

Thank you, Kristalyn Thornock. You're my favorite. Thank you, Angie Wells, for being a beta reader for me! I'm grateful for your help.

Thank you, Shannon Page, for editing my work. It's always such a pleasure to work with you!

Thank you, Robin from Wicked by Design. You provide me with covers I'm proud to show off.

Thank you, Julie from JT Formatting. You know how much I love your work!

Thank you, reader, for taking the time to read this story. I hope you enjoyed it.

ABOUT THE AUTHOR

Lindsay Paige is the author of multiple Young Adult, New Adult, and Sports romances. She also enjoys writing books with characters who deal with anxiety and depression, issues which are close to her heart. Lindsay is a North Carolinian who loves watching hockey, sharing puns, having conversations with her miniature Schnauzer, re-watching episodes of MASH, and living her dream of writing books for a living.

If you would like to hear news before anyone else, interact with Lindsay, and have a place to discuss her books with fellow fans, join Lindsay's League on Facebook.

https://www.facebook.com/groups/lindsaysleague/

Author Links:

Website:
lindsaypaige.com

Twitter:
twitter.com/lindsaypaige11

Facebook:
facebook.com/authorlindsaypaige

Facebook Group:
https://www.facebook.com/groups/lindsaysleague/

Instagram:
https://www.instagram.com/authorlindsaypaige/

Newsletter Sign Up:

Stay up-to-date on books, news, sales, and giveaways by signing up for her monthly newsletter!
http://eepurl.com/hqcTw

Coming Soon

Stay tuned because the next Rebel to get a book will be Collin Kessy! His book will tentatively release in Fall 2018.

The next book by Lindsay Paige to release will be in the Hearts in Carolina series and will feature Brent Murphy (Kayla's father) and Jamie Alexander (a college student). This book will release in the Summer of 2018.

Carolina Rebels Roster:

No.	Name	Nickname	Position
1	Collin Kessy	Thing 1	Center
2	Cal Kessy	Thing 2	Right Wing
7	Scott Boyd	Scotty	Right Wing
10	Tommy Alderson	Tommy Boy	Left Wing
11	Luukas Lathi	Luck	Center
13	Brayden Hayes	Captain Hook	Center
17	Ross Strome	Rossy	Defenseman
19	Marc Polinski	Marco Polo	Defenseman
20	Elias Bertuzzi	EJ	Center
24	Noah Ramsey	Rams	Defenseman
26	Dylan Copley	Po Po	Defenseman
29	Sergey Orlovsky	Serge	Left Wing
32	Kellan Hellberg	Hells	Center
37	Liam Irving	Savage/Sav	Goalie
41	Reid Aubry	Soda	Defenseman
44	Eric Kelly	Kel	Goalie
46	Tyler Lindberg	Lindy	Right Wing

58	Bradley Potter	Pots	Left Wing
62	Kyle McNally	Nally	Left Wing
68	Zane Landry	Z	Defenseman
74	Nathan O'Donnell	Donny	Right Wing
85	Ian Rhett	Bruiser	Defenseman
94	Jeffery Olsen	Olsey	Right Wing

Lindsay has written the following books/series:

Bending Under Pressure

Bold as Love series

Bracing for Love series

Carolina Rebels series

Don't Panic

Sanity series

Without a Doubt

You Before Me

She has cowritten the following series:

The Penalty Kill Trilogy

Oh Captain, My Captain series

The Ninth Inning series